Fang Si-Chi's First Love Paradise

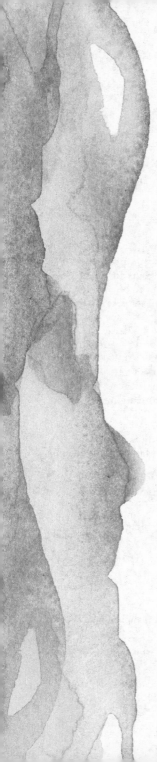

Fang Si-Chi's First Love Paradise

a novel

Lin Yi-Han

Translated from the Chinese by Jenna Tang

HarperVia

An Imprint of HarperCollins*Publishers*

FANG SI-CHI'S FIRST LOVE PARADISE. Copyright © 2017 by Lin Yi-Han. English translation © 2024 by Jenna Tang. All rights reserved. Printed in the United States of America. No part of this book may be used or reproduced in any manner whatsoever without written permission except in the case of brief quotations embodied in critical articles and reviews. For information, address HarperCollins Publishers, 195 Broadway, New York, NY 10007.

HarperCollins books may be purchased for educational, business, or sales promotional use. For information, please email the Special Markets Department at SPsales@harpercollins.com.

Originally published as *Fang Siqi de chulian leyuan* in Taiwan in 2017 by Guerrilla Publishing Co., Ltd.

FIRST HARPERVIA HARDCOVER PUBLISHED IN 2024

FIRST EDITION

Designed by Yvonne Chan
Illustrations © helgafo/Shutterstock

Library of Congress Cataloging-in-Publication Data has been applied for.

ISBN 978-0-06-331943-1
ISBN 978-0-06-341281-1 (ANZ)

24 25 26 27 28 LBC 5 4 3 2 1

Contents

PART 1

Paradise

L iu Yi-Ting knew the best thing about being a child was that nobody would take her words seriously. She could boast, break her promises, even lie. The things that come out of a child's mouth are often shiny, naked truths. Reacting instinctively out of self-defense, most adults might reassure themselves: "What do kids even know!" Out of frustration, children learn to tell the truth selectively. This freedom of self-expression is what allows them to grow up.

The only time Liu Yi-Ting ever got scolded for something she had said was at a restaurant in a high-rise hotel. These tedious adult gatherings always came with rare, uninteresting delicacies. At this particular meal, a sea cucumber lay on the big porcelain plate like a long turd deep in the toilet that the maid had scrubbed to a brilliant shine. Liu Yi-Ting let the sea cucumber slide in and out of her mouth, and then spit it back on her plate. Soon she was giggling audibly. Her mother asked what was so funny. "It's a secret," she replied. When her mother raised her voice and asked again, Liu Yi-Ting said, "It's like giving a blow job." Infuriated, her mother made her stand off to the side as punishment. When Fang Si-Chi said she wanted to stand next to her friend, Mama Liu softened her tone and turned to exchange pleasantries with Mama Fang. Liu Yi-Ting knew that compliments like "What a well-mannered child your daughter is!" were just empty praise. Their families lived in the same apartment building, on the same floor. Yi-Ting often knocked on the Fang family's door in her pajamas and slippers, and no matter what she had in her hands, be it fast food or workbooks, Mama Fang always welcomed her. They often joked that Yi-Ting was like a long-lost daughter. The girls could while away a whole night with just a piece of tissue. They were on the cusp of turning into grown adults, but they never had to hide their stuffed animals from each other. They didn't have to pretend that the only games they cared for anymore were poker and chess.

Yi-Ting and Si-Chi stood shoulder to shoulder in front of the floor-to-ceiling window. Si-Chi mouthed, Why did you even say that? Yi-Ting silently replied, It just sounded smarter than saying it looked like poop. It would take Liu Yi-Ting many years to understand that using a word you barely understood was absolutely criminal. It was like saying I love you to someone you don't love at all. Si-Chi pursed her lips, gestured at the boats below, and remarked about how many there were. They were about to return to Kaohsiung Port. Each of the whalelike cargo ships was led by a tiny shrimp of a boat. Various big and small boats aligned with each other, squeezing out V-shaped waves. The whole of Kao-hsiung Port resembled a blue blouse being ironed, smoothed over back and forth. The view made them feel sentimental and sad. They were soulmates who shared the infinite beauty of existence with one another.

The adults let them have the desserts at the dining table. Si-Chi passed Yi-Ting the flag-shaped, hard maltose candy for her ice cream, but Yi-Ting refused and mouthed, Don't give me something you don't want! Si-Chi was offended, her lips trembling as she mouthed back, You know how much I like malt-ose! Yi-Ting replied, I really don't want it! The maltose began to melt on Si-Chi's fingers, so she sucked on them. Yi-Ting began to laugh, mouthing, You look terrible! Si-Chi was about to snap back that, actually, *she* was the one who looked terrible. But Si-Chi decided to swallow those words along with the sugar so it didn't sound like she was cursing Yi-Ting. Yi-Ting noticed this and burst out laughing. A desert was suddenly smeared on the tablecloth, where a group of strange dwarves sang and danced silently in circles.

Grandpa Chien said to them, "My little sweethearts, what's on your mind?" Yi-Ting hated when people called them "little sweethearts." She hated this calculated, pitying kindness. Mama Wu said, "Kids these days hit puberty the minute they're born." Auntie Chen said, "Oh, we're about to hit menopause!" Teacher Lee added, "They're not like us. We can't even grow a single pimple!" Everyone began to spout laughter, their *hahahahahahaha* tossed all over the table. The topic of faded youth was like a can-can dance the girls never got invited to. The most faithful circle was still the most exclusive. Eventually Liu Yi-Ting understood that it was they who still had their youth to lose, not the adults.

From the next day on they became even closer, just like a clump of hard maltose candy, and would remain so forever.

———

One spring, several local households contacted the neighborhood committee to fund and offer bowls of hot sticky tangyuan to the homeless at the Lantern Festival. Their building stood out in the school district. When they rode past the area on scooters, lines and lines of Greek pillars would rush by quickly in their field of vision. Liu Yi-Ting's classmates often stood by and mocked her for living in "The Grand Palace of Kaohsiung." She was as bitter as a dog whimpering in the rain. *What do you even know?* she thought. *That's my home!* Even though she was allowed to wear her own clothes to school once a week, ever since she heard what her classmates had said, Yi-Ting put on her uniform and same pair of sneakers instead, regardless of whether she had PE class that day. She resented having to change her shoes because she'd grown.

Several mamas gathered together, talking about the tangyuan gathering. Grandma Wu noted, "The Lantern Festival is on a weekend; let the kids do it!" The mamas agreed that children should start learning about charity from a young age. Yi-Ting got chills when she heard this. It was like a hand had reached into her stomach and struck a match, engraving a few lines of poetry. She didn't know what the word *charity* meant. She read in the dictionary that "'Charity' is kindness and benevolence without judging others. The Emperor Jianwen of Liang's inscription on

4

Wu-Chun's tombstone said: 'Morals arise from kindness and stem from spiritual intuition.'" No matter how Yi-Ting looked at it, these definitions seemed quite different from what the mamas were saying.

Liu Yi-Ting learned at an early age that the best feelings one can have come with the knowledge that you would be rewarded if you tried hard enough. This idea cheered her up no matter how much she worked. She tutored her classmates in their homework, let them copy her notes, did their calligraphy assignments, and made arts and crafts for them. There was no need for her classmates to run any extra errands. In her efforts she always acted very agreeably, without a sense of mercy or superiority. Her workbook got passed around, copied by various hands. Some people's handwriting was like smooth bubbles being blown out; some were like lumps or curvy raw noodles. Every time her workbook made it back to her, she fantasized about different children being born from her notebook, each with a distinctive face. Whenever someone asked to copy Fang Si-Chi's homework, Si-Chi suggested they borrow Yi-Ting's assignment instead. "Her homework gets around." They would look at each other and smile; they didn't need anyone else to understand.

Winter lingered that year, and it remained very cold during the Lantern Festival. They put up the tent at the side of the avenue. The first child who arrived was assigned to scoop salty broth for everyone, the second was to add savory tangyuan, the third child was responsible for pouring sweet broth, and so Yi-Ting, who came fourth, was made responsible for adding sweet tangyuan. The tangyuan were obedient; once puffed, they floated up and would be ready to be dumped into the bowls. The red bean broth made the pudgy faces of the tangyuan seem fitful and pouty. What did it mean to learn about charity? Or kindness? Or benevolence, or sympathy? These questions jumbled together in Yi-Ting's mind. People gradually streamed in, their faces wrinkled by the cold wind. The first guest to arrive was an older gentleman wearing clothes that were little more than rags. When the wind blew again, the tattered cloth fluttered in the air like the paper streamers hanging at the bottom of a billboard. The older gentleman stumbled toward them, looking so exceptionally fragile, it seemed like he would be torn apart by the breeze. She then thought, *Oh, I don't have the right to think of them this way. All right, it's my turn, three tangyuan per bowl.* "Grandpa, please sit over there, wherever you want." *Teacher Lee said three was an auspicious number, a good number; he really was erudite.*

The crowd was bigger than they expected. Her thoughts about people receiving handouts, how shameful that was, simply faded away without any metaphors. She just greeted people and scooped food for them. At one point, a commotion arose at the front of the line: a middle-aged man was asking if he could get two extra tangyuan. Kwei, the boy responsible for scooping salty tangyuan, suddenly froze, face fossilized by the cold wind, or by the question itself. Yi-Ting heard him respond, "That's not something I can decide!" The uncle quietly moved along, his silence like a gemstone sunk in the noise of the red silk, heavier than ever, pressing down on them. Yi-Ting felt scared; she knew that they did prepare extra tangyuan, but she also didn't want to make Kwei look like a bad guy. Once Yi-Ting received the next bowl, she got distracted. She later realized that she had given the man an extra tangyuan—an unconscious mistake. As she glanced back, she realized that Kwei was looking at her.

Another auntie brought a plastic bag for the occasion. Unlike the rest of them, she didn't smell like the piles of garbage left behind after a typhoon. She came and said she would like to take the food away and eat at her place. Yi-Ting remembered how the post-typhoon mess smelled. She had passed by those garbage piles while in the car; although she might've forgotten how the scene looked, her nose remembered everything. Yes, these stranger uncles and aunts were swine bent over in their pens, emitting the smell of a flowing, polluted river. *I can't think about this anymore. This auntie had a home; she was not a homeless person. Stop thinking.*

Another auntie asked them for clothes. This time, Kwei spoke up immediately and with confidence replied, "Auntie, we only provide tangyuan. Only tangyuan. We can give you more of these, but that's all." The auntie paused as if in a trance, perhaps calculating whether the calories of extra tangyuan equaled the warmth of more clothes. Still visibly dazed, she carried two big bowls away into another tent. The tent became more and more crowded; the sunlight cutting through the red canvas turned people's faces a shy color.

Si-Chi was the good-looking one. She took the guests to their seats and gathered the trash from the surroundings. Yi-Ting called Si-Chi to replace her temporarily, claiming that she hadn't been able to use the toilet since the morning. Si-Chi said, "Okay, but you'll have to help me out later."

Yi-Ting walked the two blocks back home. The ceiling of the lobby was as high as paradise. Before she entered the lobby bathroom, she saw Teacher Lee's wife scolding their daughter,

Xixi, who was sitting on the sofa in the corridor leading to the bathroom. Yi-Ting took a quick glimpse and saw that a bowl of tangyuan was on the coffee table in front of the sofa. The tangyuan were on top of each other, spilling over the brim of the pink plastic bowl. She only heard Xixi cry out, "Some of the people who came weren't even homeless." Yi-Ting suddenly panicked. She rushed into the bathroom and looked in the mirror at her flat nose scattered with freckles, her nearly square face. Si-Chi always told her that she never got tired of looking at her, and Yi-Ting would reply, "You're saying that because it looks like a loaf of Chinese Northeastern flatbread, and you're getting hungry." The frames of the mirrors in the lobby bathroom were Baroque-style gold with carved flowers. At her height, her reflection in this mirror looked like a bust portrait from that era. No matter how she straightened her back, she couldn't see her breasts. She quickly washed her face, thinking how bad this would look if somebody came in and saw her! *A child who didn't look like much to begin with posing in front of a mirror. How old was Xixi? She seemed to be two or three years younger than she and Si-Chi. Teacher Lee was such a legend, and look at Xixi!* When she left the bathroom, she didn't see mother or daughter, and the bowl of tangyuan was gone.

Against the back of the sofa were two heads of curly hair, one red and one gray, wispy as clouds. The redhead had to be Auntie Chang, who lived on the tenth floor. Who the gray head of hair belonged to she didn't know. That kind of gray resembled precious metal, and Yi-Ting was unable to discern whether the hair was entirely gray or rather white strands intertwined with black. Black and white equaled gray, after all, and Yi-Ting was passionate about color theory. That was probably why she couldn't manage the piano. The more black-and-white something was, the easier it was for there to be mistakes.

The older women bowed their heads, practically disappearing into the sofa. Their voices suddenly rose, like an eagle leaving its aerie—the raptor opening its beak to cry, the prey dropping from its mouth.

"What? Such a young, beautiful wife; why would he hit her like that?"

Auntie Chang lowered her voice. "They say he only hits her where others can't see."

"How did you even find out about it?"

"Oh, I introduced the cleaning lady to them."

"So, the maids can't even keep their mouths shut; how come Chien Sheng-Sheng never intervenes?"

"That girl joined the family less than two years ago. Old Chien only cares about his business, nothing else."

Yi-Ting couldn't listen to this anymore. She felt as if she were the one being abused.

Squinting against the cold, Yi-Ting tiptoed back into the street. The bitter wind pierced her face like a full-face acupuncture treatment that a nonbeliever in Chinese medicine might resort to after no success with Western medicine. She remembered how Iwen started wearing a turtleneck while the weather was still warm. She was hiding both her bruised skin and skin that had yet to be bruised. Liu Yi-Ting felt that she'd really aged a lot in one day, had been overcooked by time.

Suddenly, Si-Chi came into sight and said, "I thought you promised to help me. I ended up coming back here alone because I couldn't find you anywhere."

"Sorry, stomachache," Yi-Ting replied, thinking what a lame excuse that was.

She changed the topic and asked Si-Chi if she was also going back to use the toilet. With tears in her eyes, Si-Chi mouthed that she wanted to go home and change; she shouldn't have worn a new coat on such a cold day. "Look at those people," Si-Chi said. "The weather reports said it would be cold today, but they wore so little. I feel like I've done something really bad." Yi-Ting hugged her tightly and said, "It's not your fault you couldn't fit into the old one." When she added, "Kids grow very fast!" both of them burst out laughing and fell into each other. Thus ended the beautiful Lantern Festival.

———

The Chien Sheng-Shengs were especially rich. The octogenarian's family business had boomed during the period of Taiwan's strongest economic growth. They were well-known for their money in Liu Yi-Ting and Fang Si-Chi's building and throughout the country. Their son had arrived late, and Chien Yi-Wei had become Yi-Ting and Si-Chi's favorite "older brother" to bump into in the elevator. In a way, their subconscious thinking about seeing him and praising his good looks showed just how much and how quickly Yi-Ting and Si-Chi wanted to grow up. Both girls ranked their neighbors secretly. Top place went to Teacher Lee, with his deep eyes and arched eyebrows carrying a hint of melancholy, his demeanor literary and intellectual, spiritual and scholarly. Yi-Wei came in second, he who spoke with a rare and authentic American East Coast accent, so tall he could reach the sky. Some men wore glasses as if simply collecting dust with their lenses; others wore thin, silvery frames as if seducing others to climb onto them. Some were tall, but seemed to have shot up too fast, and some were like wind and rainforests. The girls never put kids their age on the list; how could you talk about Proust with someone who only reads *Youth Literary*?

Chien Yi-Wei was no longer young; he was in his forties. Iwen, his wife, was only in her twenties, and also came from wealth. Hsu Iwen had been a PhD student in comparative literature before marriage completely derailed her academic career. She had a smooth oval face, big eyes, and long eyelashes; her eyes were so big that she constantly appeared shocked, and her eyelashes so long that they seemed capable of sustaining heavy weights. Her nose was so straight, it was as though spending a year in the US not only improved her English but also helped her learn how to grow a straighter nose like the Americans. Her skin was as pale as that of a fairy-tale princess, with a hint of rosy glow. Long before she had grown into a woman, she had often been asked how she did her eye makeup. She would reply that those were just her natural eyelashes. One day, Yi-Ting stared closely at Si-Chi's face and said, "You look a lot like Iwen. Or actually, Iwen looks a lot like you." Si-Chi waved the compliment away and said: "Enough with the jokes."

But the next time Si-Chi met Iwen in the elevator, she took another look, and for the first time, she realized that Iwen and she both had a face that very much resembled a tender lamb.

Chien Yi-Wei had a spectacular family background, with universal appeal and an air of American gallantry, without the American world-police self-centeredness. In the beginning, Hsu Iwen had felt wary: *How could he still be unmarried at this age?*

Chien Yi-Wei explained, "Most of the women who approached me only wanted my money. I preferred to look for someone who also came from means, and you're the kindest, most beautiful woman I've ever met." Iwen thought the explanation was too straightforward, but nonetheless it kind of made sense to her.

Chien Yi-Wei used every single line from the Love Bible verbatim; he said Hsu Iwen had a beauty beyond compare. A delighted Iwen responded, "That's quite the poetic mix of metaphors." Inside, she laughed and thought that was the best line she'd ever heard him say. A smile flickered across her face as her happiness bubbled over. Yi-Wei was obsessed: A woman who corrects my grammar. Simply sitting there, Iwen looked like one of the women on the covers of mini romance novels that sold for 49 New Taiwan dollars at convenience stores. Stunning like a goddess, lifting him with her shining radiance.

One day, Yi-Wei took her out yet again for sushi. Iwen had a petite figure and a small appetite, and a sushi dinner was one of the few occasions in which Yi-Wei could see her eat something in one big bite. After the last dish was served, before the chef cleaned up and left, Iwen sensed something was amiss, as if she were lifting a mouthful of raw ginger despite knowing it was too spicy for her. No way. Without kneeling, Yi-Wei said plainly, "You'll marry me soon, won't you?"

Iwen had heard many confessions of love, but that was her first proposal—if an imperative sentence could count as such. She ran her fingers through her hair, as if that might help untangle her feelings. They had been dating for just over two months. Did commands also count as promises? Iwen quietly said, "Mr. Chien, I'll have to think about it." Immediately she realized how stupid she was: they had been the only two customers at a popular restaurant that entire night. When Yi-Wei slowly removed a velvet jewelry box from his bag, Iwen raised her voice for the first time: "No, Yi-Wei, don't show that to me; otherwise you'll start thinking that I'm marrying you only for what's inside that box." And then she regretted it, her face as red as the chef's grilled prawns.

Yi-Wei laughed and paused. "If you think you might accept this in the future, then fine. You even called me by my full name." He put away the box, while Iwen's face remained flushed in embarrassment.

What changed her mind completely, Iwen thought later, was his attempt to surprise her after she finished her classes the day the typhoon arrived. When she stepped through the school gate, she noticed his tall silhouette standing in the headlights of a black car, holding a huge umbrella that trembled in the gusting wind. The two headlights looked like bright antennae, rain like mosquitos and flies frolicking in the beams. The light felt her out with its fingers, pierced her with its sharp gaze. She ran toward him, her rain boots splashing through puddles and producing tiny waves. "I'm really sorry. I didn't know you would come. If I had known I would've . . . Our school floods . . . very often."

In the car, she noticed that his blue dress pants were so wet they looked indigo all the way to his calves, and his leather shoes had deepened from latte to pure Americano. She thought about the folktale about the lovers at Blue Bridge. The one about the man who insisted on waiting for the woman despite the coming flood, until he eventually lost his grip on the pillar of the bridge and drowned. Iwen was reminded of the expression "tugging at the heartstrings"; at that moment she could feel a weight in her chest. Shortly thereafter, they were engaged.

After they got married, Hsu Iwen moved in with Yi-Wei and his family. His parents occupied the penthouse, while Yi-Wei and Iwen took the floor below. During this time, Yi-Ting and Si-Chi often went upstairs to borrow books, which Iwen had aplenty. Iwen would squat down to their eye level and tell them, "I have lots more books in my belly." Old Mrs. Chien, watching TV in the living room, would say, "The stomach is for having babies, not for shelving books." The TV was so loud they didn't know how Mrs. Chien even heard them speaking. Yi-Ting watched a light extinguish in Iwen's eyes.

Iwen read to them all the time. Listening to Iwen read in Mandarin, Yi-Ting felt the crispness of the words like munching on fresh cabbage, each word a single bite, nary a wasted scrap. She started to realize that Iwen was reading not only to them but to herself. So Yi-Ting and Si-Chi went upstairs even more frequently. They used a line from Du Fu's poem to describe their "conspiracy" with Iwen: "In full spring shall we come back home again." The girls were a sailcloth over the beautiful, determined, and audacious Iwen, sheltering her, pushing her, and covering her desire; they covered her so closely that it made the shape of her desire even more apparent. Every time Yi-Wei finished work and got back home, he would joke as he hung up his suit, "You're making my wife a nanny again." His clothes were just like the person who wore them, emitting the scent of freshness. Just one look from those eyes was like a promise of paradise.

For a while, they were reading Dostoyevsky. Following Iwen, they read chronologically. When they started reading *The Brothers*

Karamazov, Iwen said, "Remember Raskolnikov in *Crime and Punishment* and Duke Myshkin in *The Idiot*? They were just like Smerdyakov. They all had epilepsy. Dostoyevsky had it himself. This was to say, Dostoyevsky thought that those who were closest to Christianity were the most natural humans, yet they didn't have a place in society. That was also to say, only the unsocialized were real humans. Do you two understand the difference between being a hermit and being antisocial?"

Years later, Liu Yi-Ting still couldn't understand why Iwen would be willing to tell children that much at their age. How could she teach them about Dostoyevsky when they hadn't even started reading Giddens Ko or Hiyawu? *Maybe she was compensating for something? Did Iwen hope we would get the message that she had failed to understand at our age? By teaching us what she thought we needed to know, did she hope we would be able to put the broken parts of her back together?* One day, Iwen told them that Teacher Lee, who lived downstairs, knew they had been reading Dostoyevsky recently. He said, "Murakami once arrogantly claimed that very few people in the world could recite all three Karamazov brothers' names. The next time we bump into each other, I will test you both. Say them with me: Dmitri, Ivan, and Alexei." *Why didn't Si-Chi recite the names with us?* Yi-Ting wondered.

At that moment, Yi-Wei came home. Iwen looked over to the door, as though she could see the key chewing in the lock with that screeching sound. She glanced at the paper bag in Yi-Wei's hand as he entered, her gaze carrying both the rain of mercy and the light of doubt. She said, "That's my favorite cake! But something your mother asked me to eat less."

Yi-Wei looked at Iwen and laughed. His smile rippled his face like a pebble tossed in a pond. He said, "You mean this? Oh, it's only for the kids." Yi-Ting and Si-Chi were thrilled, but tried to appear calm. They shouldn't behave like monsters. "We were just reading Dostoyevsky. Dmitri, Ivan, and Alexei."

Yi-Wei smiled even wider. "Little girls shouldn't take food from strangers, so I might as well eat it all myself."

Iwen snatched the paper bag and said, "Stop teasing them." Yi-Ting noticed that the moment when Iwen touched Yi-Wei's hand, a strange expression appeared on her face. Yi-Ting had thought that it might be newlywed shyness, just like their feigned indifference toward the food. Food and desire are deeply connected. She later learned that Yi-Wei nurtured a little beast inside of Iwen called fear, which at that moment was dashing against the fence that was Iwen's face. It was a montage of pain that she saw. Years later, after Yi-Ting and Si-Chi entered high school and left home, they heard that Yi-Wei had beaten Iwen so hard during her pregnancy that she lost her baby. It was the grandson Mrs. Chien wanted most. Dmitri, Ivan, or Alexei. That day, they gathered around the table and ate cake, as if they were at a birthday party, only happier. Yi-Wei talked about his work in the stock market, but the girls thought he said "supermarket"; he said "stock time," but the girls thought he asked them what time it was; he said "human resources" and they thought he was quoting *Three Character Classic*, talking about human virtues and morality. They enjoyed being treated as adults, but what they liked even more was turning back into children after being adults for a while. Suddenly, Yi-Wei said, "Si-Chi does look like Iwen. Look, they're so alike! The eyebrows, the profile, and the air of elegance." Yi-Ting felt left out. The extravagant house and beautiful people in front of her looked like a family. She was indignant; there wasn't a child alive who knew as much as she did. But she would never understand how it felt to be a woman aware of her own beauty, walking on the street and holding her head low.

———

Soon it was time to enter high school, and while most of the students in their neighborhood had decided to stay in their hometown, Mama Liu and Mama Fang were talking about sending Yi-Ting and Si-Chi to Taipei. They could live in the same apartment off campus and take care of each other. The girls were watching TV in the living room, finding the programs even more interesting after taking a long, stressful entrance exam. Mama Liu said, "Teacher Lee told me he usually spends half the week in Taipei, so the girls could contact him if they need help." Yi-Ting noticed that Si-Chi slumped even more, as if her mama's sentences were crushing her. Si-Chi mouthed to Yi-Ting, Would you really want to go to Taipei? Yi-Ting said, "Yeah, I'm not against it. Taipei has so many movie theaters!"

The matter was settled by their mamas. The only thing they had yet to decide was whether to stay at the Liu family's house or the Fang family's house in Taipei.

The girls brought only a few suitcases with them. When they arrived at the apartment, dust was flying everywhere, drifting in the sunbeam that entered through the little window of their room. Several cardboard boxes lay on the floor, looking more homesick than either of them. They took their underwear out, one piece after another. But most of what they brought were books. The sunlight inside the apartment spoke the language of silence, the kind that healthy people wouldn't even dare to acknowledge. Yi-Ting broke the silence as though she were cutting open a box: "Thank god we share books; otherwise these boxes would be double the weight. Too bad we can't share our textbooks." Si-Chi was as still and quiet as the air around them. When Yi-Ting approached her, she saw that against the light, tears were tumbling and boiling in Si-Chi's eyes.

"Why are you crying?"

"Yi-Ting, would you be mad at me if I told you that I'm Teacher Lee's girlfriend?"

"What do you mean?"

"It's exactly what you just heard."

"What do you mean, his girlfriend?"

"Just what I said."

"When did this start?"

"I forget."

"Do our mamas know?"

"No."

"How far have you two gone?"

"We've done everything, even stuff we shouldn't be doing."

"Oh my god, Fang Si-Chi, he has a wife; he has Xixi. What do you think you're doing? You're so disgusting; get away from me!"

Si-Chi stared at Yi-Ting, her tears growing from seeds to beans. She suddenly lost it, wailing so hard that she seemed to expose everything, letting it all out.

"Fang Si-Chi, you know how much I admire Teacher Lee. Why are you taking him away from me?"

"I'm sorry."

"I'm not the one you should be apologizing to. Don't say sorry to me."

"But I am sorry."

"How much older than us is Teacher Lee?"

"Thirty-seven years."

"Oh my gosh, you're just so disgusting, I can't even talk to you anymore."

Liu Yi-Ting felt awful. Their freshman year started, and Si-Chi stayed out most of the time without coming home. When she was home, she wailed. Through the wall, Yi-Ting could hear Si-Chi burying her face in the pillow and screaming every night. The cotton wool began to shed from the pillow, and Yi-Ting could hear the scream turn silent like sediment settling in a water glass. They had once been twin spirits. It wasn't like one of them loved Fitzgerald while the other muddled through her feelings for Hemingway; rather, they both fell in love with Fitzgerald and hated Hemingway for the exact same reason. It wasn't like one could fill in the sentence the other forgot, but rather they would forget the same paragraph together.

Sometimes, in the afternoon, Teacher Lee would pick Si-Chi up downstairs at their apartment. Yi-Ting would peek from the curtains at the gleaming yellow roof of the taxi, her cheeks burning hot. Teacher Lee had a bald spot on the top of his head, which Yi-Ting would never be able to see clearly from any other angle. Si-Chi's hairline was straight as a highway. If you drove along it, it would lead to the most sinister truth in the world. Every time Si-Chi pulled her pale little calves into the taxi and slammed the door, Yi-Ting felt like someone had just slapped her.

"How long are you two going to keep this up?"

"I don't know."

"Are you hoping that he'll get a divorce?"

"No."

"You know this won't last, right?"

"Yeah, I know. He—He said that I'll fall in love with other boys, then we'll naturally end this. I—I'm in so much pain."

"I thought you were fucking enjoying yourself."

"Please don't talk to me like that! If I died, would you be sad?"

"Are you going to die by suicide? How? Are you going to jump off the building? Can you not jump from our family's apartment?"

They had once been twins of the mind, spirit, and soul. Back then, whenever Iwen read to them, Iwen would blurt out that she was so envious of their friendship. Together, they would reply that they were actually envious of Iwen and Yi-Wei's relationship. Iwen then said, "Falling in love, well, that kind of love is different. Plato said humans are looking for the other half of themselves that they lost; which is to say, two people come together as one to be complete, but once they're put together they become solitary again. Do you understand? For girls like you, it doesn't matter what you lack, or what you have but don't need. Because you are each other's mirror. 'Only if you never become one will you never be alone.'"

Around noon one day that summer, Fang Si-Chi skipped classes three days in a row without coming home. The bugs and birds outside were screeching. If you were to stand under the big banyan tree and listen to the cicadas, their chirps would tremble so much in the air that they would wrinkle your skin. With the cicadas hidden from sight, it was as if the banyan tree were singing.

Won—wonwonwonwon. Won—wonwonwonwon. Yi-Ting realized that her phone was buzzing. The teacher turned his head from the podium. "Whose cell phone is in heat?" Under her desk, Yi-Ting flipped her phone open: an unknown number. She hung up. *Won— wonwonwonwon.* "Damn it, they're calling me again!"

The teacher's expression turned sincere, and he suggested, "If it's urgent, then pick it up."

"Teacher, it's not urgent at all. Well, okay, they're calling me again—sorry, I'll be right back.

"Teacher, I need to head out for a bit."

Answering, she found the call was from a police station at some lake out on Mount Yangming, two hours away from the city.

Yi-Ting took a taxi up the mountain, her heart winding like the path that led to the station. She thought the shape of the mountain looked like a Christmas tree. As children, they had always stood on their tiptoes to grab the star from the top of the tree; it had been one of the things she remembered most from vacation. *Si-Chi was on the mountain, in the police station?* Yi-Ting felt her heart standing on its tiptoes. When she got out of the taxi, a police officer quickly approached and asked if she was Miss Liu Yi-Ting. Yes. "We found your friend up on the mountain." *Found,* Yi-Ting thought. *What an ominous word.*

The police asked, "Has she always been like this?"

Yi-Ting wondered what they meant. *What's going on with her?* The police station was huge, and Yi-Ting couldn't see Si-Chi. *Unless—unless—unless* that *was* her? Si-Chi's hair was clotted together, covering half of her face; her face was flaking from sunburn and bitten all over by mosquitos and other bugs. Her cheeks were sunken, her lips swollen and scabbed. Si-Chi smelled like a steaming pot of homeless people, like one of the ones they had met during the Lantern Festival so many years ago.

"Oh my gosh, why did you handcuff her?"

The police looked at her with surprise and said, "Isn't it obvious?" Yi-Ting squatted and brushed the hair away from one side of Si-Chi's face. Her neck looked like it was about to crack in half, her eyes were wide open, mucus and saliva were dripping onto her clothes. Just then, Fang Si-Chi blurted out, "Haha!"

Several doctors lived in the same apartment building as their families. Liu Yi-Ting couldn't understand what Si-Chi's doctor was talking about, but she knew Si-Chi had gone insane. Mama Fang said there was no way they could take care of Si-Chi's needs at home, nor could they even let her stay in Kaohsiung. Si-Chi couldn't go back to Taipei either; there were too many doctor parents at the elite school she attended—her family would lose face. Mama Fang compromised by sending Si-Chi to a mental health center in Taichung. Yi-Ting thought about Taiwan, their island, folded in half, with Taipei and Kaohsiung being the peaks, and Taichung as the valley. At that moment, Si-Chi had fallen into the valley. Yi-Ting's twin. Soulmate.

From that day on, Yi-Ting often jerked awake in her sleep with tears streaming down her face, and she waited to hear the weeping from the other side of the wall echo her own. Mama Fang never came to Taipei to gather Si-Chi's belongings. After the end of the semester, Yi-Ting finally opened the door to Si-Chi's room. She stroked the stuffed animal on Si-Chi's bedside, a tiny pink sheep, touched the stationery set identical to her own, and smoothed over the school number embroidered on Si-Chi's uniform. It felt like running her hands over the stone wall of an ancient ruin and suddenly touching a piece of hardened gum; it was like forgetting one simple word in the flowing lecture that is life. Yi-Ting knew something had gone wrong. She wondered when their paths had started to diverge; now they were in two completely different worlds. They used to move in parallel, living side by side. And then Si-Chi somehow took a crooked path.

Yi-Ting wilted as she stood in the middle of Si-Chi's bedroom. It looked exactly like her own. She realized that from then on, she would look like someone who had lost a child in an amusement park. Yi-Ting cried for a long time before noticing a pink notebook lying on the desk. Next to the notebook was a fountain pen with an open cap. *This must be her diary.* Yi-Ting had never seen Si-Chi write with such messy penmanship. It must have been something she had planned to keep private. The pages had turned soft and wrinkled from too much handling, which made it hard for Yi-Ting to just peek through. In the diary, Si-Chi had added footnotes to diary entries she had written long ago. Little Fang Si-Chi's writing was like the smile of a chubby kid; grown Fang Si-Chi's writing was like the face of a famous political commentator. The main text was in blue, while the footnotes were written in red, just like how Si-Chi did her homework. The first page Yi-Ting read was written several days before Si-Chi was found on the mountain. There was only one line: "It rained again today; the weather report is always lying." But this sentence wasn't what Yi-Ting was looking for. She wanted to find out when things had taken a wrong turn for Si-Chi. She decided to start from the beginning. And then she found it on the first page.

In blue: "I have to write this down so the ink can dilute my feelings, otherwise I'll go crazy. I took my essay downstairs for Teacher Lee to correct it. He took out his thing and forced me against the wall. Teacher Lee said ten words: 'If that won't work, why don't you use your mouth?' I spit out six words: 'I can't. I don't know how.' And then he stuffed it in my mouth. It felt like drowning. When I was able to talk again, I told Teacher Lee: 'I'm sorry.' It felt like I just failed my homework, even though it was not my homework. Teacher Lee asked if I would bring another essay to him next week. I lifted my head and felt like I could see through the ceiling, and could see my mama shooting the breeze with her friends, talking about my accomplishments at school. I know that whenever I don't know how to respond to adults, it's better to say yes. I saw the ceiling roll and tumble like ocean waves past Teacher Lee's shoulder. It reminded me of when I was little and ripped a dress by accident. He said, 'This is how Teacher shows you he loves you, do you understand?' He got it wrong, I'm not the kind of little kid who would mistake a penis for a popsicle. We both worshipped Teacher Lee. We said that we wanted a husband like him when we grew up. Sometimes when the joke went on for too long, we'd say we wished he *was* our husband. After thinking for days, I've figured out the only way forward. I can't just *like* Teacher Lee, I have to *love* him. Your lover can do anything to you, right? Thoughts are such powerful things! I'm a counterfeit of my past self. I have to love Teacher Lee or I'll be in too much pain."

In red: "Why did I say I didn't know how? What if I didn't want to? What if I told you that you couldn't? I didn't realize until now that everything can be boiled down to the first scene: He forced himself inside of me, and I apologized for it."

Yi-Ting continued reading as though she were a child nibbling on cookies; no matter how careful she was, there would always be more crumbs on the floor than in her mouth. She finally understood. Every pore on her body was suffocating, her eyes staring blankly through a veil of tears. So much noise in the room—she was bawling, wailing like a crow shot by a hunter's arrow and falling from the sky, entangled in its own screaming. But nobody hunts crows to begin with. *Why didn't you tell me, Si-Chi?* Staring at the date, Yi-Ting saw it was five years ago in the fall. That year, Auntie Chang's daughter finally got married. That was around the time when Iwen first moved into their apartment building. It was when Yi-Wei started beating her. Five years ago, Yi-Ting and Si-Chi had only been thirteen.

The story needs to be told again from the beginning.

PART 2

Paradise Lost

F ang Si-Chi and Liu Yi-Ting had been neighbors for a long time. The seventh floor was at an awkward height: jumping off could mean death, paralysis, or just broken arms and legs. Theirs was an era of name-brand schools and elite classes, which they had attended since they were very little, but they weren't like the neighbors' kids who could travel abroad whenever they liked. "It's hard enough to spend our whole lives mastering Chinese," they said. They seldom talked about their feelings in front of others. Si-Chi knew that it came off as hostile and threatening for a porcelain doll of a girl like herself to show off her intelligence. As for Yi-Ting, she knew that people would think an ugly girl acting all smart was just plain crazy. Thankfully they had each other; otherwise they both would have been suffocated by their thoughts about this world. They read the poet Baudelaire instead of the Baudelaires from *A Series of Unfortunate Events*. They found out about arsenic from *Madame Bovary* rather than the famous Hong Kong movie *Hail the Judge*. This was how different they were from other kids their age.

When Lee Guo-Hua and his family moved into this building, they visited all their upstairs and downstairs neighbors. They also brought a vaselike porcelain urn of an expensive seafood dish called Buddha's Temptation to every household. With one hand around the urn and the other holding their daughter Xixi's hand, Teacher Lee's wife looked like she was more afraid of losing the urn than her daughter. When they visited the Fang family, they saw rows and rows of books lining the wall. Lee Guo-Hua perused the spines of the books and complimented Mr. and Mrs. Fang's literary tastes. Teacher Lee told them that after teaching in the cram school for so long, all that seemed to matter to his students was improving a grade by a few more points or how fast they could finish a test. "And I'm but a lowly teacher."

With humility and pride, Mrs. Fang immediately responded, "These books aren't ours; they're our daughter's."

"How old is your daughter?" Teacher Lee asked.

That year, the girls were twelve years old, freshly graduated from grade school.

Teacher Lee objected. "But this must be a college student's bookshelf! Where's your daughter?"

Si-Chi wasn't at home at the time; she had gone over to Yi-Ting's place. After several days, Teacher Lee visited the Liu family, where he also found a row of books on the wall. His brownish-red fingers ran over the spines of the books as if playing a flourish on a piano. He complimented the Liu family in the same fashion. But there wasn't an opportunity to introduce Yi-Ting to him either because she happened to be over at Si-Chi's place that day. After Teacher Lee's daughter, Xixi, went back home, she stood on top of her bed and used her hands to mime making measurements against the wall: "Mommy, can you get me a bookshelf, too?"

———

Young Mr. Chien from the penthouse was getting married. The family invited everyone they knew in the building. It was said that the bride was introduced to young Mr. Chien by Auntie Chang on the tenth floor. Auntie Chang had just married her daughter off to someone else and was continuing to matchmake. Si-Chi knocked on the Liu family's door, asking if they were ready. Yi-Ting answered the door in a fluffy pink dress, looking like she had been crammed into it. Si-Chi thought she looked ridiculous but also felt a surge of pain and pity for her. Yi-Ting must have fussed for a long time before figuring out what she could wear to the wedding. Yi-Ting saw Si-Chi's look and said, "I already told my mama that dresses aren't for me. What if I outshone the bride?" Si-Chi understood that Yi-Ting was joking to assure her that there was nothing to worry about. She could finally unclench her insides.

The Fang family and the Liu family shared a table at the wedding. Young Yi-Wei stood at the end of the red carpet, the picture of a gracious and quintessential gentleman. Or maybe that was the beginning of the red carpet? Yi-Wei wore a tuxedo so black it shone with a kind of luster. The collar of his blazer cut his white shirt into the shape of a sharp pencil tip. The girls didn't know why they felt like his tuxedo was about to cut the red carpet in half. When the bride entered—so young, so beautiful—the girls saddled themselves with wordplay, throwing out phrases like *So stunning that she sank a fish* or *Send a swallow down from the sky.* But the words and metaphors they played with couldn't quite reach the grandiose meanings they had in their heads. Like a city child who spotted a butterfly and could only yell, "Butterfly!" and nothing else. That was Hsu Iwen in a nutshell: *Butterfly!* When the bride passed by their table, the bubble machines on either side of the red carpet began to spout a swarm of bubbles. The girls could see hundreds, maybe thousands, of bubbles flying around Iwen in this extravagant hall, the bride's profile reflected across their translucent surfaces. Thousands upon thousands of Iwen were spread out on these bubbles, the curve of her waist looking as though someone had squeezed her from behind. Thousands upon thousands of Iwen, rippled in rainbow, descended gracefully on every single round table and burst in front of everyone. When Yi-Wei gazed into Iwen's eyes, he looked like he wanted to drown inside of them. The symphony began to play loud music, thunderous applause arose; flashes of light made the girls feel like they were living inside a diamond. They realized later that what actually fascinated them was how much the bride looked like Si-Chi. And how the wedding was a rehearsal for their future happiness.

The bridal chamber was in the apartment right below Mr. and Mrs. Chien's penthouse. They bought the entire floor for the newlyweds and renovated the space so the two apartments came together as one. Yi-Wei waited until that night to show Iwen what he had in the velvet box: a necklace with twelve pink diamonds. Yi-Wei told her, "I don't really know jewelry, so I went to Maomao's shop and asked for his best pink diamonds."

"When was this?" Iwen laughed.

"When I met you for the first time, I noticed that everything you had in your bag was pink, so I went straight to Maomao right after that."

Iwen laughed, blossoming with joy.

"Do you buy diamonds for girls that you just met?"

"Never, only you."

"Really? How can I be so sure?" Iwen couldn't stop laughing.

"You can ask Maomao."

Iwen laughed so hard she fell out of her wedding gown. *Maomaomaomao*, she giggled, repeating the jeweler's name—it sounded like the word for "hairy."

"What kind of hair and where?" Yi-Wei's hand ran up Iwen's thigh.

"Maomao, no, no, you're so bad!" Stark naked except for the pink diamond necklace, Iwen ran around their new apartment, bending down to look at Yi-Wei's childhood pictures, hands on her waist, asking where they should put each book. Her tiny breasts standing firm like a pouty mouth, Iwen rolled herself on the Turkish carpet and sprawled her arms open, the lines under her armpits looking more naked than her breasts. The symmetrical pattern of the Arabian carpet spread out its vines and tied her up in it, a feast for the eyes. Those first several months of marriage were the golden sash in the river of Iwen's life.

Hsu Iwen's first visitors after she moved into this apartment were the two girls. They came not long after the wedding. The first thing Yi-Ting said was, "Yi-Wei told us his girlfriend knows a lot more than we do." Si-Chi laughed so hard that her stomach hurt. "Oh, Liu Yi-Ting, we're being so rude." Iwen liked them right away.

"Please come in, my little ladies."

In Yi-Wei and Iwen's apartment, one full wall served as a bookshelf. The compartments were deep enough for them to display all their books, along with an assortment of decorative objects that used to belong to old Mr. Chien. The inside of the glazed teapot reflected the colors of grapes, pomegranates, apples, and apple leaves. Fruits climbed all over the exterior of the teapot, which blocked the collected works of André Gide so they could only make out a single word from certain spines, like *Strait Is the Gate* and *The Vatican Cellars*. As they looked closer, all they could see on the books became *Narrow, Van, Tian, An, Human, Kake, Like, Du, Day*. All the Chinese characters conveyed a sense of concealment. They also read like someone desperately calling for help.

Hsu Iwen said, "I'm Hsu Iwen. *I* as in 'the beloved one on the other side of the autumn water,' *wen* as in 'tattoo,' but you can just call me Iwen." Si-Chi and Yi-Ting relaxed in front of Iwen and the books, and they replied, "Just call me Si-Chi!" and "Just call me Yi-Ting!" and then they all laughed together. Both girls were surprised that Iwen looked even more stunning than she had on her wedding day. Some people were like a masterful painting: at first they could be admired as a whole, but if you looked closer, you'd recognize that every single brushstroke and texture was part of the art. It was art that you could look at for your entire life. Seeing both girls staring at the bookshelves, Iwen said, apologetically, "We don't have all the books here. But if you'd like to read anything that's missing, I can always bring them from my parents' home." The girls pointed at the bookshelves and asked, "Isn't it hard to reach the books?" Iwen laughed and said, "If I break anything, I'll blame Gide." They broke into laughter all over again.

As they grew from girls into young women, they borrowed books and listened to Iwen read countless times. As the years went by, they never heard of Iwen breaking anything from the bookshelves. They didn't know she had to wipe her hands clean before taking down the heavy sculptures and pay attention to the slippers and the carpet, mindful not to leave sweat or fingerprints anywhere. These were exquisite tortures that came from old Mrs. Chien, who blamed Iwen for distancing her from her son. He went from being a room away to a floor away. Moreover, old Mrs. Chien didn't think Iwen was his perfect match. Back then, Iwen was still able to wear short sleeves and shorts every day.

After less than a year of marriage, Yi-Wei began to beat Iwen. Yi-Wei finished work on time at 7:00 p.m. but would get a call at 10:00 p.m. to meet up with and entertain clients. One time, Iwen was next to him peeling an apple and overheard a call that made her stop mid-slice. At 2:00 or 3:00 a.m., Yi-Wei finally got back home. Lying in bed, Iwen could see the lock and the key biting into one another. From the whiff of tobacco and alcohol, she knew that he was approaching. But there was nowhere she could run away to. The next day, right after work, he came straight back home and apologized to her, begging for forgiveness and pleasure in a drooling face. New bruises on Iwen bloomed in the colors of eggplant and red-orange shrimp; the old bruises became discolored like fox or mink hair, or over-brewed tea. When she took showers, Iwen would place her hand on top of an injury that was bigger than her palm and look at the new injuries on top of old bruises, their colors intertwining like tropical fish. Only in the shower was she able to keep her crying and murmuring away from Yi-Wei. That night, she heard Yi-Wei speaking on the phone again. Once he hung up and began to get dressed, Iwen stood outside of his changing room and asked, "Can you stay in tonight?" Yi-Wei opened the door and saw Iwen blinking, the light in her eyes faltering. He kissed her cheek and went out the door.

As Iwen had watched the staff roll out the red carpet on the day of their wedding, she had suddenly been consumed by the idea of being swallowed by a long, red tongue. It was the most beautiful moment in her life. She later realized that a wedding was always meant to be the most beautiful moment of a woman's life. This not only meant that a woman's inner and outer beauty would decline thereafter but also implied that women should automatically seal their charms and sexual desires into Pandora's box. The king-size bed shared by Iwen and Yi-Wei was the only place where Iwen could reveal her beauty again. That bed was where she died and came back to life over and over. The harshest thing she ever managed to say through gritted teeth was, "You can't fuck me in the afternoon and beat me at night!" Hearing that, Yi-Wei only laughed and unbuttoned himself. He laughed so much that the corners of his eyes squeezed into wrinkles. That pair of eyes looked like a pair of fish, swimming toward her, looking for kisses. Yi-Wei, sober, was the most adorable man in the world.

———————

Lee Guo-Hua and his wife took their daughter, Xixi, to visit Yi-Wei and Iwen. When they arrived, Iwen squatted down and greeted Xixi: "Hi, how are you?" Xixi had long hair that reached her hips, which she refused to cut no matter what. She had her mother's big eyes and her father's straight nose. She was ten at the time and insisted on buying clothes that suited her own taste. Xixi didn't respond to Iwen and just twirled her hair. Iwen brought back two cups of hot tea, poured a cup of juice and said, "Sorry my husband can't be here today; he's on a business trip in Japan right now." Xixi spun around in the swivel chair, bored by all the decor in the living room—all that culture.

Lee Guo-Hua began to talk about the living room's decor. Like a cock, his words instinctively swelled with extravagance in front of a beautiful woman. No harm in hitting on a woman in her twenties. He pointed at a jade Guanyin sculpture on the bookshelf, his index finger firm with excitement. He said, "I can tell at a glance that the stone used for this Guanyin is superb: it's crystal clear and green with luster." The Guanyin sculpture was sitting with its right foot curved and its left foot dangling in midair, its fat big toe poking out and revealing the shiny frame of its wide toenail.

Lee Guo-Hua continued. "Ah, that pose it's in is called the 'casual Guanyin.' Guan-Shi-Yin Bodhisattva is the one who looks over the world. *Guan* as in observing, *Shi* as in the world, and *Yin* as in the sound of music, which means a good man

35

looking over the world with great compassion. Casual, natural, go with the flow, all the synonyms you can think of—you read literature, you'll definitely know what I'm talking about. What's interesting about this is, in Asian cultures, men prefer a mature and plump figure; by contrast, in Western culture, they prefer youthful or childlike features. Otherwise they'd all look like Jesus, a tiny adult the minute he was born."

Xixi craned her neck and sipped her juice. She turned to her parents and grumbled, "You both know I hate orange juice." Iwen knew right away that what Xixi meant was she didn't enjoy these conversations. Iwen stood up and went to the fridge, asking, "What about grape juice?" Xixi said nothing.

Lee Guo-Hua continued looking around, but there was too much Western art that he didn't understand. If he didn't speak up about it, nobody would discover his ignorance.

"Oh, the little painting right above the fireplace, is that a real one? I've never seen a real painting from Bada Shanren before. Look at that pair of eyes on the chicken. Bada Shanren always drew eyes as a dot in a circle. It wasn't until the twenty-first century that people started to realize this painting style is more realistic and intricate than any gongbi style. Maybe you should take a look at the sales at Sotheby's, that's what I'm talking about—the ability to observe properly! Your husband is so busy, *aiya*, how I wish I were the owner of this apartment."

Lee Guo-Hua looked into Iwen's eyes. "I'm the kind of person who wants to own anything that I find beautiful." And then Lee Guo-Hua thought, *Why am I acting like this after just one drink—I only had a cup of tea. Anyway, she's safe, and I should never touch anyone or anything from the Chien family. Also, isn't she turning thirty in a few years?*

Suddenly, Xixi spoke like she had screws in her mouth. "I hate grape juice, too! I hate anything that's condensed!" Lee Guo-Hua's wife shooshed her. Iwen's temples began to throb, and she started to look forward to Si-Chi and Yi-Ting's visit in the evening.

Once Lee Guo-Hua and his family were gone, Iwen felt like the smell of antiques, history, and art had somehow been replaced by the odor of cheap mall cologne. She didn't like Teacher Lee, but it was best to stay on good terms with her neighbors. She really wished that she could simply dislike him and that would be it. Ah, how passionate this sounded, like something from a movie: *I wish I knew how to quit you.* At the thought of that, Iwen laughed, feeling like an idiot. Xixi wasn't just immature; she was too lazy to even pretend that she was mature. Such a cute little girl, long eyelashes over her big eyes. Her hair was more beautiful than a waterfall.

Iwen ran her hand along the porcelain vase. It was so smooth that she felt like she was touching the metal base inside. The touch brought a sour taste to her mouth; the feel of the azure stone reminded her of the dull fish tank she had as a kid, the rough pottery that looked like a wrinkled newborn. All these little objects, in the shape of humans, monsters, or symbols, or even gods, sat there and watched her get beaten up. Even the Guanyin Bodhisattva never helped her. Real silk was so smooth, like the mucus sliding out from her nose in the morning. Yi-Wei also had allergies. Touching this jade sculpture was like touching Yi-Wei.

Iwen didn't understand why Si-Chi and Yi-Ting liked Teacher Lee so much, especially since they hated being told what to do. Such superlative works of art were transformed into priceless cultural relics by the way he spoke. Was it because he was a teacher, and he couldn't help himself? Sometimes it was good to be ignorant. *Later, I'll read to the girls, and then Yi-Wei will get off work and come for me again.*

One day, Lee Guo-Hua finished his last class and rushed into the elevator when he arrived at his apartment building. Inside the elevator were two girls in their junior high school uniforms, the back of their necks against the golden railing in the elevator. They held back their smiles when the golden elevator door opened. Throwing his book bag over his shoulder, Lee Guo-Hua bent over and asked, "Which one of you is Yi-Ting and which one is Si-Chi?"

"How do you know our names?" Yi-Ting quickly asked back.

After entering junior high, Si-Chi was often treated to breakfast and drinks out of nowhere by boys their age. Both Si-Chi and Yi-Ting had become instinctively defensive toward the opposite gender. But this person in front of them, his age seemed to surpass that of the men they had to be wary about.

Emboldened, Si-Chi said, "I'll respond to either name, Liu Yi-Ting or Fang Si-Chi."

Lee Guo-Hua could tell that they felt safe around him, and for the first time, he was grateful to be his age. On the girls' faces, he saw traces of the two mothers living upstairs, and then he knew the answer. Fang Si-Chi had a face like a newborn lamb. Lee Guo-Hua straightened himself up.

"I'm Teacher Lee. I just moved in downstairs. I also happen to teach Chinese literature, so if you ever need any books to read, you can always borrow from me."

Yes. Try his best to play it subtle. As subtle as a literary style from the late Ming dynasty. He coughed to convey his image as a respectable older man. Why did this elevator have to travel so fast? He reached out his hand; the girls paused for a moment, then took turns shaking it. They looked like they were about to laugh, their faces on the verge of a smile. One step further and they might burst. Once he was out of the elevator, Lee Guo-Hua began to wonder if this was going too far. He wouldn't lay a finger on rich kids because that meant trouble. And based on the expression on Yi-Ting's pockmarked face, he thought that maybe the girls only had eyes for each other. The look on their faces when they shook hands with him! Their bookshelves alone announced that they wanted to be treated as adults. Their hands were soft as a mother's breasts. Palms like quail eggs, the heart of a poem. Maybe something will work out in the future; you never know.

On the weekend, the girls followed their mothers to visit Lee Guo-Hua. They changed out of their uniforms. Yi-Ting wore her long pants while Si-Chi wore her skirt, outfits that would become symbolic. Once they entered his home and changed into slippers, Si-Chi blushed and thought, *Ah, I'm wearing these shoes without socks!* When she curled up her toes, Lee Guo-Hua saw her toenails were colored pink, shiny, and somewhat shy. It was not just that the landscape was ashamed of its ruined scenery, but the landscape was also ashamed of itself. Mama Fang asked the girls to greet Teacher Lee, which they did. Mama Liu apologized for how indifferently they said the word "Teacher." The girls were much too mischievous. Lee Guo-Hua thought, *What a beautiful word, "mischievous"; nobody over fourteen could penetrate that word.* Mama Liu and Mama Fang reminded the girls to say "please," "thank you," and "excuse me" before they left them in the room.

The girls were very patient when it came to spending time with Xixi. Only two years younger than they were, Xixi was practically illiterate compared to them. In spite of this, Xixi was very opinionated about many things, like how she was supposed to read picture books out loud. If you weren't listening closely, she might have sounded like a little eunuch on the television announcing some sacred statutes. Xixi struggled to read, and once when Si-Chi was about to explain a Chinese character to her, she threw the book and yelled, "Papa is an idiot!" But all that Lee Guo-Hua saw when the picture book snapped shut was the wind lifting Si-Chi's bangs. He knew that it was even more forbidden to lift up a girl's bangs than her skirt. When Si-Chi's bangs flew up, it was as though she was dropping down from somewhere high. Her long neck supported her egg-like face; her forehead was as full as a burp from a satisfied baby. Lee Guo-Hua thought Si-Chi was like a pixie out of a fairy tale, able to understand human language and trying its best to comprehend him. Shocked by her outburst, the girls looked at Xixi, then turned toward Teacher Lee. His only hope in this moment was that he didn't look even older than he actually was. Si-Chi and Yi-Ting would understand many years later that Teacher Lee had intentionally made Xixi stupid because he knew very well what a highly literate person could do to him.

Teacher Lee said to them softly, "What about this? I have a

collection of Nobel Prize–winning literature." *Xixi, these Nobel Prize books, they're all here together at the right time and place.* He was supposed to play a good father who looked forward to his daughter's love. A teacher who occasionally revealed his soul, a nomad drifting all the way to middle age, still misunderstood in his role as a Chinese literature teacher. The entire wall of classics marked all his academic knowledge. One textbook marked his solitude; one novel represented his soul. It didn't matter if they had taken his classes or not. It didn't matter whose daughter it was.

———

Standing at the cram school podium, Lee Guo-Hua confronted an ocean of twirling black hair. The students who had finished taking notes and lifted their heads looked like swimmers trying to catch their breath. He walked back and forth in front of the blackboard, as though drawing a traditional landscape painting. He lived in the scenery he created. How curious it was, the pressure brought by college entrance exams! In his life, there was only the cram school and the female students from the elite school. Grinding it down, the pressure distilled into love letters sealed in pink, scented envelopes. Some of the girls were so ugly! Faces full of red rashes, their rough hands stretching out as though they were ready to pull back an arrow to launch letters toward him. So ugly! Even if he didn't need to force himself on them, he wouldn't want to touch some of these ugly ducklings. But it was because of them that he was able to fill that paper box at his secret apartment with love letters. Most of the beautiful girls he brought to that apartment had all fallen intoxicated into the ocean of pink envelopes. No matter how beautiful they were, though, none of them had ever gotten as many letters as him. Some of them became much more compliant after finding that paper box. As for the others, even if they resisted, he was willing to believe that they were convinced at the sight of these letters and wanted to prove their eagerness to him.

One girl stayed up from 1:00 a.m. to 2:00 a.m. to outdo her classmate; this classmate stayed up from 2:00 a.m. to 3:00 a.m. to outdo this girl. An ugly girl working hard to beat tens of thousands of exam participants. All these midnight lamps combined were hotter than the sun at high noon. Under such intense pressure, the girls' nostalgia for carefree days and delusions of future romantic fulfillment were all projected onto Teacher Lee. The girls talked about him while grading each other's exam papers, saying that it was because of Teacher Lee that they fell in love with Chinese literature. They said so without realizing that it sounded like they loved him only because they had to study for this exam. That their excitement for cram school was also tinged with desire; that this desire was actually despair. Thanks to his straight nose, and thanks to his sophisticated humor. Thanks to his whimsical handwriting on the blackboard. To stand out among tens of thousands of students required summoning as much energy as them all, distilling that power into meticulous, elegant handwriting etched onto a love letter. Those swaying ponytails were not only elegant but trembling with desire. A paper box full of so many girls' calls of the wild! If those girls were only half as beautiful as their handwriting, it would be more than enough. He shot such grand desires into these beautiful girls, along with the suffering, cruelty, and inhumanity of the Taiwanese academic system. Girls determined to stay up and study 365 days a year—for an ugly duckling, that effort multiplied by the tens of thousands of students to beat. He shot this whole load into these beautiful girls: the grandiose climax, the seduction of the epics, and the glorious ideology of getting into the right college.

Most of the students in the cram school were at least sixteen, long gone from the Island of Lolita. Fang Si-Chi was only twelve or thirteen at the time, still astride the tree branches on this island, licked over by the waves. He never touched girls from wealthy families because that would mean trouble. A porcelain girl would never break unless somebody made her fall. Having a romance with her would be great, too, very different from helping a student enter the best university; a love affair could genuinely change someone's life. It was also different from paying for sex. A girl seeing a penis for the first time, laughing at the ugly veins protruding on it; crying like a dog over how she could contain its entirety; crying with her upper face, but laughing with her lower face, as though confused about her feelings. It took a while for him to open her legs. He didn't have time to glimpse the little bow on the underwear, the one that stopped right under her navel. It was true, he did it all just for that confused facial expression. What was he looking for? What else couldn't he get? Fang Si-Chi's bookshelf was a record of her attempt to leave Lolita Island, only to be spat back out onto the beach by the ocean.

The Island of Lolita. The island he'd been trying to reach, that remained a mystery to him. The kingdom of milk and honey. Milk from her breasts, and honey in the essence of her body. He should visit her while she was still on the island. The index and middle fingers on his right hand formed 人, the character for "person," walking into her vagina. Push her down onto the Nobel Prize–winning anthologies, the entire set of books, even the spirit of Nobel, trembling along with her. Tell her that she was the pearl white hope of his chaotic middle age. First let her shatter in these words, the sea of words that junior high school boys could not yet understand. Let her feel herself growing up in these words, make her soul lie to her body. Her, a junior high school student with a mouth full of sophisticated words. Push her uniform skirt all the way up to her waist, chase the bow to her ankles, tell her he was going to push in from behind. This way, her body would be able to catch up with her soul. His upstairs neighbor, the most dangerous place, was also the safest place. A porcelain girl. A girl purer than a virgin. He hungered to see how Fang Si-Chi would laugh and cry at the same time. Otherwise it would feel like he had collected the hair ornaments of all the concubines of the Qing dynasty while still missing the empress.

The first time Lee Guo-Hua saw Fang Si-Chi was that painterly moment when the golden elevator door opened. When they spoke to each other, Si-Chi casually leaned her head sideways against the mirror and didn't even try to look at herself. How blasé. In the mirror, her cheeks appeared bright yellow, just like the imperial robes that he collected. The kind of color that only the emperor was allowed to use. The color that was noble in its essence. Maybe she didn't understand how beauty wielded the powers of destruction at the time. Underneath the school number sewn on her uniform appeared the faint edge of a pink bra. That edge without any lace, a bra that belonged to an innocent girl! A bra without any smooth wire! The white socks on her feet looked rather vulgar. *When looking for pure white, even the snow looks too dark.* How did the next sentence go? He couldn't remember in that moment. It didn't matter, anyway. It wasn't among the must-read educational materials circulated by the Ministry of Education.

———

It was getting close to autumn then, a hot autumn. During the week, Lee Guo-Hua split his time with four days in the south and three days in Taipei. One day, he went up on the Maokong Gondola to drink with a few other teachers from the same cram school. There were usually fewer people in the mountains, and it'd be easier for them to talk there.

"If I were Chen Shui-bian, I'd become a consultant for a consortium only after leaving the presidency. Who would start taking money when he was still in the position? So stupid," the English teacher said.

The math teacher said, "Earning seven hundred million dollars with the movie *Cape No. 7* is not a lot, to be honest. But Chen Shui-bian should go to jail for forty years just for saying 'One Country on Each Side' to China."

The English teacher replied, "He doesn't even have the honesty a politician should have. Before the presidency, there were the Four Noes, and by the end they became the Four Yeses. Asking for this and that, it's just like that English saying, 'Don't upset the big boss.'"

"I saw in the newspapers that many intellectuals are supporting Taiwan's independence," the physics teacher said.

"That's because most intellectuals lack common sense," Teacher Lee said.

The four of them laughed, satisfied with their own common sense.

The English teacher added, "Nowadays, I just change the channel whenever I see Chen Shui-bian on the TV, unless Diana Chen is speaking."

This made Teacher Lee laugh. "Do you like older women? I don't; she looks too much like my wife." An elegant pass, touching down on the topic of conversation that interested them most.

"Are you still with that girl, the one who wants to be a singer? How long has it been? Incredible how long it's lasted, no different from how I go home every night to my wife," the English teacher asked the physics teacher. The other two teachers burst out laughing.

The physics teacher smiled with a blossoming kindness. "She said it's too hard to become a singer," he said, sounding like he was talking about his daughter.

"So she's modeling now."

"Will she be on TV?"

The physics teacher took off his glasses and wiped away the grease on the nose pads, his eyes in a trance. Looking rather humble, he said, "She was in an ad."

The three other teachers nearly applauded together, praising the physics teacher's bravery. Teacher Lee asked, "What if someone gets jealous?" And it looked like the physics teacher was going to wipe his glasses permanently. He stayed silent.

Then, the math teacher began, "I've already fucked three honor guard captains. One more and it'll be a grand slam."

Cheers. Cheers to Chen Shui-bian's seven hundred million dollars' worth of meals in jail. Cheers to those Taiwanese independence supporters with only knowledge but no common sense. Cheers to all the young girls who diligently took notes in sex ed without having any sexual common sense. Cheers to the teachers for filling the girls' grandiose emptiness as they prepare for the college entrance exam.

"I never say no," the English teacher said. "I don't know why you guys are so set in your ways. You're more stubborn than the girls."

"You're such a player. After being with those girls for a while, you'll find that the ugliest women are also the biggest romantics. I don't have that big of a heart," Teacher Lee said. Looking at the bottom of his glass coyly, he added, "And I like to play games."

The English teacher asked, "But if you don't really care about them, isn't it exhausting to pretend?"

Lee Guo-Hua thought about it. He counted the girls he'd been with. He'd found that fucking a little girl who deeply admired you was the most efficient way to keep her close. The more attached they were, the more hurt they felt when he tossed them aside. He liked trying out sweet words on one girl so he could use them again for the next. This permanent continuity was extremely beautiful, and economical, too. The centrifugal force from the act of tossing away was even more stunning, just like in a movie. The female protagonist takes the camera, spinning in the snow. Her face blocks the lens, the background a scenery. A square courtyard streaks by like the view from a high-speed train; with force, space stretches into time, as flesh and blood blur together. So stunning. This was very hard to explain to the English teacher; he was too big-hearted. The English teacher would never understand the eternal peace Lee Guo-Hua felt when he first heard that a girl he slept with died by suicide. It was like hearing Li Bai's "Song of Purity and Peace" after a tsunami. To end your life for a man was the greatest compliment you could give to him. He didn't care if it had been for him or because of him; it made no difference.

The math teacher asked Teacher Lee, "Are you still with the sophomore in Taipei? Or was she a senior?"

Teacher Lee murmured no and sighed with his nostrils. "I'm getting worn out. But you know, the new semester hasn't started yet, and there are no new students. Might as well keep it going."

The physics teacher had put on his glasses at some point. He suddenly raised his voice and spoke as though to himself. "One day I was watching TV with my wife, and she didn't even bother to tell me that *her* ads had started airing."

The others' hands took turns slapping his shoulder like falling leaves. Cheers! Cheers to the unspoken sentimental tradition of the teacher-student romance on both sides of the Taiwan Strait. Cheers to the homewrecker who jumped from the TV into the living room. Cheers to the husband who gets home from the motel and can still have sex with his wife with the lights on. Cheers to the start of the semester.

"Both of you are bigger prudes than any of those girls," the English teacher told the physics teacher and Teacher Lee. "I don't know why you're waiting around for the incoming students."

The wire of the gondola outside the restaurant scraped layers of clouds open. The gondolas were far away and tiny. The one closest to their window slowly climbed uphill, while another gradually descended on the other side. It was like a string of Buddha beads being counted, one by one. In Teacher Lee's heart,

Li Bai's ancient "Song of Purity and Peace" suddenly began to play. The clouds reminded him of their light clothes; the flowers reminded him of their faces. Even though it was close to autumn, most trees in Taiwan were still lush with deep-green leaves. Staring at the clouds, he thought about Fang Si-Chi. Not about her clothes, but something she had said during her first visit to his home. "My mama doesn't let me drink coffee, but I know how to make it." That simple sentence was full of profound meaning. Si-Chi had reached up for the grinder on the top shelf of the cabinet. Between her shirt and her skirt, she exposed a big chunk of pale belly. It was so delicate and pale, like the skipped blank space in an exam booklet full of green grids for writing Chinese characters. A blank space for an answer you'd remember only after turning in the paper. Such a vast blankness, making the teacher wonder what the student was trying to say there. When Si-Chi got the grinder, her shirt draped down like a stage curtain. She didn't look at him, but her face was red as she ground the coffee beans. During later visits, the grinder was always on the kitchen counter, so she didn't need to reach back up to the shelf again. However, whenever she took the grinder in her hands, her face always turned even redder than before.

The final thing that had made Lee Guo-Hua take this step with determination was Fang Si-Chi's self-esteem. Such an exquisite child would never talk about it with anyone. That would be too filthy. Self-esteem had always been a needle that harmed others and oneself, but here the needle would sew her mouth shut. All that Lee Guo-Hua needed at that moment was a thorough plan. He heard that Papa and Mama Fang often went on business trips, but perhaps the trickiest thing to deal with would

be her friend Liu Yi-Ting. When performing surgery on con-
joined twins, sometimes one had to decide which twin would get
to have a single organ. He only hoped that Fang Si-Chi would
cherish herself so much that she wouldn't even tell Liu Yi-Ting.
In the end, before the plan was even fermented, all that Lee Guo-
Hua wanted was offered to him on a silver platter.

———————

Mrs. Chang on the tenth floor was at her wits' end about her
daughter's marriage. Her daughter had just turned thirty-five
and still didn't have a partner. The candles on her birthday
cake looked ill and exhausted. Mrs. Chang's maiden name was
Lee, and she had endured hard times with Mr. Chang when
they were students. Later on, after Mr. Chang became rich, she
still held on to this sense of thrift. Mr. Chang retained all his
habits. After they graduated from college, Mr. Chang scooped
up the food in his soup to take home to feed his wife, who, at
that time, was still Miss Lee. Now, even though she was Mrs.
Chang, Mr. Chang still packed up the good leftovers to bring
back to his wife whenever he went out for business gatherings.
Most of his so-called friends laughed at him for being too old
school. Mr. Chang simply smiled and replied, "Only when these
delicacies are offered to bodies that overcame hard journeys do
I feel that I am fully respecting your generosity of this meal."
Mr. Chang felt no need to hurry along his daughter's marriage.
Though she had inherited her mother's plain looks and low
self-esteem, Mr. Chang still thought his daughter was adorable.

When Yi-Wei was still single, old Mr. Chien would get drunk
and shout at Mr. Chang, "We'll take your daughter in." Mrs.

Chang would raise her wineglass with both hands and say their daughter could never be a match for the Chien family. And then back home, she would tell Mr. Chang, "I don't know how many girls Chien Yi-Wei has beaten up, but I'd rather be poor than marry Wan-Ru off to him." When she heard this, Chang Wan-Ru didn't feel that her mother was protecting her. She only felt miserable. Whenever she bumped into Chien Yi-Wei in the elevator, the lingering silence between them suffocated her. But Chien Yi-Wei was always at ease, as though he'd never heard his parents joking about the two of them. Or maybe he took it completely as a joke. Such a thought made Wan-Ru even angrier.

In the days leading up to Chang Wan-Ru's thirty-fifth birthday, Mama Chang's face looked like she was counting down to Armageddon. Mama Chang brought out pearl barley soup with pale yam and stir-fried beef with edamame to reduce edema; the dessert was purple rice that promoted blood circulation. All Wan-Ru did was lift up her bowl and gulp down everything. The lenses of her thick glasses were smothered with a layer of fog. Mama Chang was unable to see through it and tell whether her daughter was angry or sad. Maybe she felt nothing at all.

Not long after Wan-Ru's birthday, she announced to her family that she'd found a boyfriend on her business trip to Singapore. Her boyfriend was an overseas Chinese, and whenever he spoke, it reminded Si-Chi of the scents of exotic spices and tropical pitcher plants. He looked exotic, too: high eyebrows with deep eyes, a dent under his nose and a pouty upper lip. He was handsome from all angles. Like Wan-Ru, he excelled in school; he'd been her senior in the same master's program in the US. It was rumored that the betrothal came with a wooden box full of

American money. He was also good with words, saying things like, "This is all that I can give. Wan-Ru and I both studied finance, but Wan-Ru is priceless." Si-Chi and Yi-Ting didn't know the groom's name, so they just called him "The Boyfriend." For the next ten years or so, Liu Yi-Ting often heard Mrs. Chang say, "Don't judge my daughter, Wan-Ru, by her appearance! She may look quiet, but I must say that she's the one who had her pick; she wasn't waiting to be chosen by someone else." Whenever Mrs. Chang talked about opening the wooden box, she said what was inside had been greener than a fresh lawn.

After Wan-Ru got married and moved to Singapore, Mrs. Chang began to talk about how she worried about other people's marriages, and how the road toward marriage was one of perseverance. Soon she introduced Iwen to Yi-Wei.

One time, Mrs. Chang bumped into Lee Guo-Hua in the elevator. She immediately said, "Teacher Lee, it's such a pity you haven't met my Wan-Ru! Don't be fooled by her quiet appearance; she attracts all the best guys!" And then she lowered her voice. "Old Mr. Chien always wanted me to marry her off to Yi-Wei!"

"Really?" Lee Guo-Hua immediately thought of Iwen. The moment she wore her slippers to the kitchen sink, the back of her feet pink against her bones. On her calves were several mosquito bites, also pink.

"Why not?" Lee Guo-Hua asked.

"My Wan-Ru is headstrong, and Yi-Wei needs more of an obedient woman. Iwen is the one who's babysitting all day for the neighbors!"

"Whose children? Aren't they Mr. Liu's and Mr. Fang's daughters?"

"The ones who live on the seventh floor."

Hearing that, Lee Guo-Hua felt a stirring in his loins that he'd never felt before.

Mrs. Chang continued, "I don't know why kids are so into literature. Ah, Teacher Lee, you don't look like someone who gets caught up in amorous thoughts. Wan-Ru and her husband both studied business. I said of course you need to study business—it's more useful!"

Lee Guo-Hua wasn't really listening. He simply stared at Mrs. Chang's open mouth. He nodded deeply. Those nods were the shows of obedience of someone who was distracted. In his eyes was the pure gaze of someone about to confront his deepest depravity.

———

Whenever Si-Chi and Yi-Ting finished school, they headed straight to Iwen's apartment. Iwen would prepare savory snacks, sweets, and juice. The snacks would still be warm when they arrived. Lately, they'd been fascinated by literary works from China's Cultural Revolution. Today, Iwen played the Zhang Yimou film *To Live*. The wide screen in the home theater unfurled like a sacred edict, while the projector buzzed. Iwen skipped giving the girls popcorn to make the mood more solemn. The three of them curled up on the leather sofa, which was soft as warm sunshine. Before they started watching, Iwen said, "Don't just be idle spectators of other people's suffering, all right?" They both said yes, detaching their backs from the sofa and sitting straight up. Not long into the movie, in the scene when Fu-Gui is being carried back home from the casino,

Iwen lowered her voice and said to the girls, "My grandfather also used to be carried by someone to school, while other kids walked on their own feet. He felt embarrassed and told me, 'I always let the person who carried me chase me around all the time.'" And then the three of them fell into silence.

Fu-Gui's wife, Jiazhen, said, "I don't want anything. All I want is to spend quiet, peaceful days with you." The girls noticed from a side glance that Iwen was using her sleeve to wipe away tears. And then it occurred to them that autumn was arriving late that year; it was so hot that they still had the fans on. So why, at this moment, was Iwen wearing a turtleneck with long sleeves? They were drawn back to the shadow puppetry in the movie. Without turning their heads, they knew that Iwen was still crying. A series of rings at the doorbell pierced through the shadow puppets scene, then pierced through the projector screen that hung down. Iwen didn't seem to hear it. Her life was full of movies, and within the movies there were dramas. Her life was also full of dramas. Si-Chi and Yi-Ting hesitated to get Iwen's attention. On the third ring, Iwen suddenly awakened as if struck, patted her cheeks, and ran out of the home theater. Before leaving the room, she told them, "Don't wait for me. I've already seen it so many times." A trail of tears crawled down from Iwen's eyes, reflecting the lights from the movie. They looked like the colored popsicles in the amusement park, the tear marks streaming out from Iwen's iridescent eyes.

Another scene went by. The girls were having a hard time paying attention to the movie, but they felt like they couldn't talk about Iwen while they were in her home. They stared at the screen in a trance, the kind of trance that only intellectuals have when faced with a dilemma. Iwen, such a beautiful, determined, and audacious woman. Suddenly, the door to the home theater opened and the yellow lights from the outside projected into the darkness. They immediately saw that it was Teacher Lee. He was silhouetted in the doorframe, and all the girls could see was the contour of his hairline and the lint on his shirt shining silver. The fan continued blowing, sprinkling golden dust from underneath Teacher Lee's armpit. His face was buried in the shadows, and it was hard to see clearly in his direction. Like a faceless angel in an Islamic fresco. The silhouette of Teacher Lee softly approached them, while Iwen quickly followed behind. She squatted in front of them, her tears dried, colors from the projector lighting up her face. Iwen said, "Teacher Lee is here to see both of you."

Lee Guo-Hua said, "I just happen to have a lot of high school reference books. And so I thought about giving them to you girls. Not trying to compare you to other kids, but it might even be a bit too late to give you these books. I just hope that they're useful."

The girls immediately thanked him. They also had some selfish thoughts. They thought Teacher Lee had saved them from the shock of witnessing their goddess Iwen break down. Seeing her cry for the first time felt like she'd desecrated herself even more than if she had pooped in front of them. When the tears streamed down Iwen's face, it was like her face zipped open and revealed the ruined cotton beneath a shell of gold. To see Iwen cry was like finding out that a popular idol did drugs. All they wanted was to be children for now. Teacher Lee had scooped them up from the edge of the evil side of the world, spitting them out of this tense situation.

Lee Guo-Hua said, "I have a thought. How about both of you submit an essay to me every week? When I'm in Kaohsiung, that is."

Si-Chi and Yi-Ting agreed immediately.

"Let's start tomorrow then. And what if I correct your essays every other week, then we can discuss them together? My hourly rate is over ten thousand New Taiwan dollars, but of course I won't charge you girls." Iwen realized that it was a joke and laughed with them, but she still looked a bit lost in her own world. "The essay topic . . . I recently asked my other students to write about honesty, so let's write about honesty, deal? I suppose both of you girls wouldn't be interested in writing about your dreams or your future, those kinds of topics, right? The more personal the topic is, the more the students write themselves out of it."

The girls thought, *Teacher Lee is so funny.* Iwen's smile gradually faded, but the lost expression was still stranded in her eyes.

Iwen didn't like Lee Guo-Hua at all. She didn't like that he was invading her time with the girls. When they'd first met, he couldn't stop staring at her, just like any other man. It was the kind of attitude that middle-class men had when asking for a menu at a food stand that didn't have one. The kind of greediness of "just checking it out." She felt weird around him most of the time, sensing judgment in his eyes. Much later, Iwen would find out that Lee Guo-Hua was trying to get a closer look at Iwen's face so he could superimpose Si-Chi's face on her. "Girls, make sure you submit your essays on time. I'm not even this generous with my own daughter." The girls thought, *Teacher Lee is so funny, so kind.* Liu Yi-Ting was never able to finish the film *To Live* after that.

The girls each submitted their essays to Lee Guo-Hua every week. After meeting up with them and Iwen together a few times, Lee Guo-Hua suddenly said that it was hard to discuss the essays thoroughly because they kept chattering when it was all four of them. He proposed that they should meet one-on-one at his place, with Si-Chi and Yi-Ting coming once a week on different days. The girls should visit him separately right after school, before his cram school classes began. Iwen stayed silent when she heard this; she felt awkward about competing with her neighbor for the girls' attention. Under this arrangement, she would see the girls two times less each week. The girls, who fed her wounded self with positive energy. Her beloved little women.

This was what Si-Chi wrote about honesty: "One of the very few virtues I have is honesty. I enjoy honesty, the untold intimacy and self-satisfaction of being honest with someone. The true meaning of honesty is that I can still be proud after confessing to my mother that I broke a vase." Yi-Ting wrote, "Honesty is a secret love letter pressed under a pillow. A corner of the envelope unintentionally peeks out, as if enticing someone to take a look inside." Fang Si-Chi had such self-esteem, of course. Holding a red pen, Lee Guo-Hua got so excited that he forgot to write for a long time and left a huge red stain. Liu Yi-Ting also wrote very well. Their essays read like they were talking about the same thing in different ways. But that didn't matter.

It happened on a day when Si-Chi thought Teacher Lee looked particularly delighted as he explained the course materials. As their conversation moved from essay writing to the most popular restaurants, he moved his hand on hers. She immediately blushed and tried to pull away, her face growing even redder. Under the desk, the blue pen dropped from her trembling hand. She bent over to pick it up, and when she lifted her head, the yellow light in the study room shone on Teacher Lee's greasy, smiling face. She watched the teacher rub his hands in anticipation. Like the wings of a golden swan. She was shaken. Because she could imagine how she looked under the flicker of that yellow ray of light. She never thought of Teacher Lee as a man, but little did she know that Teacher Lee had taken her fully as a woman. And then Teacher Lee opened his mouth. *Would you take the book that I mentioned earlier from the bookshelf?* Si-Chi, for the first time, noticed that Teacher Lee's voice was like the Yan Kai calligraphic script, as though tendons and veins were clear on the flesh, pressing down on her.

Si-Chi stood on her tiptoes and reached her hand toward the book. Lee Guo-Hua immediately approached her from behind, surrounding her with his body, his hands, and the wall of books. He slid his hand down from the upper corner of the bookshelf onto her hand that was resting on the book spine, then all the way down to circle her waist tightly. She didn't have any physical space to break from his embrace; she could feel the breath from his nose on the top of her head, moist like the sky outside the window. She could also feel his heart beating. He said nonchalantly, *I heard Yi-Ting say that you both really like me.* They were too close; the meaning of what Yi-Ting had said got twisted.

Tearing her clothes was more painful than tearing her open, this little girl. Ah, the thighs that were like spring bamboo, the butt that resembled frosted flowers. The plain little underwear, only for changing and not for pleasure. The little bow on the underwear that stopped right underneath her navel. Everything about her was white as paper, waiting for him to leave his mark.

Si-Chi's mouth was wriggling: *No, no, no, no.* It was the signal she and Yi-Ting used whenever they were caught in difficult situations. In his eyes, it looked like: *Now now* (no no) and *Do it do it* (don't don't). He turned her around and put her face in his palms, saying, *If that's no good, why don't you use your mouth?* His face had the helpless expression of a retail employee who had resigned himself to sell something at the lowest price after failing to bargain. Si-Chi made some sounds. *I can't. I don't know how.* He took it out and, as her fearful, lamblike face looked shocked before the veiny thing, stuck it in. Her mouth was warm and red as a bridal chamber, her teeth prickly like a beaded curtain. As she was about to vomit, her throat closed up, while his voice exploded: *Ah, my god!* Liu Yi-Ting would later read from Si-Chi's diary, "My god, what an unnatural sentence. Like a stilted translation from English, the way he forced me to flip myself over."

The next week, Si-Chi went downstairs again. She saw that there were no red and blue pens, no essay. Her heart was as desolate as the empty desk. He was taking a shower while she settled on the sofa. The sound of his showering was like static from a broken television. He bent her in half and carried her over his shoulder, twirling open the buttons on her uniform, one after the other, like blowing out candles on a birthday cake. He wanted to make a wish but he didn't know what to wish for. And she was completely extinguished. The shirt and skirt of the uniform were kicked down by the bed. She looked at her clothes and felt like she herself was lying in a heap down there. As his stubble rubbed her skin red and swollen, he said, *I'm a lion, and I'm going to mark my territory.* She immediately thought that she had to write that down. The way he spoke was so outdated. It wasn't that she was fascinated by his words, but rather that it would be too painful if she didn't think about something else. Too painful.

In her head, she started to generate metaphors. Her eyes had begun to get used to the bedroom with curtains drawn on each side. Some faint light came in through the crack between the curtains. With him on top of her, she watched the ceiling tumble up and down like a canoe. That moment was like ripping her favorite dress as a kid. Trying to look into his eyes was impossible, like trying to balance between two cars of a moving train, like looking at a portrait of wriggling intestines. Branches of crystal light bulbs made a circle, circling and circling endlessly, impossible to count. He circles incessantly. Life circles endlessly. When he barked on top of her, she felt that a part of her had been pierced to death before she could even know what it was. He had one hand against the headboard, watching her cry quietly into the pillow. Her wet, lamblike face looked like she'd just come out of the shower.

Lee Guo-Hua lay on the bed like a satisfied cat, thinking, *She didn't even make a sound while crying. Not even a noise when someone raped her. Bitch. Tiny little bitch.* Si-Chi found her clothes and squatted, burying her face in her shirt and skirt. She cried for two minutes without turning her head. Then, through gritted teeth, she said, *Don't look at me when I change.* Lee Guo-Hua used his arms as a pillow, feeling a bud of desire grow in him despite the vast fatigue after coming. Even without looking, he could still see her lips, red as an apple. The milk from the apple pulp, nipples like almonds, hole like a fig. The fig that helps strengthen the spleen, lubricate the intestines, and increase the appetite in traditional Chinese medicine. The fig to help polish the gemstone of his timeless fantasy. A little girl who thought that breaking her hymen would be harder to recover from than breaking her arms and legs. The fig that banished his desire, yet also baited it further. Her fig led to forbidden depths. She was the fig. She was the forbidden.

The silhouette of her back seemed to suggest she wouldn't understand the language he spoke. It was like how she stared at the wet and sticky underwear without knowing where it belonged. She put her clothes back on, hugged herself, and stared at the ground.

Lee Guo-Hua spoke to the ceiling. *This is how your teacher loves you, do you understand? Don't be mad at me. You're someone who reads a lot of books. You should know that beauty doesn't belong to itself. You're so beautiful, but you can't belong to everyone—you can only belong to me. Do you know? You're mine. You like your teacher, and your teacher likes you. We're not doing anything wrong. This is the ultimate pleasure for two people who like each other. You can't be mad at me. You don't know how much courage it took for me to make this move.*

The first time I met you, I knew it was fated that you would be my little angel. You know, when I read your essay, you said, "In love, I often see paradise. In this paradise, there are horses with hair of white gold kissing each other in pairs, while a little bit of steam rises from the ground." I never memorize my students' essays, but I really tasted paradise in you. Whenever I held my red pen, I thought of you biting your pen and writing down this sentence. Why are you always in my head? You can blame me for going too far. You can blame me for overdoing it. But can you blame my love for you? Can you blame your own beauty? Let's not forget, it's Teacher's Day a few days from now. You're the best present for Teacher's Day.

It didn't matter if she took his words in or not. Lee Guo-Hua thought he had spoken cleverly, drawing on his lecturing skills. He knew that she would still visit next week, and the week after that.

Si-Chi woke up on the main road that night not far from her place. It was raining cats and dogs, and her uniform was soaking wet. The thin, light clothing enclosed her body, her long hair stuck to her cheeks. Standing in the middle of the road, she let the headlights of passing cars swipe past her. But she didn't know when she had left her apartment, where she had gone to, or what she had done. She thought she had gone back home after leaving Teacher Lee's place. Or maybe, Teacher Lee had left her place. That was the first time Fang Si-Chi had partial memory loss.

One day after school, the girls went to Iwen and Yi-Wei's place to listen to Iwen read again. Iwen looked sick lately. When she read Gabriel García Márquez, her voice was loose and distracted, the story's meanings dissipated. Iwen was telling them about what excrement symbolized in Márquez's works. She said, "Excrement lets characters see desolation they must face in their everyday lives; excretion and discharge lets these characters understand the desolation in our own lives."

Yi-Ting suddenly said, "I look forward to visiting Teacher Lee every day." She said it as if she were just passing through Iwen's place, as though five days at Iwen's apartment were comparable to only one day at Teacher Lee's place. Right away, Yi-Ting knew that she had said something wrong. But Iwen simply responded, "Oh really?" And then she continued talking about pee and poop in Márquez's works in a very different tone. She sounded like she was squatting on the toilet, suffering from constipation like one

of his characters. Si-Chi blushed as though she'd become constipated as well. Yi-Ting's ignorance was beyond brutal, but nobody
could blame her. Nobody ever rode on her and beat her, and having nobody ride on her and beat her made it more unbearable. By
then, the girls already knew what it meant when Iwen wore long
sleeves. Si-Chi hated how Yi-Ting tried to get closer to Iwen to
make her feel better. She hated Yi-Ting's face at that moment.
She hated that Yi-Ting was complete and intact.

After the girls left, Hsu Iwen locked herself in the bathroom,
turned on the faucet, and started to cry into her palms. *Even the
kids pity me.* The faucet sloshed and sloshed and she stayed there
and cried for a very long time. Iwen saw the light coming in between her fingers, making her wedding ring shine. It was like Yi-
Wei's eyes when he laughed.

She liked how Yi-Wei smiled all the time, how whenever
Yi-Wei saw something pink he would buy it for her, from pink
pencils to a pink sports car. She liked how Yi-Wei would hug a
family-size carton of ice cream and dig into it while watching a
movie in the home theater, patting a side of his shoulder, telling her that it was her place. She liked how Yi-Wei would buy
the same shirt in seven different colors, how he would say "I
love you" in five languages. She liked to watch Yi-Wei dancing
the waltz by himself, how he would sometimes close his eyes,
touch her face, and say he wanted to remember her that way.
She liked how Yi-Wei would lift his head and ask her how to
write a specific character and then, while she was demonstrating, take her index finger into his mouth. She liked when Yi-Wei
was happy. She liked Yi-Wei. But look how brutally Yi-Wei had
beaten her up!

———

Whenever Fang Si-Chi took a shower, she put her fingers inside herself. Pain. She didn't know how he managed to enter such a narrow space. One day, when she put her fingers in again, it dawned on her what she was doing: *He wasn't the only one capable of taking away my childhood. I could do the same. He could want something, and I could want something, too. If I gave up on myself first, then he wouldn't be able to abandon me again. We said we'd love the teacher anyway. Your lover can do whatever he wants to you, can't he?*

What is true, and what is fake? Maybe truth and lies are not opposites, and maybe absolute deception exists in this world. She had been pierced, plugged, and stabbed. But the teacher said he loved her, and if she also loved the teacher, then that was love. Making love. Making endless love in the eternal night with elegance. She remembered that she had another future, but now she was the counterfeit of her past. A counterfeit without an original. She could go on writing an angry five-character quatrain forever, until it became a tragic, elegant, ancient poem over a thousand words long. When Teacher Lee closed the door, he put his index finger on his lips, saying, *Shh, this is our secret.* She could still feel that index finger in her body like a joystick and a motor. Remotely controlling her, dominating her, happily biting her mole. Evil is such plainness and plainness is so easy. Loving a teacher isn't hard after all.

You only had one chance at life, but it didn't mean that you had to seize the moment. Teacher Lee's mole floated there; his dyed hair could remain black for the rest of his life. Having only one chance at life meant that she was already a counterfeit even when she was not. She made her stuffed animals fight Yi-Ting's; danced around the green beans she placed on top of the wet cotton, wanting them to sprout faster; pretended the piano was her mean piano teacher. Yi-Ting would pound on the lowest key while she pounded on the highest key. They saw each other's reflection in the broth of bone transfer soup, which helped them grow to the perfect height. She fantasized about finding the horn of a unicorn and the tail of a phoenix in the soup. Having only one chance at life meant it was all about learning how to wriggle teacher out of her while being careful not to hurt him. It meant that although humans only lived once, they could die many times. These days, her thoughts chased closely after her; she was like a little animal who'd been running away for its life during a hunt and got caught in the branches and finally felt some relief. She had an excuse not to survive. Everything dawned on her at once. Her mood swung from great happiness to incredible grief. Si-Chi began to laugh in the bathroom, laughing so much that she started to tear up and burst out crying.

Lee Guo-Hua didn't wait until their usual lesson day and went to ring the Fang family's doorbell. Si-Chi was bending over the table, eating her dessert. When Mama Fang led Lee Guo-Hua to the living room, Si-Chi lifted her head and her eyes became soulless. She simply stared at him. He said, "The tiny oil painting in the corridor is so beautiful. Si-Chi must have painted it." He gave Si-Chi a book and told Mama Fang that there was a great exhibition in the municipal art museum. He wondered if Mr. and Mrs. Fang had the time to bring Si-Chi there. His daughter, Xixi, would never go with him; she wouldn't be interested.

Mama Fang asked, "Well then, how about you take our Si-Chi, Teacher Lee? Both of us are busy these days."

Lee Guo-Hua pretended to contemplate this and said yes in a very generous manner. Mama Fang turned to Si-Chi. "Why didn't you say thank you? Why don't you go and change?" In an unusually formal tone, Si-Chi said, "Thank you."

Before Teacher Lee had arrived, Si-Chi and her mother were having a casual conversation; so casual, it was as if they were smearing butter onto a piece of toast.

"Our tutors seem to teach us everything but sex education."

Her mother looked at her in shock. "Sex education? That's only for people who need to have sex, isn't it? Isn't *this* the real education?" Si-Chi understood better now. Her parents would be absent forever in this story. They skipped the classes and thought that the courses had never even taken place.

Si-Chi took the book Teacher Lee gave her and went back to her bedroom. She locked the door, standing behind it and frantically flipping the pages. She found a flier at the back of the book. She concentrated hard on this piece of paper, as though trying to pierce through life with her gaze. The flier came with the cutout of a tiny person, probably from the media section of the newspaper. It was a beautiful girl with long black hair. Si-Chi found herself laughing soundlessly. A book by Liu Yong, one of the most well-known authors based in Taiwan, with an image of an actress bookmarked inside. *This man is funnier than I thought.*

Much later, Yi-Ting would read from the diary: "If it hadn't been for Liu Yong and the cutout, maybe I would feel better. Let's say he even quoted some dramatic lines, like what Abélard wrote to Héloïse: 'You destroyed my sense of security and ruined my courage for philosophy.' I hate that he didn't even bother to cover up his vulgarity. I hate that he's no different than the boys from junior high school, hate that he thinks I'm just like any girl in junior high. He can't win me over with just a book from Liu Yong and some clippings from the newspaper. But it's too late. I'm already contaminated. There's another kind of happiness in being dirty. It's too painful to think about erasing that filth."

Si-Chi buried herself in the closet with her twirling thoughts. She couldn't wear something too fancy. She had to save some good outfits for future occasions. But then she thought, *Future?* Si-Chi knelt in front of an array of small dresses, thinking that she was an island surrounded by soft waves. Before heading out, Mama Fang told Si-Chi her teacher was waiting for her at the convenience store on the corner. She didn't remind her not to come home too late. When she went out of the building, heavy rain was coming down. She would be soaking wet when she reached the convenience store. Whatever. The farther she walked, the heavier her clothes weighed. Her feet felt like she was stepping in shoddily made paper boats. Trying to walk in pouring rain was like trying to sweep aside a beaded curtain. And then she saw a taxi at the corner of the road, the top of the car splashed with drops of rain that looked like crystal. When she entered the back seat, she first put her feet outside the car and dumped two cupfuls of water from her shoes. As for Lee Guo-Hua, he was sitting quietly without a single drop of rain on him.

Teacher Lee looked like he was very fond of her. The wrinkles from his smile looked like ripples in a puddle. Lee Guo-Hua said, "Remember what I told you about the history of Chinese figure painting? You're like the painter Tsao Zhongda with the tight garments, and I'm Wu Daozi with the floaty clothes."

Si-Chi squeezed out a smile.

"We're a dynasty apart ourselves."

Teacher Lee bent over the front seat and said, "Look, a rainbow!"

When Si-Chi looked forward, she only saw the young driver glimpse them through the rearview mirror. His eyes looked like a pair of blunt knives. The distance between them resembled the vast, separate landscapes in their eyes. The taxi brought them to a tiny hotel.

Lee Guo-Hua lay on the bed, hands creating a pillow behind his head. Si-Chi had already put on her clothes and sat on the carpet, fiddling with the fibers. When she smoothed the carpet through, it turned blue; when she smoothed it back, it became yellow. So many obscene memories weighing down such a beautiful carpet! She started to cry. He said, *I'm just looking for a smart and sensitive girl to talk to.* She snorted coldly with laughter. *You're lying to yourself.* He added, *Or maybe every little girl who wants to write well should experience a forbidden romance.* She laughed again, saying, *What an excuse.* He said, *Of course it's an excuse. Without any excuses, how could you and I go on living with it?* Lee Guo-Hua thought about how he liked her shame, and the morality that couldn't be washed away from her body. If their story were turned into a film, the narrator would describe her shame as the deep, dark lair of his shameless pleasure. He would come in the depths of her upbringing, rubbing her shame hard, rubbing it into a shape of shyness.

The following day, Si-Chi went downstairs and submitted her essay as usual. From that point on, Lee Guo-Hua often went upstairs to invite Si-Chi to various exhibitions.

Yi-Ting enjoyed her weekly private lessons. She got to spend time with Teacher Lee alone and listen to his anecdotes about important figures in Chinese literature. She felt like she was standing before a buffet, not knowing where to start the feast. She didn't want her time alone with Teacher Lee to be interrupted, so whenever it was Si-Chi's turn, by the same logic, she never knocked on Teacher Lee's door. The only time she interrupted their sessions was when Mama Fang insisted that Yi-Ting bring herbal drinks to soothe Teacher Lee's throat. Hell knows where Lee Guo-Hua actually needed soothing.

Teacher Lee looked gentler than usual when he answered the door. His face broadcast eternal peace. Bent over the table, Si-Chi lifted her head abruptly and gave Yi-Ting a purposeful look. Yi-Ting noticed that there were no pens and papers on the table, and Si-Chi looked weathered from battle. In this stuffy place, Si-Chi's hair looked rather frizzy. Lee Guo-Hua looked at Si-Chi, then at Yi-Ting, and smiled. "Is there something Si-Chi would like to tell Yi-Ting?" Si-Chi bit her trembling lips and then mouthed toward Yi-Ting, I'm all right. Yi-Ting replied, also mouthing, All right. I thought you were sick, silly. Lee Guo-Hua couldn't read their lips, but he was confident he would be able to brew a sense of shame from what he had done to Si-Chi.

The three of them sat around the table. Lee Guo-Hua smiled again and said, "I forgot where we were." He turned and looked at Si-Chi with gentleness. Si-Chi said, "Me too." They started to make small talk. Si-Chi thought, *If I grew up and walked outside all day in makeup . . . the oil surfacing beneath my blush might be a conversation like this, shallow and loose.* Growing up? Wearing makeup? Her hands fell at the thought. Sometimes, she thought she had died on Teacher's Day a year back. Sitting in front of Teacher Lee, she felt something between them, some kind of secret happiness that was going to burst out of the floorboard. She had to stomp down to keep it in check.

Yi-Ting said, "Confucius and his disciples are all bedfellows from the same school of philosophy."

Teacher Lee replied, "I can't say that in the classroom. Parents would complain."

Yi-Ting continued with reluctance, "Plato and the philosophers from the same school are also bedfellows or whatever you want to call it, aren't they, Si-Chi?"

Listening to both of them, Si-Chi realized that happiness could be everywhere, but none of it belonged to her.

"Si-Chi?"

"Oh, I'm sorry! I didn't hear what you said." Si-Chi felt her face rusting and her eyes burning. Lee Guo-Hua also noticed it and found an excuse to send Yi-Ting away.

Happiness to Fang Si-Chi was letting the teacher crush her body until she squeaked. It was letting the teacher watch her toss around the bed like a wave. The Buddha said happiness was floating in the sky of thoughts. As for her, happiness was drifting in the sky full of love. Her happiness was not a paradise full of love. It wasn't unlove, but it also wasn't hatred. It certainly wasn't indifference. She just hated everything involved. Whatever he gave her was for him to take away. Whatever he took away was for him to give back with full passion. Whenever Si-Chi thought of her teacher, she thought how the sun and the stars are the same thing. She was so happy, but so in pain. After locking the door, Lee Guo-Hua came back to suck her mouth. *Aren't you always asking if I love you?* Si-Chi pulled her lips away from him and put a metal spoon in her mouth. The smell was like the time she fell asleep and drooled all over the pencil traces on her sheet of paper. The essays she wrote during those two years without anyone actually reading and correcting them.

He tore her clothes off, thrusting against her and growling, *Ask me! Ask me if I love you! Ask!* Lee Guo-Hua casually lay down and closed his eyes. Not knowing when she had put her clothes back on, Si-Chi murmured, *I only remember this sentence, when Iwen read* One Hundred Years of Solitude *to us, "If he started to knock on the door, he would need to keep knocking on it—,"* to which Lee Guo-Hua replied, *I opened the door already.* Si-Chi said, *I know. I'm talking about myself.* In Lee Guo-Hua's head, he heard and saw Iwen, and felt an unprecedented peacefulness. A calm sea. He thought about how stunning Hsu Iwen was. But he had never come twice in such a short time. It was better to take the younger one.

One time, after Yi-Ting finished her essay, Teacher Lee happened to be out. She headed back upstairs, knocking on the Fang family's door. Si-Chi opened the door. There was nobody else. Still, they mouthed at each other. Yi-Ting said, Teacher Lee looks good with his face deep in sorrow.

"What?"

"He looks good with his face deep in sorrow!"

"I don't understand."

"Sorrow like he's grieving. His face looks like a Greek sculpture."

Si-Chi didn't reply.

"Don't you think?"

"I still don't understand."

Yi-Ting tore a page from her notebook and showed Si-Chi. "'Eyes plunged in deep sorrow. Deep eyes and arched eyebrows, looking sorrowful and full of deep thoughts.' Haven't you read this part of the book?" Yi-Ting stared at Si-Chi, her eyes full of triumph.

"Not yet."

"Teacher Lee is good-looking with those sorrowful eyes of his. Really! You'll probably get to that part next week!"

"Maybe. Probably next week."

Si-Chi and Yi-Ting were scheduled to spend days reviewing their essays with Teacher Lee throughout junior high. These days were like mile markers in the tedious repetition of student life. For Yi-Ting, these lessons were a hopeful start to every week. As for Si-Chi, her lessons were intrusive deep nights that broke into the long daylight, again and again.

Autumn arrived. One day, Yi-Ting visited Lee Guo-Hua while Si-Chi visited Iwen. When Iwen answered the door, she was watery-eyed. She looked like she had been pierced by a beam of sunlight after walking in the darkness for a long time. Iwen looked surprised, like a solitary person suddenly asked to speak to someone. She seemed unable to gather her words. She was so sheepish and vulnerable. It was the first time Si-Chi saw that Iwen had marks on her face. She didn't know that the scratches came from Yi-Wei's wedding ring. Their beautiful, determined, and audacious Iwen.

The two of them sat in the living room. A woman and a little girl. They were so beautiful, so alike, a smaller Russian doll taken from a bigger Russian doll. Iwen broke the ice and said, with a dimpled smile, "How about we sneak some coffee?"

Si-Chi replied, "I didn't know you had coffee at your place."

Iwen said, her dimples deepened, "My mother-in-law doesn't let me drink it. Chi-Chi, my dear, you know where I put everything. Should I be worried?"

It was the first time Si-Chi heard Iwen call her Chi-Chi. She didn't know if Iwen was trying to appeal to her or her own youth.

Iwen took Si-Chi for a ride in her pink sports car. She lowered the top of the convertible. The fresh air that swept over the car was so clean that it didn't feel like city air. Si-Chi realized she would never be able to discover the beauty of this world alone. After Teacher's Day in her first year in junior high school, she had stopped growing up. Lee Guo-Hua had been pressing against her, not letting her do so. Her hope and passion for life, her curiosity about existence, no matter what she called it, everything had been destroyed the moment someone entered inside her, completely squeezed her out. It was not nihilism, nor was it the nothingness of Taoism or Buddhism. It was the nothingness of math. Zero. Iwen noticed the tear streaks on Si-Chi's face in the blowing wind. She thought, *Ah, she looks just like me, lying in bed crying.*

Iwen opened her mouth. Her voice was full of sand and wind. It was not dusty sand or little rocks, but sand from a gold mine. "Do you want to talk about it?"

Iwen tried not to call her Chi-Chi again. When she did that earlier, she realized that she sounded motherly. They remained silent for two blocks, two green lights and two red lights. And then Si-Chi spoke, "Iwen, I'm sorry. I can't talk about this now."

The city with its vigorous construction sites, all excavators and gravel cars, surrounded and overlooked them. Iwen said,

"Don't be sorry. It's me who should be sorry. I don't make you feel comfortable enough to open up."

This made Si-Chi cry even harder. Her tears were so heavy that the wind couldn't even lift them. She spat back, "You also never tell me about what you're going through!"

Just then, Iwen's face became so sad that she looked like a doll with cotton stuffing coming out.

She replied, "I understand. There are some things we just can't talk about."

Si-Chi yelled, "Why do you have scratches on your face?"

Iwen slowly explained, one word after another, "I fell down. I was just being silly."

It shocked Si-Chi. She knew that Iwen was trying to tell her the truth. Iwen had uncovered her metaphorical clothes and exposed her metaphorical, ugly naked body. She knew that Iwen knew she would understand right away. The scratches on her face were like deep tear marks. Si-Chi thought she had just done something awful.

Mindlessly bending her fingers, Si-Chi lowered her voice to a volume that would let her words reach Iwen's ear and then get blown away right after. She said, "Iwen, I'm so sorry."

Placing one hand on the steering wheel, Iwen locked her eyes on the road ahead, straightened her hair, and said, "There's no need to apologize. It's not us who should be apologizing."

They parked the car right across from the shopping area. Every shopfront seemed luxurious. They sat in the sports car with their seat belts on. They were so safe, sitting there with their seat belts attached. So secure and so tight that their hearts buckled dead.

"Iwen, I didn't know it would be this easy to decide to fall in love with someone," Si-Chi said.

Iwen looked at her, staring into her eyes; they were like a fish tank filled with shimmering water. She unbuckled her seat belt and hugged Si-Chi. "I didn't know about this before. My poor Chi-Chi."

They were big and small Russian dolls. And they both knew that if they kept opening up, digging down to the smallest Russian doll, they'd eventually find a doll no bigger than a pinkie finger. Because it was so small, and the paintbrush too thick, the brushstrokes would be loose, the face blurry as if sobbing.

They didn't enter a coffee shop but a jewelry store. Si-Chi squinted her eyes. All of the cabinets around the shop were full of sparkling gemstones, like blinking elf eyes. The fake hands and necks in the display cases made one think of fairy tales. There was an old woman sitting right behind the display window. She was wearing a knitted magenta dress, the kind of color and material that people couldn't really explain or remember, as if to say, *I can do everything. I am absolutely nothing.* The old woman with the magenta dress saw Iwen, and soon after, she took her glasses off and put down the gemstone and loupe in her hand. "Oh, it's Mrs. Chien!" she said. "I'm going to call Maomao downstairs." She went away so fast that Si-Chi didn't even have time to see where the stairs were. Si-Chi also noticed that the old woman didn't put the gemstones away. Iwen said to Si-Chi in a low voice, "This is our secret base. They even have a cold drip coffee maker your size!"

A blue shadow appeared, and then a man with a round face and full-rimmed glasses came up to them. For some reason, Si-Chi thought at first glimpse that his pale skin was the color of tooth-paste and not of stardust. His knitted sweater was the blue of a computer screen, and not the blue of the ocean. Above his upper lip and below his lower lip, he kept tiny pinches of facial hair, so even that it looked like it was trying to half-cover his lips. Si-Chi noticed that when Iwen turned her head toward him, the beard appeared to be waiting for someone to lie in its lawn. Mr. Mao-mao immersed himself in the rain of the gemstone elves' glimpses. Everything about his posture and clothes was trying to say, *I know everything. I can do anything. I am nothing.* That was the first and last time Fang Si-Chi had the right instinct about someone after she stopped growing up.

————

Before the last summer vacation of junior high, Si-Chi and Yi-Ting took the entrance exams for the local First Girls High School and Taipei First Girls High School. They both applied for the elite language class and got accepted. Mama Fang and Mama Liu told each other that as long as their daughters had one an-other, they wouldn't have to worry about them living away from home. At the reunion dinner, Lee Guo-Hua said nonchalantly, "I'm kind of busy, but I might be able to look after them from time to time in Taipei." The reassurance Teacher Lee spoon-fed Mama Fang and Mama Liu was enough, and Si-Chi didn't make any faces at the round table. She quietly ate the decorative paper next to her sushi.

Throughout that summer vacation, Teacher Lee kindly took Si-Chi to exhibitions. One day before visiting an exhibition, they met at a coffee shop far away from the building they lived in. Lee

Guo-Hua had been in Taipei, so Si-Chi went to the coffee shop to wait for him. Sitting there, she realized she looked desperate. She imagined that she looked like a man waiting for his lover to no avail. After waiting for a long time, the man would order a bottle of wine and start drinking by himself. When he finished the wine, all he could do was order another bottle. And when the woman arrived, it would be hard for him to explain why his face was blushing and his heart was beating, as though he were simply desperate.

The little round table in front of Si-Chi was dotted with a tiny black shadow. Slowly, the shadow moved toward her coffee mug. She noticed a fly on the other side of the tall window, its shadow projected on the table because of the sun. It was in the shape of a heart. It must have been the pair of opening wings on the fly. The floral pattern on the tablecloth was as neat and clean as rows of planted seedlings. As if playing games among the flowers, the shadow swam all the way to her coffee tray and, with a little struggle, wriggled and jumped into the coffee. She picked up the teaspoon, stirring the milky foam, trying to shoo away the shadow. It simply stopped there and refused to move. It made her think about how Lee Guo-Hua would hug her and tell her how Zhao Feiyan's breasts were the tender domain for Emperor Cheng of Han. Initially she'd thought to herself, *Or maybe it was actually Zhao Feiyan's sister Zhao Hede?* She didn't know what she rejected more were his claws. Sitting in the coffee shop in a trance, Si-Chi thought what Teacher was looking for was a home. A home that only listened without speaking, one that is a little silly, but silly in a way that reassured him, though he would never admit it. That kind of domain? She didn't know when the shadow had swum out of her coffee mug. It quickly moved toward her, then jumped off from the edge of the table. She closed her thighs re-flexively. She was wearing a black skirt, so she wasn't able to spot that shadow anymore. When she looked up at the window, the fly was already gone.

Si-Chi carefully took out her diary from the bag, wanting to write down this short-lived romance between her and the fly. When she looked up, she saw that on the other side of the cof-fee shop, there was a man crawling on the floor, trying to pick something up. Because of his size, his flannel shirt rode up his belly as he leaned down, exposing a ring of flesh. What surprised her was that the underwear showing at the top of his pants had a border of Chinese-red lace! She casually moved her gaze away, showing no signs of laughter. She didn't laugh because in her heart, she was full of hazy anticipation for love. Even if it wasn't love from "unloved." There was an essential part of love that was always connected to this world. She had long given up on her self-esteem; if she were not to keep any love, she would never be able to keep on living. When she moved her pen, she caught a glimpse of the fly again, stopping at the window on her right side. The fly looked like it would live forever, which gave her a sense of gratitude. She was grateful that she still remembered how to be so grateful. Later, Yi-Ting would find this paragraph in Si-Chi's diary: "No matter what kind of love it is, his most violent love or my most innocent love, love teaches us to forgive someone outside of love. Although I can no longer eat up the macarons in front of me—'the crisp, soft, pale breast of a young woman'—I already know that association, symbolism, and metaphor are the most dangerous things in the world."

The next day, in a tiny hotel, Si-Chi finished dressing, and for the first time she didn't wilt on the ground. She simply stood there, bending over to look at the wet spot on the bedsheet. She asked, *Who did this?*

That was you.

Me?

You.

Really? And then she looked at the bedsheet in awe. *It must be Teacher's?*

It was you.

Si-Chi knew that Lee Guo-Hua was trying to look innocent; even the hair on his chest looked triumphant. He pulled out his arms from behind his head and touched the wet spot with her. After a while, he grabbed her hand. With a mixture of pride and desolation, he said, *Being with you makes me feel like all emotions have lost their names.* Fang Si-Chi laughed; that was a line from the writer Hu Lancheng. She asked him, *Hu Lancheng and Eileen Chang. Who else are you going to quote? Lu Xun and Xu Guanping? Shen Tsongwen and Zhang Zhaohe? Abélard and Héloïse? Heidegger and Hannah Arendt?* He only laughed in response. *You forgot Tsai Yuanpei and Zhou Jun.* Si-Chi's voice began to heat up. *I don't think so. More precisely, I don't want that. I don't want Teacher to pursue that. Is this what you wanted?* Lee Guo-Hua didn't answer. Eventually Si-Chi sat on the floor, thinking that Lee Guo-Hua had fallen asleep again. And then suddenly, he said, *In matters of love, I never had the opportunity to use my talents.* Si-Chi thought, *Really?*

———

Twenty years ago, Lee Guo-Hua was in his thirties and had already been married for ten years. That was when he became very popular at a cram school in Kaohsiung. His classes instantly filled up.

In that year's entrance-exam preparation class for those looking to retake the test, there was a girl who asked a lot of questions during the break. Without looking too closely, he could tell that she was beautiful. During each break, she would snuggle against the podium, holding her thick reference books with her tiny hands. She would point at the page and ask in a soft voice, "Teacher, why is the answer A to this question?" Her fingers were so pale that they looked childlike. At first glance, Lee Guo-Hua had an urge to break them. Such a thought scared him, so he murmured something in his head: *Gentleness, respect, and humility. Gentleness, respect, and humility.* It was like reading Buddhist scripture. The female student laughed and said, "Everyone calls me Cookie. My last name is Wang. Teacher can call me Cookie Wang." He almost burst out, *I'd prefer to call you candy. Tiny sugar cane. Honey. Gentleness, respect, and humility.* Cookie's questions were always silly, and she had plenty of questions because she was so stupid. His luck in love came as quickly as his fame and money. Sometimes, he had delusions that fame and profit were just bonuses, and the real purpose of teaching was to get those pink love letters. Bronze money stank, while love letters were fragrant.

He didn't need any self-criticism. It was easy to take another step. It had nothing to do with having a wife. The students loved him, and he shouldn't waste his chance. Sincere relationships exist rarely in this world. One day, he simply asked, "Would you let Teacher show you something after class?" To him, it was the very sentence that had been used in American movies a hundred times, the sentence evil people used when they tried to lure kids away from the park. The most outdated words were always the truth. Cookie said yes, exposing her canine teeth.

Two days before, he'd checked out a tiny hotel not far from cram school. When he checked, his heart was not cold, but also not boiling hot. He simply thought that everything had its right place. That was the first metaphor that came to his mind. It was from the Tang-era literature on the natural world. This type of writing always talked about how the hill was tens of steps away to the east, the forest tens of steps away to the northwest, a cave tens of steps away to the south, and a fountain in the cave. It read like a description of pursuit, and even more like the private parts of a little girl. So beautiful. The tiny hotel was in an alley. The alley was on the right side of the main road. Outside the window of the room were trees; on the trees were leaves; inside the underwear was a penis. Such a beautiful thing, it would be a waste to not take it away.

At the entrance of the hotel, Cookie smiled and asked, "What are we going to do, Teacher?" He pulled the curtain shut after entering the room. The light was faint like the smoldering tip of a cigarette, and the canines in Cookie's mouth began to tremble, asking again, even changing the way she addressed him, "*Teacher, what are you doing?*"

What else did she think I'm going to do? He took off all his clothes, and everything flashed in front of Cookie. She started to cry. "No, no, I have a boyfriend."

"Why did you say you like Teacher if you have a boyfriend, huh?"

"It's not the same."

"Why did you keep coming to me when you have a boyfriend?" He pushed her onto the bed.

"No, no."

"Why did you even come here with me? You led me on!"

"No."

Tearing her uniform will attract attention, so just take her underwear off. He admired his own clear thought process. *Gentleness, respect, and humility.*

"No! No!"

He slapped her with the same open-palm motion he used to throw chalk back into the metal holder at the bottom of the blackboard, the kind of motion that fascinated the female students. Cookie stopped talking. She knew that he was being serious, and that he had to finish this business today, just like how they progressed through lessons in class. Her underwear was peach pink with polka dots. At first, he thought, *Damn it! She already has a boyfriend. But I hope she's still a virgin.* He didn't know a girl could be so strong. He had to punch her eyes, her nose, and her mouth. When he saw her mouth was bleeding, he thought it must be a cut from her cute canine teeth. She still wouldn't open her mouth. He had no choice but to risk leaving bruises on her with one more blow. One, two, three. Three was an auspicious number, meaning multiplicity. *Gentleness, respect, and humility.* When Cookie pressed her hands to her nose, her thighs loosened. He was surprised to find out that he was just as excited by the blood coming out of her mouth as the blood on her inner thighs.

In his class of two hundred students, the boys always sat on the left side of the room and girls on the right. He discovered that half the world would open their thighs for him. How innocent his past was! It had taken so much effort to win a national teaching award back when he was still teaching at a senior high school.

In his student days, he had never gotten into any fights. Fighting provoked his peers and upset his teachers, not worth it. After being in a relationship for a few years with his first love, he got married. It was only then that he realized how loose, yet constrictive, his wife's vagina was. But, on the other hand, how tight but vast were the little cunts of the tiny female students! *Gentleness, respect, and humility.*

Cookie stopped coming to class for the next two weeks. He was indifferent. There were still lines of students waiting to ask their questions at the podium! Half of the line was boys, but even so the line was still long. He was afraid that his life would only be this long. The week after, Cookie was waiting for him downstairs. She said, "Teacher, can you bring me to that place again, please?" As soon as Lee Guo-Hua saw her, he thought about how he tore her underwear that day. She must have walked back home without wearing anything underneath. He felt a sacred stirring in his loins, remembering that scene.

Cookie's boyfriend was her childhood sweetheart. Cookie's family sold yimien, flat egg noodles, while her boyfriend's family sold bantiao, wide rice noodles, next door. After her encounter with Teacher Lee, she'd gone home and offered herself to her boyfriend. They used to stop at her bra, and now all of a sudden they flew past that. Her boyfriend was clumsily stunned. But after he saw the tears in Cookie's eyes, he asked her what happened. Cookie's boyfriend smoked, and in three cigarettes' time, he decided to break up with her. Crying harder than she had in the tiny hotel, Cookie begged him to tell her why. Her boyfriend tossed the fourth cigarette on the floor, only finishing a quarter of it. Cigarettes were the only luxury Cookie's boyfriend indulged.

"How can I still be with you when you've been dirtied?" Cookie pleaded with him to stay. "So that's why you gave it up to me just now? So disgusting, holy fuck!" Like the cigarette on the floor, Cookie began to shrivel, shrink, and slowly extinguish.

Nobody liked Cookie anymore. But if Teacher still liked her, that counted for something. She would do anything for Teacher. They could be together. When such a young and beautiful girl put her arms around his neck, he felt prouder than he would wearing an actual diamond-studded chain. He started making an effort to earn more money and bought secret small apartments in both Taipei and Kaohsiung. A year later, in the new school year, he picked another girl from the question-asking line who was more beautiful than Cookie. Cookie begged him not to break up with her, and even slept one night on the side of the road in desperation.

In the twenty years that followed, Lee Guo-Hua discovered that there would always be young girls who supported, admired, and loved him. He discovered that social taboos about sex were all too convenient for him. After he raped a girl, the whole world would point at her and tell her that it was her own fault. And then this girl would actually think it was her fault. A sense of guilt would chase her back to him. His sense of guilt was that of a noble, purebred shepherd dog. The little girls were lambs that were forced to run before they even learned to walk properly. Then what was he? He was the most frequented, most inviting cliff for the girls to climb up and jump down from. He could have any girl. The ones with big eyes who looked like they were constantly alarmed; those with flat chests like little boys; those who were skinny because of their weak stomachs; those who stuttered and were slow to react. Despite this abundance, that first throbbing he felt when he tore open Cookie's underwear eluded him. Maybe that feeling was what people generally called first love. He finally felt it again more than ten years later, when his baby daughter, Xixi, called him Daddy for the first time. And then, another ten years later, the throbbing returned when he saw that girl framed in a golden door, the girl with a gentle lamb's face. Fang Si-Chi.

———

Before Si-Chi and Yi-Ting entered high school, Mama Fang and Mama Liu headed north to Taipei to take a look at the dormitory. They hesitated over whether they should let the girls stay in an apartment instead. Eventually Teacher Lee told them absentmindedly, "I will take care of the girls in Taipei." And with that in mind, the two mamas decided to let the girls stay in one of the Liu family's apartments there. It would only take them fifteen minutes to walk to school.

During summer vacation, Si-Chi and Yi-Ting traveled back and forth between Kaohsiung and Taipei to visit their extended families and purchase household necessities for the apartment. Once, while packing her suitcase at home, Si-Chi said in an innocent tone to her mother, "I heard there's a student who's in a relationship with a teacher."

"Who?"

"I don't know her."

"Already a seductress at such a young age."

Si-Chi stopped talking. She decided then that she would never talk about it again. The innocence on her face tore open the dessert on the table. When her mama had her back turned, Si-Chi dumped all the crumbs into the crevice in the back of the leather armchair. Later on, when Teacher asked for her photo, she found a family photo from her drawer. Her father stood on the right, her mom on the left, and she was squeezed between them in a white spaghetti-strap dress with a blue floral print, an awkward juvenile smile on her face. She cut her parents out of the picture and took just the slippery sliver of herself to Teacher Lee. In the photo there remained one hand on either of her shoulders, big soft palms that she wasn't able to cut away.

Si-Chi and Yi-Ting were used to taking the high-speed rail. Even when something was new to them, they tried not to show it. Lee Guo-Hua was smart and could always find some spare time to take Si-Chi out for a while. He didn't need that much time any-way. In Lee Guo-Hua's eyes, a huge island like Taiwan was, con-trary to popular belief, not full of coffee shops and convenience stores but, rather, tiny motels. One time, Si-Chi told him cheer-fully, "Teacher, if you keep following me every which way, I'm afraid my body will be so disoriented that everything including this bed will be beyond recognition." Of course, it wasn't because of the beds that she didn't sleep well. It was because she dreamt of a penis dangling in front of her every night, forcing itself under-neath her. In her dreams, she always felt like someone outside the dream was stuffing something into her body. After entering senior high school, she even grew afraid of falling asleep. She downed coffee at midnight from age thirteen to eighteen. Five years, two thousand nights, the same dream over and over.

One time when Si-Chi and Yi-Ting went up to Taipei on the train, there was a mother and a daughter sitting across the aisle. The daughter seemed to be only three or four years old. They weren't good at guessing kids' ages. On and off, the little girl kept opening and closing the lid of her water bottle with cartoon drawings on it. Whenever she opened it, she would yell at her mama, "I love you!" When she closed it, she would scream even louder, "I don't love you!" She wouldn't stop making noise or using her tiny hands to smack her mama's face. Every now and then, someone would look in the direction of this pair. Watching them, Si-Chi found herself suddenly tearing. She was so envious of love that could be shouted out loud. Love could feed itself, but it made a person insatiable. *I love him!* Yi-Ting used her finger to dab Si-Chi's cheeks and spoke to the teardrop dew on her fingertip. "Is this what they call homesickness?"

"Yi-Ting, I'm no longer myself. I'm homesick for myself." Si-Chi's voice was like a dish that had gone cold.

If only she were mad at him. It would be even better if she were mad at herself. Melancholy was a mirror, and anger was a window. But she couldn't live without liking herself. Which was to say, she couldn't stop liking Teacher Lee. If it were truly rape, the situation wouldn't be as difficult as this.

For a very long time after this was all over, Liu Yi-Ting would think about Si-Chi, the Si-Chi who wasn't even able to control her pooping and peeing at the psychiatric hospital. *Her* Si-Chi. She would think about Si-Chi whenever she made a long stroke with her highlighter, just like the red lines on the sides of the road, in her thick foreign language textbook; when a boy that Yi-Ting liked pressed his lips on hers; when her grandmother passed away and she sang the Heart Sutra with the undertaker at the funeral. She would think about Si-Chi no matter what she did, about how Si-Chi wouldn't be able to experience all these things. A low-brow soap opera, a new title from a Nobel Prize winner, a super-mini tablet, a super-huge cell phone, bubble tea that tasted like plastic, waffles that smelled like newspapers. Every minute, every second, her thoughts were with Si-Chi. When that boy moved his lips from her mouth to her breast; when the mall had sales that jumped from 30 to 50 percent off; on days with sun and days with rain, she constantly thought about Si-Chi. Yi-Ting thought about how she got to enjoy everything that her twin of the soul would always be destined to miss. She was always thinking of Si-Chi. A very long time after what happened, she would finally realize what Si-Chi meant that day on the train. Every single thing in this world belonged to a hometown that Si-Chi would never know again.

A few days before the girls moved to their apartment in Taipei, Iwen asked Si-Chi to make some time for her during her packing, no matter what. This time, Iwen didn't lower the convertible top on her sports car. The summer lasted longer than average that year before they entered high school, so the mornings were as hot as midday. Si-Chi thought about this season, and about herself. She realized she wasn't just boiling early in the morning, but she was scalding, like in the dark of night. Of all the dark nights in Fang Si-Chi's life, Teacher's Day that year was the darkest of them all. She realized she thought about Teacher Lee all the time. It was not that she missed him, nor was she mulling him over. He was running rampant in her head.

Throughout junior high school, she had rejected many junior high and high school guys, and even a few college guys. Whenever she rejected them, she would say, "I'm sorry, but I can't make myself like you." She'd feel a fire surging beneath her numb, wooden face when she said this. Those boys barely knew her. Their crooked handwriting, their childish words. Their letters with drawings of little animals that told her she was a rose or a thick, comforting soup for the soul to help them pull all-nighters. Standing before her pursuers' whirl of courtship dances, she felt like these little boys were practically pleading. She wasn't able to say, *Actually, I don't think I'm good enough for any of you. I'm orange juice and cream soup gone sour. I'm a rose and a water lily infested with bug eggs. I'm a north star in a city full of light, unseen and unneeded.* These boys' innocent and audacious love was the most precious feeling in this world. Besides what she felt for Teacher Lee.

Iwen parked in front of the jewelry shop, unbuckled her seat belt, and patted Si-Chi's head. When they entered, they found Mr. Maomao sitting behind the counter in an egg-yellow shirt. To Si-Chi, he looked the same as when he had worn a blue knit sweater the first time they'd met. He immediately stood up and said, "Mrs. Chien, welcome."

"Hello, Mr. Mao," Iwen said simultaneously.

Mr. Maomao immediately replied, "Just call me Maomao!"

"Just call me Miss Hsu," Iwen said.

Si-Chi was shocked. In just four sentences, she knew right away that the two of them had gone through this routine a number of times before. She didn't know that so few words could contain so much of their feelings for one another. She realized that Iwen was indulging herself subconsciously. Someone like Iwen would definitely understand what Mr. Maomao meant with that tone.

Everything Iwen wore was gray, from her turtleneck to cropped pants. For other people, these were the colors of dust and haze, but for Iwen, they were clouds and fog. She said somewhat apologetically, "This is my favorite little friend. She's going to senior high school in Taipei, so I'd like to buy a souvenir for her." She turned toward Si-Chi. "Yi-Ting said she didn't have time, so I'll give you both the same thing. She won't mind, right?"

Si-Chi panicked and said, "Iwen, we absolutely can't accept such expensive gifts."

Iwen chuckled in response. "You can refuse expensive gifts from boys, but this is a gift from me. You have to take it. Just take it for my sake—I'm not going to see much of either of you for the next three years."

Mr. Maomao laughed, which made his already-round face close to a perfect circle. He said, "Mrs. Chien is making herself sound so old." Si-Chi thought Iwen should have responded, *It's because Mr. Mao keeps calling me "Mrs."* Yi-Wei treated her so horribly, but all Iwen did was run her fingers over broken glass.

Si-Chi began looking at jewelry with her head held low. In the sea of sparkles and fog, she wasn't able to concentrate on Iwen and Mr. Maomao's conversation. Actually, they barely said anything to each other. Then, Iwen pointed at a pendant, one with a platinum rose that contained an aqua-blue gemstone at its heart; it was the color of water at a shallow beach. She said, "What about this one? Paraíba isn't that expensive." Si-Chi accepted.

Mr. Maomao found matching chains for the pendants. He

brushed them clean, then placed them each in a velvet box. The heavy, expensive metal and the thick boxes looked light and effortless in his hands. Si-Chi thought this person radiated cleanliness.

Iwen and Si-Chi drove back home. At a red light, Iwen turned her head and noticed Si-Chi's eyes were filmy with tears. "Do you want to talk about it?" she asked. "It's okay if you don't. But I want you to know that you can tell me anything, even if you feel like you can't talk about it. You can pretend that I'm nobody."

Si-Chi lowered her voice and spoke in a tone beyond her age. "I think Teacher Lee is acting weird." Iwen looked at her and saw that her tears were drying, replaced by a hardened gaze.

The light turned green. Iwen's thoughts ran like a marquee. She thought about Lee Guo-Hua. She thought about that moment when she'd turned her back to him but could still feel his eyes staring hot at her ankles. Another time, when Yi-Wei threw a birthday party for her, Lee Guo-Hua gave her the first edition of an English book that she had always wanted. He carried a glass of pink champagne but didn't even drink from it. In front of Yi-Wei, he looked ridiculously humble. The book was a rarity, but thinking back to it now, she couldn't remember where she even put it. Perhaps that was because she secretly hated him. When Teacher Lee first started teaching the girls to write in her home, he always interrupted her and said, "Mrs. Chien, if the girls use your methods to write, they'd definitely get a zero on their compositions." He had said this and stared infinitely at her in the face. When he said he wanted to take the pink balloons from her birthday party home for Xixi, she instinctively felt he was lying, though she couldn't say why. He was probably going to pop the balloons right after getting out of the elevator and stuff them in a public trash can. She thought how his gaze would wander around her face, as though trying to memorize a poem from the Tang dynasty.

Iwen asked Si-Chi, "What do you mean by 'weird'? He just seems absent-minded to me." She held back from saying he always looked like he was scheming.

"You're right; he's just preoccupied. I don't think Teacher Lee really does anything he says he'll do." Si-Chi held back from saying the opposite was true.

Iwen said, "I've been thinking about Teacher Lee's attitude. Let me give you an example . . . um, it's like a wooden cabin before the sun comes up in the morning. If you brush your hands on the wood, you can feel its obedient pattern. But walking barefoot, you always feel like you need to watch your step. It always feels like there's a loose board somewhere. If you step on it, you might wake something or other in the house."

Si-Chi thought, *Fang Si-Chi, just one step further. Stick your feet forward so you can rewind and come back from the edge of the cliff. Just one step, one word, that's all you need.* Just as she was about to say something, she felt a set of teeth biting her feet tucked under the front seat. The evening before, at Lee Guo-Hua's place, he'd lifted her legs up to his shoulders and bitten her heels. Mr. Maomao and Iwen both looked clean. If Iwen was a cloud, then Mr. Maomao was rain. If Iwen was fog, then Mr. Maomao was dew. Si-Chi felt a poignant sense of grief from her contamination. She laughed at the thought of it, savagely. Her face looked like a fierce wind had blown all her features out of order.

Hearing Si-Chi's wild laughter, Iwen continued, "I used to

tell both of you why I like sonnets so much. It's because of their shape, iambic pentameter and ten syllables. Every sonnet looks like the shape of a square, like a handkerchief one might wave when parting ways with an ex forever. Sometimes I wonder if I accidentally hurt you both with what I said. At my age, I know that no matter how many books I read, they won't be of any use in my life. *Is there something the matter with Teacher Lee?*"

But Si-Chi's eyes had become her mouth, and her mouth had become eyes.

In her first year of junior high, all Si-Chi could see had been Teacher Lee's chest. Now she was about to enter senior high school. She'd grown taller, and these days all she could see were the dents of Teacher Lee's shoulders. She laughed out loud and said to Iwen, "Nothing's the matter with him. Actually, he treats me too well!" She understood why Teacher Lee never asked her if she loved him. It was because when she asked him *Do you love me?*, they both knew she meant, "I love you." Everything was constructed by his words, relentless as shark teeth devouring from front to back. What a house of promise!

That was the last time Fang Si-Chi saw Iwen before she went mad. She didn't know that the platinum pendant would become a memento of Iwen. That precious time they'd shared.

After Si-Chi and Yi-Ting got on the high-speed rail, Si-Chi gave Yi-Ting the jewelry box and said, "I think Teacher Lee is weird." She hoped that the heaviness of the jewelry box would make her words seem light. Yi-Ting joked, "Iwen's weirder. She gave us jewelry—it's like she's about to die or something."

The girls and Iwen, their time precious as jewelry.

———

After Si-Chi and Yi-Ting moved to Taipei, Lee Guo-Hua would come pick up Si-Chi from their apartment whenever he was in town. When Si-Chi and Teacher Lee walked down the street, she would feel the gaze of strangers on them even though they never held hands. Passersby, receptionists, the billboard at the corner of the road that showed a model with a set of very clean teeth. The canvas would flip up in the wind and reveal the upturned, tiny windproof triangles behind the frames. The model would lose a lot of teeth this way, cheering Si-Chi up. Teacher Lee asked her what she was laughing about; she'd say it was nothing.

She had no interest in visiting Taipei 101. The place she wanted to go the most was Longshan Temple. She could see Longshan Temple's curved cornices waiting for her from a distance. It was very crowded, and everyone had sticks of incense in their hands. When they walked forward with incense, the smoke would drift back into their faces. It was as though people were simply following the smoke instead of carrying it. There were separate gods in charge of everything: romance and marriage, having kids, academic careers, or anything in general. Si-Chi's ears brushed against the shoulder line of Lee Guo-Hua's shirt. She seemed to understand that none of this would ever mean anything to her. What happened between them was something beyond the reach of any god. Hidden beneath the covers, even the gods couldn't see it.

Throughout junior high school, she hadn't been any good at making friends. Rumor had it that she was conceited. The only person whom she could call her friend was Yi-Ting. But Yi-Ting had also changed now that they were in senior high school. Yi-Ting said it was Si-Chi who'd changed. Yi-Ting didn't know that while other kids were playing around, a man was frolicking with Si-Chi's body. Her classmates often joked and matched all the beautiful girls in their class to the boys from the First Boys High School. Si-Chi always made a face as though she'd been pierced by a knife, and then her classmates would say, *Look at her, so stuck-up*. No, it wasn't like that. She didn't know that falling in love meant at first flirting with possibilities, getting some tea at the school gate, reading a little note a boy put in the bag with her drink. She didn't know that only after some back-and-forth signals would the boy verbalize his feelings and ask her out, bowing at a right angle like the boys in Japanese movies. Once they confessed their feelings for each other, a couple could hold hands and graze fingers on the lawn. The green lawn in the middle of campus was surrounded by a brick-red track, a whole universe to itself. After holding hands, they would kiss each other in the alley, the girl standing on her tiptoes, her calves poking out of her white socks and flushed with embarrassment. Their tongues spoke more than their mouths. Every time Si-Chi felt this way about a boy her age, she imagined her diary surfacing on her skin and tattooing her with its words. A type of lupus in the shape of a map. She thought the boys stole their words from her Teacher Lee, that they imitated, practiced, and inherited from him.

She could see that desire stayed at the back of Teacher Lee's mind, like a tail that refused to recede. What she had with him was not love. But apart from this, she didn't know any other kind of love. She looked at the tiny paper notes drenched by the sweat of cold beverages, at the boys who bent their waists ninety degrees in front of someone. She really couldn't understand. All she knew of love was someone cleaning up the blood for you after doing it. Love meant tearing off your clothes without losing a button. Love meant you apologized to someone after that person thrust his thing inside your mouth.

One time, Lee Guo-Hua placed his arms behind his head, his eyes closed, and told her, *I've been thinking about how you look in your new uniform.*

Disgusted yet flattered, Si-Chi said, *Your mind is in the gutter.*

And then he began to lecture, *Don't you know that thinking very deeply about something is a Buddhist practice?*

Of course, Si-Chi replied with unusual conviction.

He laughed. *Are you telling me not to lecture you then?*

Yup, Si-Chi responded lightly.

Longshan Temple was full of words at every corner. All the pillars were engraved with poems or dictums. The characters written in clerical and regular script were in square, lantern-like blocks; as for the characters in cursive and semicursive script, they streamed downward like falling rain. Some of the people in the temple had fallen asleep, leaning against the pillars. She thought, *I wonder if sleeping like this will make the nightmares go away.* Other people sat on the stairs, staring at the sculptures of deities in their alcoves that were as red as a newlywed couple's bedroom. The expressions in these people's eyes were more like the Dead Sea than the ocean. On the wall were embossed sculptures at chest level, dyed the color of orange juice under the sun. There were plump monkeys and deer, ostentatious like the meat sold by weight in a traditional market. Their flesh looked like it could wobble and shake. Lee Guo-Hua pointed his finger toward them, saying, "You know, it's 侯 (ho) and 祿 (luh)." *Here came another lecture. A man who didn't give proper lectures in his class but would lecture others incessantly anywhere else.* Si-Chi started laughing. Her fingers traced the joints of the bamboo carved into the stone windows.

"This is a bamboo window, and each window has five joints. It's an auspicious number, a good one," he said.

Loyalty, filial piety, chastity, and righteousness poured down on her like rain.

They passed by the temple janitor's door, which was slightly ajar. A cigarette dangled from the janitor's mouth as he drained a big bucket of marinated longan. With the bucket between his thighs, it was like he was huddling protectively over a fat little kid. Everyone at the temple was following incense smoke, but the janitor's smoke came from a cigarette. This scene reminded Si-Chi of how Teacher Lee had explained the origins of chastity engraved on the wall earlier. Everything here was so ridiculous that it became all the more beautiful.

She asked Teacher Lee if he prayed on a regular basis. He said yes, so she asked, "Then why not do it today?" He said he was not in the right state of mind to pray. *God,* Si-Chi thought, *never came when you sought Him. And when you had no need for Him, He didn't show up, either.*

She asked, "Teacher Lee, do you love your wife?"

He sliced the air with his hand and said, "I don't want to talk about this. This is a fact that won't change."

A hurt expression came over her, as though pressing a bleeding wound.

"Teacher Lee, do you *love* your wife?" she asked again.

He stretched and said openhandedly, "When we were both young, very, very young, around eighteen or nineteen years old, she treated me very well—so well that later, people pointed at me and said I should be responsible for her. So I did, I married her, in order to be responsible." He paused for a moment, and then continued, "But humans are assholes. Love is love; when you lose it, you just don't feel it anymore. These days, even if someone pointed a gun at me, I still wouldn't deny that I like you a lot."

"So there were no other girls," Si-Chi said. "Your sweet-talking is impressive for someone who hasn't done it in thirty years. It's incredible."

Lee Guo-Hua wanted to throw pebbles into the abyss of Si-Chi's voice.

"I'm Sleeping Beauty, and you woke me with your kiss," he answered. At the same time, he thought to himself: *I knew I couldn't have both of them in Taipei. I have to finish with Guo Hsiao-Chi.*

As they left, Si-Chi took another glance at the temple behind them. He explained that the colorful sculptures on top of the roof were called "cut and paste," a type of mosaic decoration. She lifted her head and saw the decorations of red and yellow cubes, the fish scales reflecting the sunlight. She thought, *Cut and paste. What a good name for a paste decoration. It's like a folktale that tells a full story with very few words.*

They entered the tiny lobby back at their tiny motel. A few tiny round tables were scattered around the space, one of them taken by a couple. A man and a woman sat face-to-face with each other. The man's jeans were split at the knees; the pads of one sneakered foot rested on top of his other foot under the table. The woman gently placed one leg between the man's thighs, letting them hold her. Si-Chi instantly spotted the scars at the woman's ankles from the constant scraping of high heels. The scene left her with a feeling of tenderness and pity. She knew Teacher Lee didn't want her to pay attention to other people, was afraid that somebody might notice her. She took another glance at them before going upstairs. She thought the love she witnessed in that lobby was the truly beautiful kind.

He kept saying, *I need to relieve some of my stress on your body. This is how I love you.* Why did he have so much to say? She noticed that his sentences often ended with a period, as if he was dead sure about something. Every period from Teacher Lee's mouth was a well that she could look into and see her reflection in; how she wished she could plunge herself into its depths. She hugged herself and sat rooted on the floor, watching him sleep. Once he started snoring, she could see his nostrils blow pink bubbles. Soon after, the entire room would sprout with aquatic plants in multiple colors. Si-Chi thought, *How beautiful are the snores of the man I love. This is a secret I'll keep to myself.*

———

Guo Hsiao-Chi was in her second year in college. She'd always had average to above-average grades, athletic ability, and height. To her, the world was an apple that she could pick if she gathered all her strength to jump for it. In her last year at senior high school, there had been a lingering sense of crisis around campus because of the college entrance exam; it smelled like 2B pencil graphite mixed with cold bento boxes. As long as the bentos provided enough energy for the students to study until 10:00 p.m. at school, they didn't have to taste good. Hsiao-Chi had gone to cram school for every single subject that year; like the chicken leg in her bento, it was better to have it than go without. Hsiao-Chi's beauty was not the kind that people understood right away. Her pale face was not a multiple-choice question, but rather a short essay prompt. The number of guys who were after her was also average to above-average, ill-timed like bento side dishes gone cold.

The first time Lee Guo-Hua noticed Hsiao-Chi at the cram school was not when she came to ask him questions. It was well before; he was surprised a girl who sat so far in the back of his class could catch his attention. He was an expert at reading people. When Hsiao-Chi locked eyes with him, her open and inquisitive eyes told him that she couldn't believe he would notice her in such a big classroom. He quickly moved the microphone away from the side of his mouth to let out a laugh. After class, he went to Tsai Liang, the manager of the cram school, and asked for her name. Tsai Liang was all too familiar with helping the male teachers make moves on the female students. Sometimes, out of loneliness, she too would go to Lee Guo-Hua's apartment to spend the night.

Nobody understood the power of stepping behind the podium more than Tsai Liang. Nobody knew how messy these male teachers, who had bumbled their way to middle age, could be when they let themselves go. It was as though they wanted to compensate for the vast empty nights that were the first half of their lives. Tsai Liang called Hsiao-Chi aside while she was waiting for her tuition fee receipt at the front desk.

"Teacher Lee Guo-Hua would like to help you with your schoolwork," Tsai had said to her. "He saw your exam papers and thinks you're the top student in this school." She then lowered her voice and said, "But please don't tell anyone else. Other students might think it's unfair, all right?"

For Guo Hsiao-Chi, who was average at everything in life, this had been the most remarkable thing that ever happened to her. After school, Tsai Liang gave Hsiao-Chi a ride straight to Lee Guo-Hua's secret little apartment in Taipei.

At first, Guo Hsiao-Chi had cried and claimed she wanted to kill herself, but she grew quiet after those first few visits. Sometimes they finished too early, so Lee Guo-Hua would actually tutor her. She always had an especially serious expression on her face, as though she were really coming there for private lessons. Soon her pale face began to constantly look ill, turning from the white of a towel to the white of a candle. Whenever somebody saw her, they would say, "The last year of high school is such torture." In the end, even Hsiao-Chi herself said, "Teacher Lee, if you really love me, then everything's okay."

Lee Guo-Hua had leaned in to nibble on her collarbone and said, "Never in my wildest dreams did I think I'd be in my fifties and sharing a bed with someone like you. Where did you come from? Did you fall from the blade of the moon and the needles of stars? Where have you been my whole life? What took you so long? I need to marry you in my next life; I can't wait for it. Can you make sure to find me sooner? You're mine, you know. I love you more than anyone in this life. Sometimes I think I love you more than I love my own daughter. I don't even feel sorry for my daughter. This is all your fault; you're too beautiful."

Hsiao-Chi had smiled after he said all this.

Tsai Liang was a short woman with boyish cropped hair who

enjoyed teasing the top male students. She would boast about all the boys who got the best grades in the entrance exam like they were her relatives. Lee Guo-Hua never got jealous, even when she blithely brought up those male students as if they were her own nephews while they were in bed. He simply saw her as a woman halfway to old age, for whom every stroke of the boys' names on the Outstanding Student Board was woven into a black veil to cover the cellulite under her buttocks. Lee Guo-Hua knew that in Tsai Liang's mind, "halfway to old age" meant "halfway to youth." The only thing about her that dissatisfied him was her short hair. To keep her happy, all he had to do was teach the boys from the elite class in First Boys High School well, then scatter them near her. For them, the glow of entering the best school was like an angel's halo, and she was paradise herself. Very few grown women were so easily satisfied. He guessed she knew that he, the English teacher, the physics teacher, and the math teacher didn't bother to talk about her behind her back. But whenever they got bored, she could still tease them with the near-youthful vigor that she absorbed from spending time with the male students.

Tsai Liang was worth the effort. After all, every little female student whom Tsai Liang drove to Lee Guo-Hua's tiny apartment thought women would definitely protect each other. They cheerfully buckled themselves into the front seat. She practically took off half their clothes on the road between the school and Lee's apartment. There was no one as responsible as his manager.

Little did Lee Guo-Hua know that every time Tsai Liang went out with another male student, she resented the fact that the boy's name wasn't in any of the Outstanding Student fliers that were delivered everywhere. She hated when those boys used wax to spike up their hair; she hated when those boys didn't tuck their shirts inside their pants. *You're already wearing the uniforms from the worst high school—how dare you not tuck in your shirts!* For Tsai Liang, there was nothing more attractive than the scent of summer on the elite boys' bodies. From the top high school to the top university, admission into the best schools was only the start of their journeys toward fulfilling their lifelong dreams. But the female students already had so many demands before they'd even sacrificed anything. They were either the top students themselves or they found boys who were the top students to be their boyfriends. Silver and bronze, they wanted all of them. They never left any of these boys for her. Nobody understood that Tsai Liang hadn't chosen to be satisfied but rather gave up and accepted dissatisfaction. She kept telling herself every old man who sucked the nipple of a little girl was standing at the pole of the world, downing the summer solstice of youth. The girls she drew toward those teachers' apartments were princesses, and it was they who kissed the youth of these teachers awake. The teachers needed energy to give lectures. It was not that she sacrificed those female students; rather, she was trying to benefit a much wider range of students. This was the moral choice Tsai Liang made after self-reflection. This was her way of getting justice.

Guo Hsiao-Chi opened the door to Lee Guo-Hua's apartment using the key he had given her. On the table he'd set out five types of drinks. Hsiao-Chi knew that he would make a silly face and say to her, *I didn't know which one you liked, so I bought all of them.* She felt grateful and didn't let herself think that his perverse virtue was all that remained for her.

When Teacher Lee got home, he asked her if everything was

all right at school. She told him cheerfully that she'd joined a new student club and they'd had a famous guest lecturer today. She also bought a new telescope, and a senior had taken her to the mountains for stargazing the other day.

"Just the two of you?" Lee Guo-Hua asked.

"Yeah."

Lee Guo-Hua sighed deeply; when he cracked open his can of soda, it seemed to sigh, too. He took a sip and said, "I knew this day would come, but I just didn't know that it would be so soon."

"Teacher, what are you talking about?"

"If a guy wasn't interested in a girl, he wouldn't let her ride on his motorcycle into the mountains. If a girl wasn't interested in this guy, she wouldn't take the ride at midnight, into the wilderness."

"It was club-related," Hsiao-Chi said.

"You've mentioned this Chen guy a few times already."

"That's because he invited me to join the club!" Hsiao-Chi's voice went flat, like crumpled paper turned into scraps.

Lee Guo-Hua's eyes were like those of a dog standing in the rain. He said, "It's all right. Either way, there's someone else. It's always just a matter of time. Thanks for telling me. At least I'm not dying not knowing how."

Hsiao-Chi's voice began to rise. "Teacher Lee, it's not like that! He's just a regular upperclassman at school."

Lee Guo-Hua told her, "Being with you was just like a dream. The sooner you leave, the sooner I can wake up." His puppy eyes looked like he was holding back tears.

"There's nothing between us!" Hsiao-Chi whimpered. "You're the only one I love, Teacher!"

Lee Guo-Hua said solemnly, "You just said 'us.' Just return the key to me."

He pushed her out the door and threw her purse outside.

"Please," Hsiao-Chi begged him. Lee Guo-Hua watched her sit outside like a dog and wondered how long this begging scene would last. It was so beautiful. He stood up straight and tall and spoke to Hsiao-Chi.

"Before you came, I was alone, and once you leave I'll just be alone again. I will remember you and love you always." He quickly closed the door before she could reach out her hand, locked the first and second locks, then slid the security chain into place. He felt like a girl going into a panic after realizing someone was stalking her. The thought brought a smile to his face. What a sense of humor he had.

Hsiao-Chi's frantic knock on the door sounded like a thunderstorm. Through the thick door, he could hear the drone of her voice. *Teacher Lee, I love you. I only love you, Teacher Lee, I love you so much . . .* Lee Guo-Hua figured she would walk back to school after crying for two hours, just like before. She had lost even before she was slapped with defeat. And then he turned on the television to watch the news: Ma Ying-Jeou was running for reelection, and his wife Chow Mei-Ching was helping him gain extra support. He turned the volume up to cover the noise from outside his door. He just had to put up with it a little longer and it would be over. At this point, Guo Hsiao-Chi knew when to stop, too; she knew her limits: they were just like Chow Mei-Ching's dress, not too long and not too short.

That afternoon Lee Guo-Hua went to pick up Si-Chi at her

apartment. Inside the taxi, he gave her the key to his apartment, placing it in her little palm and covering it with her fingers.

"I got this key for you."

"Really?" Si-Chi held the key tight, and it was not until they arrived at the apartment that she realized the key had left a mark on her palm, like teeth marks from a baby. From then on he'd always ask her, *Coming home?* Was his little apartment her home? In her heart she never felt any emotions tumbling; she just faintly felt a baby gnawing on her palm.

Lee Guo-Hua and some other teachers from the cram school went on a trip together to Singapore. After school, Si-Chi had nowhere else to go, so she decided to go to a coffee shop to write in her diary and listen to music to kill time. She sat by the window, where light filtered in through the trees outside and onto her pink diary. The spots it made were round and shiny, and when she reached her hand into this dance of light and shadow, it was as if leopard spots appeared on her skin. She thought about Iwen and Mr. Maomao as she drank her coffee. *There was probably nothing between them.* But Iwen was holding that conjunction in her mouth, and there was no way Si-Chi could conjugate Yi-Wei's name next to Iwen anymore. It was Yi-Wei who first loosened his fingers from her grasp, turning them into slaps and fists.

Over the half hour that Si-Chi sat by the window, at least six men approached and tried to strike up a conversation with her. Some of them brought their business cards, while others brought beverages and even international accents. Millennia ago, the earliest Chinese poems used flowers as a metaphor for women.

Whenever someone said Si-Chi was a flower, she felt like she was being thrown into the wide and crashing river of platitudes: *Long live the emperor*, anti-communist slogans, and textbook sample essays. It was only when Teacher Lee said she was a flower that she believed he could be referring to another kind of flower. The type that nobody had ever seen.

Men were such a headache. The most annoying part was how she felt she couldn't live up to their expectations. She couldn't write anymore. She could only wander the streets.

What kind of a relationship could be called *normal*? In a society where everyone looked at everyone, what was considered correct was nothing more than doing as other people did. Whenever she came across a sentence that sounded like it described Teacher Lee and her, she would copy it down and read it a few times. *As long as somebody wrote it, it meant somebody approved*, she thought. One time, a boy wrote a letter to her, "I go to cram school every Tuesday, and every time I brush past your shoulder while riding my bike, I start to feel like that day's light begins to spread. My whole week brightens up." Of course she knew where that sentence was copied from, but even copying was a luxury. She really hated him. She wanted to tell him to his face that she wasn't the saint that he saw. *I'm just the mistress of a cram school teacher you take classes with.* She wanted to bite his mouth hard. Gradually, she understood what Iwen meant when she said, *Simplicity is the most romantic thing.* She also understood the vicissitudes in this sentence. How could she compare herself with others, stay simple and proper when it came to unspeakable love? All she could do was take in ample ancient Chinese poems and Western novels. Taiwan didn't have a narrative tradition of over a thousand years.

What kind of tradition did Taiwan have? The kind of tradition left by colonization, a sudden change in languages and names. She was just like their little island. She never belonged to herself.

Every once in a while, a memoir by a survivor of kidnapping and sexual assault would appear in translation. Touching the book covers as smooth as the face of a little girl, Si-Chi enjoyed visiting bookstores more than anything. She would read from the beginning, pinning her feet to the ground and standing there for a long time. She read about handcuffs, guns, washbasins where people were drowned, thick twisted ropes. She read these books like they were crime fiction. What surprised her was that after these girls escaped, there was always justice, rebirth amidst desolation, flowers blooming from concrete, carp leaping over a dragon's gate. Despite having escaped, after being imprisoned and tortured for years, these women would never be just regular customers at a convenience store, fans of the color pink, daughters, mothers. They would always be survivors. Si-Chi thought, *Even though I'm in a different situation, seeing other people being kidnapped and sexually assaulted feels reassuring.* And then, she thought, *Maybe I'm one of the most despicable survivors around.*

She had asked Teacher Lee before, *Who am I to you? Your mistress?*

Of course not; you're my babe, my female best friend, my little woman, my girlfriend, and someone I love the most in life. With that single sentence, he had pierced her open completely. She was shattered.

But Teacher Lee, the world calls this "cheating," the kind with a raw-fish smell—our situation stinks of it. She couldn't bring herself to say this. Instead she continued her question, *But I've met your wife, and I know Xixi, too. Do you know what I mean, Teacher Lee? I've seen their faces. This is very painful for me. It's a very real pain. I can't even go home for winter and summer breaks anymore.*

In response, he lightheartedly said but a single sentence: *Love always requires sacrifice.* Right away, she knew he was practicing his speech about supreme love again, spouting his pithy observations. She stopped talking, turning the world into silent mode. She watched him lying on the bed, his mouth twisting in different shapes. Outside the apartment, the winter birds were chirping in the frost while leaves fell from the trees. A chill of premonition ran down her spine. She was cheerful, but she could feel her head and hands still tangled up in confusion. It was she who had broken the unbreakable water of her own mother, the touch soft and scented. For the first time, she understood what mortality meant.

Teacher Lee often said, *It's like a miracle when somebody you like likes you back.* So God had visited them. He had entered the building where Teacher Lee lived with his wife and his child on the sixth floor; God then came to the seventh floor, where the girls and their parents lived. Teacher Lee loved writing in her palm, saying, *We could make a plaque with the line "Sky and land are unable to contain each other."*

Drawing strokes here and there, he laughed as he wrote 人, the character for "human," and said that it didn't really matter if the sky and the Earth could level with each other; it's humans who can't level with one another. The soft and gentle touch of Teacher Lee's index finger inside her palm resembled those leopard spots of light. Unraveling a sense of guilt didn't relieve one of guilt. Rather, Teacher Lee savored the sensation of it. The passersby who came to talk to her only saw her eyelashes curving toward the sky; nobody saw her inverted, messy, and incestuous love. It belonged to an infatuation with the lowest kind of language. She had been a beautiful girl before she became Teacher Lee's secret.

He often said, *We won't end in tragedy, but it definitely won't be a comedy, either. I only hope you'll think about the happiness you once had. When you meet a good guy, just go with him.*

Si-Chi was shocked whenever she heard this. *He really thinks he's so benevolent. You did this to my body but still want me to believe there's love in this world? You want me to pretend not to know there are girls who were torn apart, and that they still walk around the school playground hand in hand? Can you order my brain not to dream about you every night, so much so that I'm afraid to fall asleep? You want a good guy to accept a girl like me, even though I can't even accept myself? You want me to learn another kind of love besides the love between us?* In the end, Si-Chi never spoke about these things. She simply closed her eyes and waited for his lips to press onto hers.

Si-Chi heard a screeching noise from a hard brake. Somebody pulled her backward with great force, and she fell into that person. The driver rolled down the car window; his anger turned courteous when he noticed she was a sickly young girl.

"Aiya, girl, please watch out!"

"I'm so sorry," Si-Chi said. The car drove away. The man who pulled her to the sidewalk was wearing a silver mink suit. *I might have seen him somewhere before. Ah, he was one of the six guys who came to talk to me.*

"I'm sorry," the guy in the silver mink suit said. "You seemed to be a bit distracted, so I followed you."

"Really?" She didn't feel any appreciation for his rescue. She only felt faintly apologetic toward the whole world.

"I'll hold your book bag for you."

"There's really no need."

He snatched her book bag away regardless. She didn't want to snatch it back, in case passersby might think it was a robbery.

"Are you all right?" he asked.

"Yeah."

"Did you just get out of school?"

She thought, *Yeah, so?* She didn't respond. With his eyes naturally widened in surprise and his long, tapir-like nose, the guy looked like a manga caricature.

"You look so much like that Japanese pop star . . . W-what's her name again?"

Si-Chi thought about the tiny sliver of a picture in Liu Yong's book and laughed. He thought she laughed because of what he said, so his voice grew confident.

"Has anyone ever told you how elegant you are?"

"Does everyone in Taipei talk like this?" She laughed out loud again.

"Like what?"

I have a paper box in my house just to keep business cards from guys like you. She held back from saying that, but he did take out his business card and gave it to her. He held a respectable title at a famous company.

"Surely you must have other things to do, Mr. Manager?" Si-Chi asked.

He took out his phone to cancel an appointment for that day and said, "I really want to get to know you." She watched the velvety, finger-like branches on the pine tree at the side of the road sway suggestively. "I want to know you. Can we have dinner?"

She saw God slice through the fruit of her remaining rationality with a knife called pain and then bite into it nonchalantly. From the side of God's mouth, some juice that looked like blood dripped out. She accepted the invitation.

"How about we see a movie after dinner?" the guy asked.

She agreed again.

There was nobody in the movie theater. It was cold, and Si-Chi's left hand snaked up her right hand, and then vice versa. The guy with the silver mink suit put his jacket on her. The silver mink suit looked like a huge coat. When she saw the black shirt he was wearing beneath the suit, she laughed with boundless misery.

"Oh, my—uh—boyfriend also always wears black."

"Maybe I'm your next boyfriend. What does he do?"

It's none of your business. She held that back.

"You look very young. I'm guessing your boyfriend must be older than you?"

"Thirty-seven."

"Ah, he's in his thirties. As someone who's also in his thirties, I've got a pretty decent social standing."

She laughed and cried at the same time.

"I meant he's thirty-seven years older than me."

His eyes grew bigger. "Does he have a wife?"

Si-Chi's smile disappeared, leaving only tears on her face.

"I thought you said he treats you really well. How come you're crying?"

Si-Chi suddenly thought of one time when Teacher Lee took

her to a stir-fry restaurant after they left the motel. She had her own vegetable dish, while he had a plate of meat for himself. She watched him eat with gentle determination. She didn't want to look puffy, so she refused to eat any fat from the meat. She said she could enjoy the dish by simply watching him eat. He commented that her figure was perfect just the way it was. She forgot to remind him that most girls loved hearing, *You never look fat.* And then she thought, *Who would he say that to if I taught him this?* Thinking about it, Si-Chi smiled in the movie theater. In ancient history, *carnivores* had always meant society's upper class. *Being on top* had such a perfect double meaning. Amid the buzzing inside her head, she heard the guy in the silver mink suit talk about work, saying how they didn't treat him as a human and his boss was fucking him like a dog. It occurred to Si-Chi right away, *Do they know what it's like to not be treated as a human? Do they really know what it means to be fucked like a dog? I mean, being fucked like a dog.*

She didn't remember how she left the guy in the silver mink suit. She went back to Yi-Ting and her home. The doorman at the front desk always stared at her. She couldn't just tell him not to stare; she might sound too arrogant. The doorman must have been under thirty. Every time she came home, as soon as she appeared on the street, he would cast his eyeballs right on her body; those eyeballs would be glued on her the whole walk home.

She loved Teacher Lee. This love was like finding a fire source in all the darkness of the world, something that couldn't be seen by outsiders. She would close her palms around that fire, puff up her cheeks, and blow air to make it spread. Squatting at the corner of the street was exhausting, her uniform skirt dragging on the ground like an impatient tail waking up after a long sleep. But it was Teacher Lee who had darkened the world. The wounds her body carried formed a huge ravine, isolating her from everyone and everything. It was then that she realized she had subconsciously tried to kill herself earlier at the side of the road.

Si-Chi searched her drawers and found the rose necklace Iwen had given her, quietly blossoming in the jewelry box. Whenever she wore that necklace, the pendant always stopped at a lower place, which she measured by the tiny black mole on her collarbone. She had grown even skinnier. Putting on the dress she'd bought with Iwen, the blue one with roses in bloom, she cried. Her shoulders moved up and down. She hadn't thought she would put it on at a moment like this. Writing a suicide note would be too melodramatic. If she wrote it, it would contain only one line: *This love makes me so uncomfortable.*

Pulling the curtain open, she saw darkness spread throughout the sky. Clusters of lights, near and far, were as fluid and familiar as the Tang poems she had memorized since childhood. Si-Chi walked onto the balcony, looked down, watched the screeching scooter outside the convenience store. The steam evaporating all the way to the seventh floor felt like a kind of mercy. Some people were walking around with cigarettes in their mouths, their burning ends waving in front of their faces, as though they were fireflies. She climbed over the balcony railing, her hands gripping tightly, her feet stepping on the bottom rail, her toes absorbing the smell of blood from the metal underneath. She thought, *All I have to do is lose my grip, or let my footing slip. Both would be equally stupid.* The wind from high up blew her skirt fat, blowing the roses on her dress alive. *Do only those who enjoy life continue to live?* Si-Chi was consumed by grief. She was about to die. She saw the building manager looking at her from below. His feet nailed to the ground, his neck tilted to one side with no compulsion to call the police or shout up at her, as though he was simply watching the rain or the clouds above. There was only one thought on Si-Chi's mind. *This is too shameful.* She climbed straight back onto her balcony, her movements so swift she didn't feel like herself. She was only sixteen years old, but she already knew this was the most shameful scene of her life.

On the balcony, she sobbed so hard her organs felt like they were disintegrating. She sent an international text message to Teacher: *This love makes me feel so uncomfortable.* Even after Lee Guo-Hua came back to Taiwan, he never replied to her message. Teacher Lee was doom cloaked in love, or its metaphor. Society judges everyone by the way they dress themselves. Later, in Si-Chi's diary, Yi-Ting would come to this sentence: *There's so much that can happen in a night.* However, Si-Chi had made a mistake. The most shameful scene in her life was yet to come.

———

Lee Guo-Hua and his colleagues went to Singapore and slept late every morning. They visited tourist spots to take pictures, then wandered all the way to the red-light district. The photos were for his wife and daughter.

Living up to its name, the red-light district in Singapore was full of big red lanterns strung high up in the air. The lanterns reminded Lee Guo-Hua of a certain book, but then he thought, *Here, nobody has read Su Tong. There's no point in thinking about him.*

The physics teacher said, "Should we meet here again in an hour?"

The English teacher's glasses were trembling with lasciviousness, and he laughed.

"An hour is not enough for me."

They all laughed. The math teacher patted the English teacher's shoulder.

"Men should enjoy being young while it lasts. By the way, I rarely pay to be *serviced*," he said.

"I rarely do, either," said Teacher Lee.

Nobody admitted their thoughts: if a girl wasn't tricked, they wouldn't know if she'd be good at it.

This made the English teacher laugh.

"You still complain about girls with *superior techniques?*"

As for Lee Guo-Hua, he thought, *It's not like the English teacher to be so forgiving; it's more like he's too impatient. He'll never understand the achievement of having a little girl who didn't even know how to spread her legs wriggle you out of her. This is the kind of knowledge that we're letting our students walk away with. This is what we call the "spirit of a teacher"; we shower our students with care, like spring wind turning to rain.* The laughter deep within Teacher Lee rose to his face and broke open, and everyone wanted to know what he was laughing about. He shook his head, said nothing, then turned toward the physics teacher.

"I hope you won't feel guilty about your little actress."

To which he replied, "This is separate."

Teacher Lee laughed again.

"Your wife is the soul, and prostitutes are the flesh. An obedient little actress is flesh and soul together. You're so lucky."

The physics teacher began silently cleaning his glasses.

Teacher Lee realized he was talking too much, as though he were jealous of his colleagues. He spoke again with great confidence.

"I just broke up with my student."

Everyone was shocked, not because they felt for him, but because they were skeptical of who else would offer herself to him.

"The one that I have now is great, amazing—too amazing for me to accommodate two at the same time," Teacher Lee said.

"How old is she?" the teachers asked, and when Teacher Lee simply chuckled, they concluded she was under sixteen, not even legal yet. All the teachers looked at him with envy, while Teacher Lee simply showed nonchalance.

"Who doesn't get old, though?" the math teacher said loudly.

Teacher Lee replied, "We do, but *they* don't." What Teacher Lee said would remain deeply engraved in the teachers' hearts.

They laughed out loud, using the mineral water provided by the hotel for a toast. *Here's to men who age and shrink like cobblestones; here's to school years that stream past everlastingly fresh like a river; here's to birds of a feather who flock together; here's to all the pebbles who lived without fear and faced the hit of the river, despite knowing they would need Viagra one day; here's to counting down to the millennium of Viagra, like an atomic bomb; here's to the countries with legal red-light districts and Chinese-speaking populations; here's to the family dictatorship that has kept these districts up and running.*

In the end, they promised each other they would come back to the same spot in an hour.

This was the third time Lee Guo-Hua had participated in a hunting trip with his cram school colleagues. He didn't remember much from the two previous trips. This time he found a place with a well-decorated entrance and big red lanterns hanging above his head, as if Chinese New Year were imminent. When he entered, a middle-aged woman in a cheongsam came to greet him. A sturdily built man in a black suit followed her wherever she went. The woman glanced at Lee Guo-Hua's name-brand bag and, seemingly satisfied, led him to the lobby, where she gestured dramatically with her right arm at a line of young women spread across the space like a fan. It was a dazzling sight to behold. A feast for the eyes. Disorienting, dizzying, destabilizing.

Lee Guo-Hua thought to himself, *Just like I thought, a big place like this has its own advantages. I was right not to pick somebody up from the roadside like I did the last two times. Big stores have their own stocks.* All the young women here stood in a 丁 shape, the size of the character varying on the size of the women's feet. Each one of them smiled, teeth squeezed between two red lips. Six big teeth and six small teeth.

He lowered his voice and told the middle-aged woman, "I want someone young."

"Of course, young ones, young ones." There was a hint of spiciness as she spoke in fluent Mandarin.

She called two young women forward. Lee Guo-Hua pictured these girls with their makeup off. They were both around eighteen. He lowered his voice even more and asked, "Are there even younger ones?" This made the middle-aged woman laugh. She waved the women back with her hand. Their voluptuous figures receded into the curtain like a fan folding up.

"Sir, please wait for me," the middle-aged woman said in that spicy tone. She placed her hands gently on his shoulder and gave him a pinch. Between his hips and thighs was a wish too easily satisfied. It was a feeling he grew exhausted from before his wish could even be granted. However, Madam Spicy never disappointed any of her clients.

She led out a little girl, who wore light makeup that looked like it had just been applied. She couldn't have been more than fifteen years old.

"From China," Madam Spicy said.

"I'll take her."

As they climbed up the narrow stairway, for whatever reason, another row of women were lined up on the narrow stairs, each of them occupying a step. The women seemed to stare with their well-trained red lips and white teeth, as if supervising them. Lee Guo-Hua suddenly felt protective of the girl.

The room was medium-size with a piercingly bright-green tropical print wallpaper. The little girl helped him take off his clothes and cleaned his lower body with soap. She was petite, everything about her tiny. Her face, pale with too much makeup, looked like it had been stuck right on top of her dark neck. Her movements were swift. She asked him where he was from, just like the other girls. The professional yet rudimentary question, asked in an accent as tender as a slice of cake, conveyed a sense of desolation. As she rode him, her rhythm was like that of a corny song; anyone would be able to follow it right away.

Lee Guo-Hua suddenly thought about Fang Si-Chi. One time he'd hunted for her in the little apartment in Taipei. She was already stripped half-naked and running around, trying to escape from him in the room. The real pleasure of hunting was the chase, knowing he would be rewarded no matter what. There was a sparkling eye between her buttocks as she ran; that was what he was hunting for, that flash of fluorescent light. Just when he almost had her, she ran away again, as though playing a game. In less than five minutes, she tripped on her underwear and fell to the ground, face to the floor, her uniform ballooned and landed around her waist. Her flat butt on the blue carpet looked a lot like a corpse you'd see floating in a river in a movie, showing only its bottom. He passed the bed and walked toward her. On the bed, he pressed one of his feet deep into the mattress, while the other stayed level to the surface. *Sometimes, having such a soft mattress could be a disadvantage.* He was surprised.

He needed something more. He flipped the little Chinese girl over and spanked her ass as he thought about missing out on the flash of light in between Fang Si-Chi's thighs and letting her escape. He knew what it was! It was like back in his childhood, when he saw fireflies for the first time and caught one after much effort. But the moment he loosened his grip, the firefly shook its sparkling butt and flew away from him. That must have been the first time he discovered the truth about life. He was satiated and doubled the little Chinese girl's tip, even though none of his slaps left a mark on her dark ass.

But he'd forgotten there were no fireflies in his hometown. He'd forgotten that he'd never seen any fireflies in his life. Anyway, he was a busy man, so it was normal for him to forget things.

————

School started right after Lee Guo-Hua returned to Taiwan. As usual, he waited by Si-Chi's building for the girls to come home from school; she would meet him under the arcade outside the building. It was the first time he'd waited on the street by someone's place. He didn't know how time could be so slow. He always thought that patience was his greatest virtue.

Fang Si-Chi realized the motel was different that day. The room was extravagant with a sheen of gold, golden pillars on either side of the golden bed frames. In between the pillars was a wide red tapestry spitting out tiny golden tassels. There was also a large gold-framed mirror in front of the bed, but a different kind from that in her home. The bathroom partition was transparent. When he went for a shower, she turned her back to the bathroom, waxed on the floor.

He pulled her face up from behind, making her look up at him. Si-Chi said, *Teacher Lee, are there many other girls like me?*

No, never, just you. You and I are a lot alike.

Alike how?

I'm a neat freak when it comes to love.

Are you?

I told you about me getting a lot of love letters, and that was true. But I've never met the right person. Do you know what I mean? You know Teacher Wu and Teacher Chuang? What I said is true, about both of them and their things with a load of female students. But I'm different. I'm a refined intellectual in need of a soulmate. I'm lonely. I lived comfortably with loneliness for a long time until you broke through, when I saw you writing with your head low.

Si-Chi thought about it and said, *Teacher, should I apologize to you? Even though it's you who should apologize to me.* Lee Guo-Hua was exploiting her body. Si-Chi asked again, *Teacher Lee, do you really love me?*

Of course, I'd find you from among ten thousand people.

He slung her over his shoulder and carried her to bed. Si-Chi, like a caterpillar, curled up on Lee Guo-Hua's body, sobbing. *I can't do this today.*

Why not?

This place makes me feel like a prostitute.

Just relax.

No, please.

Just look at me.

I really can't.

He forced both her arms and feet out of place, as though he was an occupational therapist helping a patient after a stroke.

I don't want to do this.

I have to go to class soon. Can we stop wasting each other's time?

Si-Chi gradually felt like she had just entered a turbid hot spring where she couldn't see her hands or feet; gradually, she felt her arms and legs no longer belonged to her anymore. On Teacher Lee's chest was a red bud. Every time it shook up and down, it looked strangely religious, like a string of Buddha beads. As Si-Chi shifted her gaze, she couldn't feel her body anymore. She found herself standing outside of the big, red tapestry, watching Teacher under the garment, her body pressed beneath Teacher. She watched her own flesh cry, her soul shedding tears.

That was the two hundredth or three hundredth time Si-Chi's soul left her body, ever since the first time she'd lost her memory on Teacher's Day in her freshman year of junior high school.

————

When Si-Chi woke up, she found herself rushing to get dressed as usual. But this time, Teacher Lee didn't pretend to be asleep with his arms propped behind his head. He hopped out of bed to hug her, tracing her hair near her ears with his thumb. She could feel his heavy breath against her scalp, exhaling heavily while smelling her hair. He said just one thing before he loosened his grip. *You're spoiling me, right?* Too romantic. She was so afraid. This was too close to love.

Si-Chi thought about the time he gave her a new phone, telling her it would make it more convenient for them to meet up. The first time she heard Teacher Lee's voice from that phone, she was sitting near the entrance of a convenience store.

"Where are you?" he asked. "I keep hearing *ding-dong, ding-dong.*"

"Oh, I'm in a convenience store," she replied, casually. And then she realized this made it sound like she had rushed out the door and into a store. Maybe he hadn't thought much of it, but she had felt ridiculously embarrassed, more so than ever before. She wondered why she thought about this at all.

Sitting on the ground in the room, Si-Chi's thoughts went in all directions. Teacher Lee's snore was as clear as Yan Kai–style calligraphy, distinctive like veins protruding under flesh. Teacher Lee always wanted *it*, and even though he had wanted it a thousand times, she still felt shocked whenever it happened. It was too much work for Teacher. One man fighting against long-lasting social mores and traditions, that was too much. She stood up and climbed inside the quilt from the edge of the bed. Sitting there, she watched Teacher Lee and thought this was the same brown-black color that most books were referring to. Teacher Lee jolted awake and patted her head as though she were a basketball. She couldn't speak for a long while. There was nothing they could do about this. Nothing. His naked body looked exceptionally frail and elderly. It shocked her to hear him say he was "getting old." She wasn't going to waste her energy pitying him. It was too self-conscious of her to do that. There was no way she could tell him that she hadn't anticipated they would do it properly that day. After all, now that she had initiated it a few times, he wouldn't have to carry the cross of desire on his own anymore. Half-satisfied and half-dismal, she slowly crept off the bed with small, catlike steps, then picked up her clothes and said, "You're just exhausted."

———

Mrs. Chang had introduced Mr. Maomao's jewelry shop to Iwen when she had first moved into the building. Besides reading to Si-Chi and Yi-Ting, Iwen didn't have any other diversions. If she let old Mrs. Chien catch her reading a book, she would be scolded again.

Mr. Maomao's real name was Mao Jing-Yuan. He couldn't remember when exactly the rich ladies started to call him Mr. Maomao. Spending time with a younger guy made them feel young again. Mr. Maomao understood that mentality; he was an easygoing person to begin with. Gradually, nobody knew his actual name anymore—even he appeared to have forgotten it.

The first time Iwen visited the jewelry shop, it happened to be Mr. Maomao's shift. Normally, it was his mother who handled the shop while Mr. Maomao designed jewelry and selected gemstones upstairs. The shop was neither too extravagant nor too plain; it was just a jewelry shop, nothing more and nothing less.

Iwen had long forgotten the first time she met Mr. Maomao. She simply got used to seeing him every once in a while. But Mr. Maomao remembered everything. That first day they met, Iwen had worn a sleeveless dress with white flowers scattered all over, a wide-brim straw hat with a ribbon tied around it, and white T-strap sandals. She pressed the doorbell and pushed the door open, walking like the monsoon had pushed her in. Her dress, blown up by the wind, deflated not long after she entered the shop, the wrinkles pressing tight against her body. She had looked especially girlish as she took her hat off and ran a hand through her hair. Even though Iwen always came and went, sitting there, Maomao couldn't fight his feelings anymore. Iwen was as pale as a freshly painted, doorless room, walls so white that he salivated as she approached little by little, pressing closer to him, laying siege to Mr. Maomao's entire life.

That first day, Mr. Maomao had greeted Iwen good afternoon, to which she bowed and murmured that she was just looking around.

"May I know your name?" he asked.

"Just call me Miss Hsu."

Newly married at the time, Iwen had already witnessed on multiple occasions the influence Mrs. Chien's name exerted. Therefore, when she was alone, she simply liked to be called Miss Hsu. Mr. Maomao instinctively took a glance at the jewelry on Iwen. She was wearing a simple twisted ring. Maybe she only had a boyfriend. And then Mr. Maomao got scared by his thoughts.

"Are you looking for anything specific?"

"Oh, um, I don't know!" With an angelic smile, Iwen laughed the kind of innocent laughter that only someone who easily obtained full marks in statistics could, laughter that showed she had never been wounded.

"Would you like coffee or tea?"

125

"Ah, coffee, please! Coffee would be great." Iwen smiled so big that her eyes squinted. Her eyelashes resembled Marie Antoinette's favored fan. Mr. Maomao felt a chill sweep over him, the chill of hail, rather than ice in a glass of alcohol. Such a beautiful smile, a smile that would surely be wounded were it not protected by a snow globe.

Smoothing her dress, Iwen sat down and said she would like to look at the pair of earrings shaped like tree branches. They were platinum earrings the length of a pinky finger, engraved with winding patterns and circular branches, attached with tiny diamonds like snowflakes. Iwen was surrounded by a universe of platinum. She enjoyed every season of the year; she embraced life and life embraced her. But if she really had to choose, she preferred winter over summer, when she could look up and see a thin withered hand of a branch pointing toward the blue sky. It always felt like she pressed the sky with her left hand, while taking a pencil with her right hand to draw something upon it. She held her coffee with both hands in an unusual position, looking like she was trying to warm herself. Like a lamb sipping milk, she pouted her mouth to sip her coffee, showing a slightly embarrassed smile as though she wasn't wearing enough in front of the snow-covered branches. Never had anyone gotten so immersed in the design process of Mr. Maomao's jewelry.

Examining the jewelry in front of the mirror, Iwen forgot to look at herself. She simply looked at those little branches from another angle, murmuring that they looked a lot like Stendhal. Mr. Maomao said the branch was made of crystal salt from Salzburg. Iwen laughed and her ears, little teeth, long neck, and armpits all moved in tandem.

"This is the first time someone has understood my references—Salzburg, Stendhal's theory of love. This pair of earrings came from that theory."

"Oh, really?" Iwen might've exposed Maomao's agenda, but at that moment, it felt like it was Maomao who had seen right through her. He was incredibly moved, as though he were the one that had fallen into the salt mine and gotten covered in crystal salt. Iwen was the crystal salt right on top of him. To Maomao, she was an allusion. His allusion. Iwen no longer felt embarrassed. Fresh off her wedding, she was still in her honeymoon phase; everything in the world felt saturated with love and respect. Iwen became a regular at Maomao's shop from that day forward. Sometimes during her visits, they would spend two or three hours talking about literature. From time to time, she would bring a few literature-inspired accessories home with her, feeling like she had just walked out of Utopia. Out of the Magic Mountain. Out of a candy house. Little did she know that, for Maomao, her visits didn't feel like being in a candy house; they were like being inside a sweet piece of candy.

At first, Mr. Maomao only knew her as Miss Hsu. Later, upstairs, standing in front of the mirror, he secretly practiced calling her Iwen. *Just call me Iwen*, she had said.

Often, Iwen would bring three pieces of lemon cake to Maomao. One for his mother, the other for Mr. Maomao, and one for herself. Whenever they shared the cakes, she would say to Mr. Maomao stubbornly, *You can't blame me. It would be such a waste if we didn't have a cake to pair with such good coffee.*

"I wouldn't even buy strawberry shortcake during strawberry season, Mr. Mao. Do you know why?" Iwen said.

"I have no idea." *You smile like the heart of a strawberry.*

"Because strawberries are seasonal. I worry too much about the risks and rewards. But lemon cake is always there, and I like something that's everlasting."

Iwen continued, "When I was a student, I became friends with the girl sitting next to me. But whenever I thought about it later, I was deeply afraid to consider if we wouldn't have become friends had she not sat beside me. Sometimes I feel ashamed by such thoughts."

"So Miss Hsu isn't just passing by?" Maomao asked.

This made Iwen laugh again. "No, not just passing by."

Your twisted ring sparkles whenever you cut the cake. Maomao never asked: *Do you know how much the sound weighed on me the first time you rang the doorbell and walked in? And if you did know, would you even have pressed the doorbell?*

Iwen continued, "So, I like things that existed before me. I like cards more than emails. I like blind dates more than flirting."

You prefer Mencius over Zhuangzi, and you also like Hello Kitty. I really made you laugh. Your laughter is like the sunrise I would see after drafting jewelry designs all night long. At that moment, the sun only belongs to me. I'm older than you. I started to exist before you. Does that mean you could like me?

Lowering his head, Maomao scooped up some coffee beans, noticing a line of her hair on the glass counter. He felt a surge of sorrow. *I would have liked to pick that hair up and carry a part of you from the other shore of the counter to my shore. I would have liked to place that hair in my bed, pretending that you'd visited. That you'd visited me.*

In front of the jewelry and Maomao, Iwen was always laid-back. She was used to being around jewelry, and he seemed to grow used to her visiting. It was rare for Iwen to meet a man who was not too nervous or too generous in front of her. For that, she appreciated Maomao, thinking he was just like the coffee mug she had been using since her very first visit. Even if others used the mug when she wasn't there, it was always clean and shiny whenever she came back to it. She didn't know Maomao hadn't let anyone else touch it since then. Very few people knew as much as she did, but even fewer people were able to speak without a hint of humility or arrogance. Maomao could engrave the decade a writer spent writing a novel onto a brooch. No matter how little those rich ladies understood of his jewelry, he never felt downtrodden or lonely. He simply carried a mirror in front of those ladies with a big smile.

Sometimes, Mr. Maomao stayed upstairs working on the designs. During the process, he would instinctively move his hand to the margin of his paper and begin drawing a woman's size nine ring, twisted in the shape of sweet fried dough. On the ring, he would draw a ring finger. *I would think about the way you called me Mr. Mao, cutting it off to just Mao and then replaying that sound twice: Mao. Mao. That was the first time I realized how magnificent my nickname could sound.* He added a middle finger and a pinkie next to the ring finger, the oval fingernails looking like an ecliptic of the Earth orbiting the sun. *Which galaxy do you belong to? Surely you would be able to forgive me for noticing a star still sparkling in the sky, despite the city lights, when I drove back home after closing the shop at night. I thought about my unfinished design and the night that awaited me. I thought about staying up to finish the design and reentering the shop at dawn. I stared at the electronic calendar in the shop and tore a calendar page from my heart. And then I would think about how I would be able to see you again the next day. In the end, whenever I saw the stars and the sun, I thought about you. With these thoughts, my hand would begin drawing an index finger and a thumb, along with the wrinkles on each finger and the light hair on the back of your hand. I couldn't keep drawing this. All I needed was to see that you were doing well each week, and that would be enough.*

Iwen brought three puff pastries to the shop one day. Mr. Mao's mother saw her and asked her to wait. "I'm calling Mao-mao to come downstairs."

On top of the mille-feuille was a pile of vanilla custard. When Iwen took the pastries out, she confessed to Maomao, "We can eat vanilla cakes throughout the year because the Europeans colonized Latin America. But I still love vanilla-flavored desserts, so I must be very ignorant." Mr. Maomao laughed light-heartedly, his smile so shallow it looked like it could be scooped up with a spoon. Iwen didn't know why, but no matter how much cream there was in the dessert she brought, it never got onto Mr. Maomao's little mustache. The two of them talked about everything from colonization to Joseph Conrad.

Maomao was clearing the table when Iwen said, "I don't see how Joseph Conrad belittles women in his works, and I'm a woman." All of a sudden, Mrs. Chang rang the doorbell and walked in. It was strange that they hadn't noticed her coming, since she had red curly hair. Mrs. Chang's voice was emotional and rushed forth like the cold winter current.

"Aiya, Mrs. Chien, you're also here! How come you didn't invite me? We could've had a party in our building, right, Maomao?"

Mrs. Chien. Maomao's heart turned into a lemon. Bitter and sour, peeled and squeezed into juice. *I thought you looked familiar simply because we had instant chemistry, like out of a popular romance novel. I felt some kind of déjà vu from a previous life. But actually, it turns out I had seen you before. The bride at the wedding, whom nobody could look at directly. I just realized the pink diamond I'd selected in Hong Kong is around your neck.*

Iwen's smile was like a ghostly optical illusion. Mr. Maomao's smile was stranded at the edges of his lips, while Mrs. Chang's voice became as loud as an election truck. It was so loud, but he couldn't remember a single word.

After Mrs. Chang left, Iwen smiled apologetically.

"Sorry, I always feel a bit shy about calling myself Mrs. Chien."

Slowly, gently, Maomao said, "It's totally all right." *When you smile at me like that, how can I not forgive you? I'm nobody to you, anyway, a complete outsider.*

And then summer came. Besides Si-Chi and Yi-Ting, Mr. Maomao was the only person who noticed Iwen didn't change her long sleeves. He scolded himself, asking if he simply wanted to see Iwen's exposed arms. But apart from the unseasonal long sleeves, a new, fearful coldness surrounded her. When he asked if she wanted coffee, she seemed shocked and her voice jittered, *Yeah?* He knew that when she lowered her head, she was not looking at accessories; she was simply afraid of showing her tears. He also knew she wasn't trying to look at him when she lifted her head. She just didn't want her tears to drip down.

What's going on? he asked himself. *If only I weren't your jewelry designer. How I wish I could just be a tine on your comb, the pump of your hand soap. What's going on with you? What's going on? What happened?*

One day, Mrs. Chang, Mama Wu, and Mrs. Chen came together to look at a new line of jewelry. That was ostensibly the reason, but they spent most of their time gossiping. Everybody knew Maomao and his mother could keep secrets. Mr. Maomao's mother greeted them, while Mr. Maomao brought to them a freshly printed design, the paper hot like bread fresh out of the oven. When he went downstairs, he heard Mrs. Chang say, "So he always hit her somewhere no one could see."

"Does he beat her that often?"

"Of course! Young Mr. Chien was a green beret, just like my young cousin! They got some rough training there!"

Mr. Maomao's mother heard her son's footsteps stop, so she excused herself with a bow and shuffled upstairs. She saw Maomao roll the design print into a ball and throw it against the wall. As though murmuring to herself, she said in a tone as plain as white rice and thin noodles, "Don't be silly. She wouldn't marry you even if she got a divorce." Then she went downstairs. Mr. Maomao's mother knew. Maybe she'd known about it even before him.

He thought about how Iwen looked closely at a cocktail ring one time and said, *I must have seen this somewhere before.* He had immediately brought out all the accessories she had looked at during her first visit. He could remember everything about her outfit from that day, just like he'd quietly and confidently memorized the Tang poem "Ascending White Stork Tower." He thought about Iwen's surprised smile, a kind of smile that seemed also distant, as though she couldn't see anything that was happening at the moment.

After driving home that night, Mr. Maomao turned on his

laptop to watch the news. Corruption. Burglary. Marriage. He thought the blank background of the news seemed paler than usual, and the black fonts seemed darker. He unbuttoned his pants and thought about Iwen: the way her eyelashes knit together when she laughed; the summer day he first met her, a wine-red bra strap on her shoulder underneath her tank top. When she leaned over to examine the jewelry in the glass counter, her cleavage exposed. When she read in French, her little red tongue hopped up and down between her teeth. He masturbated while thinking about Iwen. The room was completely dark, and the light from the laptop screen fell on Maomao's body. His pants were paralyzed at his calves. He couldn't do it anymore. Naked from the waist down, Maomao cried for the first time since graduating from elementary school.

———

At Lee Guo-Hua's little apartment in Taipei, Si-Chi sat on the floor, caressing a corner of the flannel curled up from the sofa arm, and asked, *Teacher Lee, can you take me to a doctor?*

What happened?

I—I think I'm probably sick.

Are you feeling sick right now? Don't tell me you're pregnant?

No.

Then what is it?

I often forget things.

Forgetting things isn't an illness.

I mean, like I'm really forgetting things.

I don't understand.

Of course you don't understand, she whispered.

Then Lee Guo-Hua said, *You're being disrespectful, Si-Chi.*

She pointed at her clothes on the floor and said, *This is disrespectful of you to do to your student.*

Lee Guo-Hua remained silent. His silence was as long as a glacier. He finally said, *I love you, but I also feel guilty. Can you stop making me feel this way?*

I'm sick.

What kind of illness are you talking about?

I often can't remember if I've gone to school or not.

I don't understand.

Si-Chi inhaled deeply, mustering up patience, and said, *I often wake up at a weird time in a weird place. But I don't remember where I've been. Sometimes, I wake up in my bed without remembering what I did yesterday. Yi-Ting often tells me I was mean to her, but I can't remember what I said to her at all. Yi-Ting told me I walked out of class one time. But I didn't even know that I went to school that day. I forgot everything.*

What Si-Chi didn't say was that she wasn't even able to fall asleep. Even napping at her desk for ten minutes, she would dream about him inserting himself into her, so every time she fell asleep, she felt like she would die of suffocation. All she could do was to keep downing coffee. Yi-Ting would be woken up by the coffee grinder and walk out with great irritation. And every time that happened, she would see Si-Chi making coffee under the moonlight, shiny snot dangling from her nose. Yi-Ting would say, "Do you really have to do this? You're like a zombie, copying my homework and spending time with Teacher. Now you're not letting me sleep, either?" Si-Chi also didn't remember taking the coffee grinder and throwing it at Yi-Ting. She only recalled that she didn't walk home with Yi-Ting one day. When she got home, she didn't even know how to open the door and kept trying to use the key to Teacher Lee's apartment without success. When she finally managed to open it, she saw coffee grounds spilled all over the living room floor.

Throughout her three years in senior high school, Si-Chi also dreamt about men other than Lee Guo-Hua forcing themselves on her. One time, it was the teaching assistant in math class, who was as skinny as the lead of a mechanical pencil, his Adam's apple protruding from his dark skin. When he was on top of her, he said, "It's all your fault. You're too beautiful," and his Adam's apple trembled and wriggled as he swallowed. It looked like an opal-colored beetle, the kind that could drill under human skin in a horror movie. His words of love would slip inside his Adam's apple, and then into his throat, and then into Si-Chi. For a very long time, she couldn't be sure if it was really just a dream. In every math class, when Si-Chi exchanged and graded test papers with her classmate, she would stare at the teaching assistant as he chanted a series of answers: ABCD. A was an order, B was a curse word, C was a way to tell her to be quiet, and D was a satisfied smile. Then one day, the teaching assistant bent over at the podium, which allowed Si-Chi to see all the way into his shirt. She noticed he never wore any necklaces, but in the dream, he always wore a tiny jade Guanyin pendant. It must have been a dream. And another time, she dreamt of Kwei. That also took her a long time to figure out if it was a dream or not, until one day Iwen spoke on the phone about how Kwei was studying in the US and had not come back to Taiwan for three years. It must have been a dream. She even dreamt of Papa Liu and her own papa.

135

Lee Guo-Hua thought of a book he read about PTSD, which used to be called a veteran's disease. One of the symptoms of PTSD was that the victims would blame themselves and feel guilty. *That is too convenient,* he thought. *It's not that I don't feel any guilt; it's that these girls have exhausted my sense of guilt. Little girls' labias also look like wounds. It's too beautiful, this transfer of guilt. It is one of the most extreme rhetorical methods.*

Lee Guo-Hua asked Si-Chi, *Would you like to go to a counseling session? Do you want to tell the psychiatrist something? What would the psychiatrist learn from you?*

I won't say anything, Si-Chi said. *All I want is to be able to sleep well and remember things.*

How long has this been going on?

Maybe three to four years.

How come you said nothing about it these past years, and now you want to see a psychiatrist? From what you've told me, you're completely abnormal! Lee Guo-Hua said.

Si-Chi replied slowly, *Because I didn't know if it was just me.*

This made Lee Guo-Hua laugh. *Normal people aren't like that!*

Staring at her fingernails, Si-Chi continued, *Normal people also don't do what we do.*

Lee Guo-Hua fell into silence again. Silence was just the tip of an iceberg; underneath it were words that were ten times colder.

Are you trying to pick a fight with me? Why are you so disobedient today?

Putting her white socks on, Si-Chi said, *I just want a good night's sleep.* And then she stopped talking. They never talked about this again.

Walking out of the apartment, they came upon a homeless

person at the gate of the building under the arcade. He had a steel lunch box in front of him with coins scattered inside, like sesame seeds on top of a bowl of white rice. The homeless person used his hands to drag his disabled legs. Si-Chi flattened her skirt and then squatted down, leveling her gaze with the homeless person. Then she dumped all of the coins from her purse into her hands and placed them in his palms. Holding Si-Chi's money, the homeless person bent and wriggled his body, right leg thudding loudly on the ground. He kept saying, "Such a good girl. You will certainly be blessed with everlasting happiness and a long life." *Ah, everlasting happiness and a long life.* Si-Chi smiled. The wind lifted up her hair. Her lip gloss glowed on her lips, and she thanked the homeless person, feeling utterly convinced.

After getting in the taxi, Lee Guo-Hua told her, "Good, your parents taught you well. You don't know how many Black kids Xixi has adopted so far. But please stop donating money to that beggar. For better or worse, I'm somewhat known around here. If we keep lingering at the gate together, it's not going to do us any good." Si-Chi didn't say anything. She simply moved the hair that stuck to her lips, gnawing at the tip of it. The hair, damp from saliva, made faint noises in her mouth. She started day-dreaming and thought, *Ah, this noise! In this season of fallen leaves, the road becomes a long river fully covered in yellow teardrops, and I allow my body to drift along this river. It must be this sound.* Teacher Lee was still talking about Xixi adopting some kids, saying he had already become a grandfather. Si-Chi burst out laughing, and he asked what she was laughing about.

Nothing.

Are you listening to me?

Yup. Gnawing on her hair, Si-Chi thought, *Do you really want me to listen to you?*

In Lee Guo-Hua's little apartment there was a storage room, and the villa that belonged to Teacher Lee had a storehouse. He was the kind of person who would buy every single item he liked from the supermarket. Sometimes he thought he should collect antiques since he earned enough money. And that was the perfect metaphor for the other side of his life. He always told the little girls, "I have something fun to show you." And he would grow extremely excited, because nobody ever caught on to the double meaning, no matter how obvious it was. He would point toward the Eastern Chinese gouache portraits of ladies on the wall when he brought these little girls to his apartment. The ladies in the portraits were always reading, their eyebrows curved like a moon on the verge of an eclipse. When the girls studied the painting, he would tie up their arms and legs from behind, reaching out one hand and telling them, "Look at that. That's you. Do you know how much I missed you before you appeared in my life?" They always cried when he carried them to his bedroom. As for the portraits in the living room, red, timid smiles remained on the ladies' faces, as though it wasn't clear to them what had just happened.

Lee Guo-Hua had only brought Si-Chi to his villa in Nei-hu once. The storeroom was full of antiques. Once he pushed the door open, sunlight streamed in and stretched out a golden parallelogram on the floor. Many of the wooden Guanyin sculptures were the size of children, falling against one another, some of them with chipped noses. Years of dust separated the numerous Guanyin statues that sat between the shell dividers from the embroidered portraits depicting hundreds of children. They all smiled toward Si-Chi from the room's darkest corners. Feeling a sense of humiliation, Si-Chi said quietly, *I don't understand.*

He was sneaky and asked her, *I gave you some lessons in our essay class, and you're such a smart girl. How come you don't understand?*

After thinking about it, Si-Chi said, *I think someone who thinks they can turn an obedient person into an immoral person has a very evil sort of confidence. Maybe I did feel something was off, but I kept telling myself what I felt wasn't normal. And then I stopped feeling anything.* Her righteous voice faltered and froze. *But maybe the most evil thing about it was that in my naivete, I walked down those stairs.*

Taking her to the villa meant bringing her to the bed in the second-floor guest room. He took a nap while Si-Chi talked. For the first time, words poured out of her without pause. *I always knew I was a special kid, but I never wanted to be special because of my appearance. I want to be like Yi-Ting. At least when people compliment her intelligence, we know they're being genuine about it. Nobody actually sees me because of the way I look. I used to tell Yi-Ting I really like Teacher Lee, because we both think Teacher Lee is able to "see." I don't know. We trusted someone who had memorized the entire "Song of Everlasting Regret."*

On Monday, he dragged her to a motel with a big 喜 (happiness) character in the signpost. Tuesday, they visited another motel with the character 滿 (satisfaction); Wednesday, it was 金 (wealth). 喜滿金 are great characters; they're auspicious in any order. Leaving that longing on the island was like sleepwalking at home; nothing was dangerous. He could talk about books until they penetrated her. The magic of literature!

Si-Chi asked him one time what she meant to him. He only replied four words, *Thousands of pointed fingers*. She asked if that mattered to him and remembered him replying, *It did matter at the beginning, but now there's just one thing I want. So it doesn't matter anymore*. After that, he held her hand on the street for the first time, as though it were an act of infinite bravery. It was midnight down in the old alley and, of course, nobody would see them. When they lifted up their heads, there was a full moon. She thought of that saying about letting heaven and Earth be witness. Walking back to the apartment, he bent over her, and all she felt was the heat of the moonlight on the back of her hand, imprinted with the outline of Teacher Lee's hand. She thought about the cheesiness of the expression "thousands of pointed fingers." It could be easily replaced with other words such as "thousands of gazes" or even "thousands of knife slashes"; he simply drew expressions from his own dictionary, after all. Si-Chi was cheerful.

When Lee Guo-Hua went back to Kaohsiung, Si-Chi sent him text messages every night to say good night. She turned off the light, settling herself on the pillow in the darkness of her room. The light from her phone projected on her face, carving out the contour of her eyebrows, nose, and dimples. Whenever she weighed the words she tried to use, she would instinctively tilt her head, her hair tumbling against the pillow, making swishing noises, like what a flowing river or golden sand would make. Her head sank deeper and deeper into the pillow. The tone she used in the text messages recalled the essays she wrote in junior high school. After wishing him good night, she couldn't fall asleep, afraid of dreaming. She stared at her hands under the quilt, holding the luminous pearls that he gave her, saying it would help her sleep. The pearls looked like the full moon plucked from the dark branches in the night sky, green like jade, emitting faint light. But the full moon was too close to her, making all the dents and scars on it too visible to her.

Lately, whenever Lee Guo-Hua went back to Kaohsiung, he brought gifts for his wife and his daughter, Xixi. What he brought most often were the dragon robes from the Qing dynasty, which he found in antique shops. One day he spread a robe on the floor, showing stretched silk lines and a big yellow 人 character. It was extravagant and rare, like a tiger-skin carpet. At the sight of it, Xixi said, "Daddy wants to collect things himself and is just using Mommy and me as an excuse." As for Teacher Lee's wife, she felt that tinge of sorrow. She thought she would never be able to understand the person sleeping next to her. Clothes from the dead! Some of these people had even been decapitated in public! She laughed bitterly and said, "I don't understand anything about this stuff. You should take them back and do the research yourself." Little did Teacher Lee's wife know that what she felt was another kind of sadness, a premonition of getting hurt. Seeing their reactions, Lee Guo-Hua would always look sheepish and defeated. He put the dragon robes away. The next time he brought a gift for his wife, he almost believed she might actually like it. If she didn't like the bright yellow of an empress, what about the golden yellow of a princess? If not, what about the fragrant color of a concubine, tinged with desire? One robe after another, he put them back into the storage room in the apartment, on the verge of getting angry. He was mad about how his wife would never be satisfied with his gifts. But with a quick shift of thought, he still nobly forgave her.

Whenever Mrs. Lee received her gifts, the fear living inside her came out as sadness. For her, the sadness was at least healthy because it meant she was still in love with her husband. Since he was a teenager, he'd never been good at giving gifts to anyone. They rarely went abroad together, but one time he'd picked up a tiny antique she thought looked like a piece of junk at the local market and brought it home. This was even during their honeymoon. When he became instantly famous at the cram school that year, he brought back a Tang Sancai glazed sculpture. "Sancai sculptures mainly come in yellow, green, and white. But of course, those are not the only colors they come in. Three means multiplicity." He waited until she repeated after him: "Yellow, green, and white." Then he loosened his grip and said, "This is for you."

For so many years, Mrs. Lee was incredulous of how much he spoiled Xixi. When Xixi was ten years old, she started buying jeans that cost over ten thousand New Taiwan dollars. And when she entered junior high school, she started carrying brand-name purses. Mrs. Lee didn't show her anger. If she did, she would become the mean parent. She once asked her husband if he could ask other teachers in the cram school to help Xixi with her schoolwork, to which he only replied, "It's not the best." She got the sense he meant those people weren't the best, not that the idea was awful.

"Do you mean those people aren't the best?" she asked when they were in bed together.

"How so? They're like me. All regular people." He ran a hand through her hair, which felt like rice husks after years of perming. He smiled at her. "I'm getting old."

"If you're old, then I am, too."

"You have beautiful eyes."

"I'm just an old woman."

Lee Guo-Hua smiled again, thinking at least Xixi's eyes looked like her mother's. Her hair was the texture of rice husks and rice bran. As for those girls, their hair was soft-cooked, fragrant white rice. *His rice*. His main sustenance. All Mrs. Lee knew was that his poor gift giving stayed consistent. The closer Si-Chi tried to stay with him, the more he wanted to head back to Kaohsiung with the gifts. It was not to compensate for his sense of guilt; he was simply too happy.

———

After Si-Chi and Yi-Ting started their semester in Taipei, Iwen became paler. In the beginning, she would tag along with Yi-Wei on his business trips. She especially enjoyed flying to Japan. Whenever Yi-Wei went to work, she would walk out of their apartment in Ginza, wandering around for half the day. Japan was such a nice place; everyone looked like they had a to-do list written across their faces. All pedestrians rushed as though they were on the way to a family wedding or a funeral. The Japanese could cross a street with a ninety-second "Walk" light in ten seconds. As for Iwen, she would walk slowly, taking up that ninety seconds, thinking about how her worries could be diluted in the midst of the crowd, thinking about how she could always cross the street for that full ninety seconds. Black, white, black, white. How much time had she wasted? She had an entire life waiting for her to waste!

Whenever Yi-Wei went to Japan, he would visit a good friend,

Jimmy, who studied in the US with him. They always spoke English. Each time before Jimmy visited them, Iwen would purchase three bento boxes from the nearby sushi shop. She would communicate in Japanese mixed with English and receive the bentos in cinnabar-colored lacquerware containers. On the bento boxes were printed golden pine, bamboo, and plum flower trees. The golden pine needles were curled just like Yi-Wei's chest hair; the bamboo was as straight and discernable as Yi-Wei's fingers; as for the plum tree, the last flower that was about to fall from the curved branches was like Yi-Wei's smile.

Jimmy was a short and skinny man. Even though he had been living in Japan for a long time, she could tell his mannerisms and voice were still very Western. She couldn't quite explain it. Perhaps it was because the top two buttons of his shirt were unbuttoned, or he could never fully bow. Maybe it was because he always called her Iwen directly. One day Yi-Wei told Iwen, "I thought about hiring Jimmy right after graduation, but he's too smart. I don't think he would be happy working under me." In Japan, all Iwen had to do was be a good wife without questioning. And there, Yi-Wei let her be. One day Yi-Wei brought a big bottle of Junmai Daiginjo sake home with him. When Iwen saw the long wooden box, her expression changed as though she were looking at the coffin of a family member. That night, Jimmy came to visit them. At the sight of a table full of a variety of dishes, he exclaimed in English: "Bro, why don't you visit Japan more often?" Yi-Wei laughed a lot, like a trembling tree branch, not knowing he was the last plum flower of the season. They called each other "bro," patted each other's shoulders, bumped fists. This all looked beautiful to Iwen. She was witnessing foreign culture in a foreign country. It was not until they finished dinner, when Yi-Wei asked her to bring out the drinks, that Iwen suddenly felt awake.

Yi-Wei went upstairs to fetch a souvenir from Taiwan. Iwen excused herself from the dining table, walking from the dining area to the kitchen. The wooden box in her hand still looked surprisingly like a baby-size coffin. Jimmy sat at the table. From above, Yi-Wei noticed Jimmy was staring at Iwen's back. When Iwen squatted down to unpack the wooden box, the white skin of her lower back was partially exposed, where the joints of her spine were faintly visible. Stretch that gaze further and he could almost imagine her crotch. This was Yi-Wei's territory. Here and there were all parts of his territory. When Yi-Wei walked down the stairs, the railings felt like his crutch, but he pretended nothing had happened. The drinks were poured, and the side dishes were all on the table. They talked about everything from their university fraternity to the yakuza, from sushi to collective suicide in Okinawa during World War II. Yi-Wei's voice grew louder and louder, and whenever they toasted, Iwen thought the glasses were going to shatter.

They talked until midnight, and Iwen started to feel exhausted. She excused herself again, dragging her slippered feet into the bedroom to look for her eye drops. Yi-Wei waved at Jimmy and followed her. Yi-Wei hugged Iwen from behind, reaching his hands all over her. Iwen whispered, *No, no, Yi-Wei, not now.* Yi-Wei snaked his hands elsewhere. *No, Yi-Wei, not here; I really can't.* Yi-Wei moved his palms with all his fingers, kissed her with his lips and his tongue. *No, Yi-Wei. We can't do this, not now.* Yi-Wei began to unzip himself. *Let me close*

145

the door at least. Yi-Wei, please. Yi-Wei knew Jimmy could hear everything.

Jimmy sat at the dining area, listening to Iwen. He leaned his head lazily against the high chair. A middle-aged Taiwanese guy who lingered in the golden mile of the Japanese capital deep into the night. Through the glass roof in this 350-square-foot dining room, he could see an early night sky, just like the ones they had seen on the American east coast. He listened to his friend's wife. He walked unsteadily out of their apartment. On the side of the road was the sign of an izakaya written in Chinese characters, just like in Taiwan. Inside the display window, where the heads of the mannequins should have been, were hooks shaped like question marks.

Three months later, Yi-Wei had to take a trip to Japan again. Iwen sat by, listening to a phone conversation between Yi-Wei and Jimmy. She could no longer focus on the news on the TV right in front of her.

Sometimes, Si-Chi would call Iwen from Taipei, but the way she talked was like water gurgling as it boiled. She would talk for half an hour, but Iwen couldn't understand anything she said. One day, Mama Fang complained half-jokingly that Si-Chi never really called home. Iwen's face turned stiff. Next time Si-Chi called, she wouldn't dare ask how school was going, how her classmates were, or how she was feeling physically and emotionally; that was too much like mothering. She knew Si-Chi didn't want anyone to nag, but Iwen didn't know what Si-Chi wanted to say exactly. Whenever she talked to her on the phone, Si-Chi always talked about how heavy the rain in Taipei was and how much homework she had. But when Iwen pushed her to tell her more about these things, she couldn't describe them in detail. It was as if her student life in Taipei was something from a TV show. Iwen faintly suspected that Si-Chi was hiding some kind of rotten wound, something so big that she couldn't take it, like moldy sores all over her body. But she couldn't get her to say anything more. Whenever she tried, Si-Chi would start talking about the rain. Only one time did Si-Chi say that the rain was so heavy it was like "a god scooping up water with the Taipei basin to shower with." Hearing that, Iwen realized Si-Chi might already have surrendered herself to the mysteries of her trauma.

On the other end of things, Yi-Ting barely called Iwen. She was hesitant to ask Mama Liu if Yi-Ting had called them or had said anything.

Iwen disliked summer. Although nobody ever questioned her about it, she felt uncomfortable when strangers stared at her turtleneck. She thought those stares were like the hook of a question mark that people were desperate to tug at her collar with. Back in Tokyo again, she ordered some sushi from the shop she frequented. The vermilion container outlined in thin gold still looked like Yi-Wei. After they had ordered so many times from this shop, the containers piled up all around, which resembled their loft apartment. They emitted some kind of sorrow in the glow of sunset. The more meticulous the art was, the duller it looked in repetition. In a trance, Iwen thought about how Yi-Wei would be sixty years old when she was forty. By then, he might not try to beg her for his own pleasure. But he might continue to beat her. It seemed more bearable if he simply beat her up. Better in the afternoon than in the evening. She started crying while thinking about it. Her tears fell to the floor, splashing the dust-covered tiles. It was as if even the dust was disgusted by her.

Yi-Wei and Jimmy skipped drinking tonight. They had been talking about Ma Ying-Jeou's presidential reelection all night already. Iwen didn't know how scared she looked when Yi-Wei called her name. Jimmy thanked Iwen for hosting him and asked Yi-Wei if he would walk with him for a bit. Yi-Wei laughed and said it was like escorting a girl back to her dorm.

Once they stepped outside, the wind blew against Jimmy's face and made him squint. The hot wind lingered on his polo shirt, revealing his thin frame. Yi-Wei put his arm around Jimmy's neck, inadvertently showing how he was greater than him physically and in many other different ways. Jimmy turned to Yi-Wei, still squinting, and spoke in English: "Bro, you hit her, right?" Yi-Wei was unable to retract his smile.

"Sorry, what?"

"You really did hit her, right?"

Yi-Wei let go of Jimmy's neck and said lightly, "Did I fly here for you to lecture me?"

Jimmy gave Yi-Wei a shove. The sight of Yi-Wei's brand-new, clean collar reminded him of how he saw Iwen hug a big heap of dirty laundry, struggling to push all the clothes into the washing machine. That thought stopped Jimmy from pushing Yi-Wei all the way up against the wall. "Not cool, man! Who do you think you are?"

Yi-Wei didn't push back but only stood there rooted to the ground, so he couldn't be jostled any further. "Mind your own business."

"Fuck you. You're a real asshole! Do you think she's like all the other girls you dated and will just shut up, take your money, and leave? She really loves you!"

Yi-Wei paused, like he was contemplating something. And then he spoke again with a smile. "I saw you staring at her."

"What the fuck are you talking about?" Jimmy said.

"What I'm saying is, I saw you *staring* at my wife." Yi-Wei continued, "It's like how you always used to chase after the same woman as me back in school."

Jimmy's face dropped like water dripping from an air conditioner. Drip, drop, drip, drop. He sighed. "You're worse than I thought."

And then he turned away. Yi-Wei noticed they were standing in a street full of people. The sun shone on all their dark-haired heads, which looked sleek and smooth in the light. When Yi-Wei looked again, he found Jimmy was long gone.

The first time Iwen had met Jimmy was at the party after her wedding. The wedding ceremony was for the older generation, but the party was for theirs. Iwen liked the way Yi-Wei said *wo men* (we), the way he pouted his lips when he said *wo*, as if he were about to lean over and kiss her, and how he pronounced *men* like putting on a smile. Yi-Wei was so adorable.

At their wedding, there were politicians and media press groups. But that didn't matter. When Iwen and Yi-Wei visited the wedding dress shop for a custom gown, Iwen drew her ideal dress: a tube top made of a very fluffy veiled dress with a line of pearl buttons at the back.

"I didn't know you draw," Yi-Wei had said.

"You don't know a lot of things."

He reached out his hand and touched her bare waist. "Then when will you tell me these things I don't know? You're so mean."

Iwen had laughed so hard that the paintbrush in her hand trembled, creating more and more wrinkles in the veiled dress on paper. Once Yi-Wei got home, old Mrs. Chien instantly rejected the design. *She may as well just take out her boobs to show everyone.* With that, they changed the design to a laced high collar with long sleeves and a fishtail. Iwen struggled with the idea for a bit, but thought, *Never mind. The wedding is just one day. In the future, I can wear whatever I want, even get naked at home.* She laughed loudly at the thought of this, her eyelashes clustered like they were about to throw a revolution, her big eyes submerged in the sea of lashes.

For the reception, they had rented the entire top floor of a hotel, including a restaurant with an outdoor dining area and a pool. All the guests were Yi-Wei's friends, and everyone spoke English. Iwen just stood there, like a statue in wax, letting guests pat her and take pictures. For her, it was just a day to wear her new favorite clothes. They opened champagne, red and white wine, one bottle after another. One guy drank so much he walked straight into the pool. He burst his head out of the water and yelled, "Shit, I can get wet, but my phone can't!" Everyone laughed out loud.

Yi-Wei had joined his university's fraternity when he was studying in the US. There were two types of people allowed in: the very rich ones and the very smart ones. Iwen never asked how Yi-Wei was admitted to the group. When Yi-Wei started drinking, he made a lot of noise, shouting into the microphone, "Jimmy, where the hell are you? Come up to the stage!"

"Who is it?" Iwen asked.

"I'm going to introduce you to my buddy."

Standing on the stage, Iwen watched groups of people greet each other and separate. The gathering and separating were faster than the toasts. One person walked here, and the other walked over there, as though knitting something complicated. One person went through the other while another person came straight into this knot. The guests who took off their blazers didn't look any different from the catering staff with their bowties. *Jimmy who?* A short little man walked toward them and was blocked by a big fat shadow. The big fat man went away. Everyone was facing sideways as if they were in an ancient Egyptian mural. Only that short little man continued walking toward them. Another person blocked him. Iwen began to feel her concentration fading away, and finally, that short little man was very close to them, revealing himself entirely. He walked onto the stage and hugged Yi-Wei. In Yi-Wei's arms, he looked like a little kid.

"Oh, this is Jimmy," Yi-Wei said. "The smartest guy from our college. He's too smart. I didn't dare ask him to work for our company."

"Hi, Jimmy. Just call me Iwen."

Partying late into the night, Iwen had been so exhausted she sneaked indoors and fell asleep sprawled on a long table. When Jimmy saw her while looking for the restroom, he was fascinated. It was very dark in the room, and all the gold and silver looked like abandoned metal. Two long tables, each for sixty people, were parallel to each other. They were so long that, from where he stood, everything on the other end of the table looked like dots. It was like the perspective technique they had learned about in art class. A tiny bride was sprawled over the far end of the table; her back, shoulders, neck, and arms exposed from her pink dress. She was so pale that she practically merged with the white tablecloth. The lights from outside entered through the square windows, stretching shadows into diamond shapes on the table like exotic and sparkling fish scales. It was as though the bride were sleeping on a gigantic mythical monster, about to be carried away any minute.

Yi-Wei entered the room. "Hey."

"Hey."

They looked at the scene together, watching Iwen's back breathing up and down.

"Bro, be good to her, you know what I mean?" Jimmy had said quietly. And with that, he stuck his hands in his pockets and left for the restroom.

Yi-Wei covered Iwen with his blazer. Coming back to the outdoor area, he took the microphone and said in English, "All right, guys, it's bedtime!"

The craziest guy from the college fraternity raised a wine bottle high and howled, "Oh, come on! The whole world knows what you're gonna do when you get home!"

Yi-Wei laughed. "Fuck you, Ted!"

Ted spilled the wine from his glass. "Oh, you're not fucking me!" And then he made some dirty gestures, making everyone laugh very hard. Inside, Iwen was sleeping quietly. When the lights moved around outside the window, she grew shiny scales like a dragon, as though she could fly away any minute.

Whenever Fang Si-Chi finished school, she was always taken back to Lee Guo-Hua's apartment. On the table there would be a row of beverages, and Teacher Lee would show a weirdly humble expression, saying: *I don't know what you like, so I bought everything.* She replied, *I drink everything. This is such a waste.* He said, *It's all right. Just pick what you like, and I'll take the rest.*

Si-Chi thought the conversations were strange, strangely gentle as though they were almost a married couple.

Si-Chi picked up a can of coffee, but it had a weird flavor. *Compared to pour-over coffee, the canned version you buy at convenience stores is like coffee you'd trick a kid with—which is exactly my situation.* Si-Chi couldn't help but laugh out loud thinking about it.

What's so funny?

Nothing.

Why are you laughing then?

Teacher Lee, do you love me?

Of course, I love you more than anyone in the world. I never thought that I could find a soulmate at this age. I love you more than I love my daughter. I can't believe I don't even feel bad saying that. It's all your fault. You're too beautiful.

He took out a stack of cash from his bag. Wrapped around the cash was a currency strap from the bank. With one glance, Si-Chi was able to tell it was around a hundred thousand dollars. He casually stacked all the cash by the beverages, as though it was one of the things that Si-Chi could pick up as she liked. *It's for you.*

Si-Chi seethed. *I'm not a prostitute.*

Of course you're not. But I won't be able to be with you for half of the week. I feel really bad about it. I would love to stay by your side, take care of you and your daily needs. It's just a little cash. I hope you eat better and think of me when you buy something you like, all right? This isn't money, but a concrete expression of my love.

Si-Chi felt her eyes grow hot. How could this guy be so stupid? She said, *No matter what, I won't take it. I'm good with my mama's pocket money.*

Lee Guo-Hua asked her, *Since we don't have class today, why don't we go shopping?*

Why?

Don't you need a new pair of shoes?

I can borrow Yi-Ting's first.

We can go window shopping.

Si-Chi didn't speak and quietly followed him to the taxi. Looking out at the passing roads, she thought, *There's nothing but malls in Taipei.* They entered a well-known store for flat shoes, the brand Si-Chi usually bought. She was hesitant to ask how he knew the brand. Trying on a pair of white shoes next to Lee Guo-Hua, the clerk was so attentive that her face seemed almost contorted by all the directions it went in. Si-Chi understood why and thought she was inside one of those model displays, brightened beautifully by a halogen lamp. Lee Guo-Hua also noticed and whispered, "The clerks here love it when an old guy like me brings in a beautiful young lady."

Si-Chi looked at him incredulously and said, "Let's go."

He said, "Nonono." Picking up the pair of shoes, he went to pay for them. Si-Chi felt as though something shattered inside her, the fragments a piercing pain. The next day, when she would return to Yi-Ting and her apartment, she would discover that he'd simply stuffed the stack of cash into her book bag. She would think, *This guy really enjoys stuffing things into people. He wants them to act overjoyed about it.* She would laugh in spite of her pain.

When they returned to the apartment from the mall, Si-Chi was still furious. Teacher Lee asked her, *Can you stop being mad at me? These are very beautiful things; why don't you want them? I told you it's not about money or shoes. It's about my love for you. Isn't that the best thing about presents? Aren't presents a way to give love to someone you like, as an expression of your love?* Half-squatting and half-kneeling, he opened his palms upward.

Si-Chi thought, *It's like he's one of those little eunuchs who had to do the rain-dance prayer with the emperor way back when. Actually, he looks more like he's begging for something. Begging for what? For me?*

His apartment was located close to the shore of the Tamsui River, farther from the noisier side. The sun set later in the summer, and at dusk the sky turned from a bright golden color to warm orange. Pressed against the window by him, Si-Chi watched the scenery become foggy then clear again, and clear and then foggy. She didn't know why it felt like the sun was a full egg yolk about to be pierced and flow out over everything, scorching the entire city.

When she got dressed again, he casually lay on the bed and asked, *How's the sunset?*

Absolutely stunning. There was some kind of violence in its beauty, but she resisted saying that out loud.

He lazily continued, *I don't like the word* stunning; *it's too cliché.*

Buttoning the last button, Si-Chi slowly turned toward him, watching him display his body confidently, as though he were a sculpture that had been in the center of a plaza for hundreds of years. She said, *Really? Then why does Teacher Lee tell me I'm stunning then?*

He simply said brightly, *I wish I could stop teaching for a month and only mess around with you.*

You'll get tired of me.

He waved his hand and asked her to come to the bedside.

Picking up her tiny hand, he wrote in her palm, *It's like the fatigue you feel after drowning*.

Mustering up the courage, she asked him, *What do you like most about me when we make love?*

He replied, *Your timidity and you faintly coming out of breath*.

Si-Chi was surprised, recognizing this phrase as the opening description of Lin Daiyu in *Dream of the Red Chamber*. She almost burst out crying but asked, *Is this what* Dream of the Red Chamber *means to Teacher?*

Without hesitation, he said, Dream of the Red Chamber, The Songs of Chu, The Records of the Grand Historian, *and* Zhuangzi *all mean this to me.*

In that instant, she suddenly understood much more about this relationship: greed, chaos, life and destruction, filth and cleanliness, fantasies and curses. It was all clear to her now.

The sky turned dark without them noticing. From this side of the Tamsui River, overlooking the more populated side, they could see the Guandu Grand Bridge stretching out thin like a beautiful woman, her leg in a red stocking, toes tapping at the border of the other side of the city. Deeper into the night, the red stockings slowly wove into golden horizontal lines. It was raining heavily outside, as though God were showering with all the water from the Taipei basin. So much water was dumped that the canvas of the night became clusters of ashen flowers; the flowers were perpendicular to the woman's red foot, blossoming along the Tamsui River. *So beautiful*, Si-Chi thought. *I wonder how Iwen would describe this scenery.* And then she thought, *I probably can't tell Iwen this on the phone. This type of beauty is so lonesome. Beautiful things are always lonely.* She couldn't find herself in this kind of love. Her solitude was not from being alone, but from having nobody at all.

Si-Chi kept thinking that if the story of her and Teacher Lee were to turn into a movie, the director might be overly worried about the dullness of each scene. They were always in an apartment or a motel room, the darkness of night pressing her against the window until her face began drooping with grief. Teacher Lee would turn off all the lights except for the dim one by the bedside. The moment he turned off these lights, the night would swim its way inside, filling the entire room. Night would squat down and use its hands to surround the dim light, as though about to extinguish it or perhaps just warming itself. It wasn't pornography; from beginning to end, it was just a man on top of a girl, in and out, over and over. There was no plot at all. Her existence simply occupied space, living as though dead. She thought about how much Teacher Lee liked fantasizing that they were filming a movie and felt how deeply Teacher Lee had planted a root inside her body.

Whenever they spoke on the phone, Teacher Lee had a hard time telling her he loved her. It was only at the very end of the call that he would burst out, *I love you*. Those three words contained a rotten sorrow. She knew he said it so he could hang up.

After that day, whenever Si-Chi saw those white shoes from the department store on the shoe rack at the apartment she shared with Yi-Ting, she would think about how they were once stranded at the side of the bed with four legs dangling over the mattress.

Ever since Mrs. Chang's visit, Iwen hadn't come back to Maomao's store. Mr. Maomao tore off one page from his mental calendar each day, like he was tearing off dead skin. *Every single day of not seeing you feels like taking out one marinated fruit from the jar. It's never fresh.* The cicadas sang all summer like electric drills. Iwen never showed up. The lemon cake felt like forever ago to Mr. Maomao.

One day while on his cell phone near the entrance, Mr. Maomao suddenly saw Iwen crossing the street at a distance. He hung up right away and ran toward her. *White top and long pants, it must be you. Even if it turns out not to be you, I have to run.* It was the first time he felt that the street went on forever. "Mrs. Chien, Mrs. Chien!" It seemed to take her a while to realize he was calling her, and she slowly turned toward him. It was like a movie scene in slow motion.

It's you.

She was wearing a pair of dark sunglasses, so Maomao couldn't be sure if Iwen was looking at him. He stopped in front of her, trying to catch his breath. "Mrs. Chien, long time no see!"

"Ah, Mr. Mao, good to see you again."

"What brings Mrs. Chien to these parts today?"

"Ah, um, I forgot what I was going to do." She laughed, squeezing out her adorable dimples, dimples that looked like they were there to be filled.

"Can I walk with you for a bit?" Mr. Maomao asked.

"What's that?"

"I can drive you. My car is right there." Gesturing toward the distance with his hand, he said, "In the parking lot over there."

"All right then." In silence, they lowered their heads and went toward the parking lot. *It's hard for me not to look at the wrinkles of the white pants by your knees. They're like tides. It's hard for me not to notice you balling the hand closest to me into a fist. Every single bone in the back of your hand looks so tense, as if you know that I have the urge to hold it. It's hard for me not to think about the marks left behind by fists under your sunglasses.*

Maomao opened the door on the passenger's side. It was a relief the weather had gotten cooler; otherwise the car would be baking hot. Maomao sat in the driver's seat.

"Where are you heading to?"

"I completely forgot." Smiling with a hint of apology, Iwen bit away the lip gloss on her lower lip. Neither of them fastened their seat belts.

"Mrs. Chien."

"Call me Miss Hsu, please."

"Iwen." Maomao spoke her name as though someone had been repeatedly teaching him how to do it since birth. It was unforgettable. He saw tears streaming down under her sunglasses. She immediately took her glasses off, turning her head to the side to wipe away her tears. Maomao saw her eyes were swollen, not from being beaten, but from crying. The color of her blood vessels was more heart-stopping than her bruises, the color of black clouds.

Maomao began speaking as though mumbling to himself. He was gentle as a pack of tissues. Iwen had never heard him speak this much.

"Iwen, you might have forgotten the first time you met me. But I haven't. It seems silly for a man in his thirties to talk about love at first sight. I'm not a greedy person, but the more I got to know you, the more I wanted to know you. Whenever I got back home late, I would think about what you said during the day. Actually, the first time I met you was at your wedding, but you probably didn't notice me at that time. I thought about the way you looked at Mr. Chien when you exchanged vows that day—I would give anything for you to look at me that way." Maomao paused and then continued, "Sometimes I thought, maybe I'm really not your type. I don't have that noble bloodline in me."

Iwen had chewed off all the lip gloss on her upper lip. He had only just noticed Iwen had taken off her sunglasses. She remained silent for a long time, making both of them feel like they were looking for a palm-size maple leaf they'd pressed between the pages of a large Chinese dictionary as kids. It was a thick kind of silence, tumbling over and over. It was the silence of a golden-framed Bible with brittle pages. Iwen only replied with one sentence, unsure if it counted as an answer. She lifted her head, stared hard at Maomao with her puffy, rabbit-red eyes, and said, "I'm pregnant."

———

At home in Kaohsiung, Iwen always watched the news on TV at 10:00 p.m. Rather than actually watching the news, she had a nightly ritual of counting down the minutes to see if anyone would call Yi-Wei to come out and join them for drinks. The music at the start of the news was full of energy, like the theme song for a magical girl's transformation sequence in a cartoon. One night, the phone rang, and Iwen noticed she was trembling along with the phone. She saw Yi-Wei say yes and heard him enter the changing room. She heard the hangers move in the closet like the dangling handrails in Japan's subway, swinging back and forth when the train pulled into the station.

Yi-Wei saw Iwen's face the moment he opened the changing

room door. She was so close that her face was practically stuck to the door. Yi-Wei laughed and said, "You scared me."

Iwen blocked his way with her body, not letting him out.

"What's going on with you?"

Tears began to drop from Iwen's cheeks. "Yi-Wei, do you love me?"

"My sweetheart, my baby, what's going on? Of course I love you. Stop crying and tell me what happened."

Iwen tumbled to the floor, her legs spread out like a kid; she arched her back and buried her face in her hands, like a child who died crying.

Squatting down, Yi-Wei asked, "What's going on with you, my baby?" He had never heard her cry so loud. "Don't ever give me a reason to stop loving you, okay?"

Iwen took the diamond watch from her wrist and smashed it on the floor. The hands came off, the surface looking like a blank face. She said, "I like you, love you, and worship you with all my heart. I'll be a fool for you if you want me to. I'll swallow anything you want me to. Didn't you say you would protect me and take care of me? Why do you beat me?" Without stopping, Iwen kicked her feet like a child having wet herself. She cried until she couldn't breathe, then crawled over to the bed, her fingers clinging to the grids of bookshelves on the wall to get her asthma inhaler. She sat up and hugged herself, convulsing and crying. Yi-Wei reached out to pat her, but she thought he was going to hit her and fell back on the floor. Her milky arms and legs flung all over.

"Iwen. Iwen, Iwen my dear, I won't go. I won't go today, or ever again, all right? I love you, and it's all my fault. I love you so much. I'll stop drinking, all right?"

That whole night, whenever Yi-Wei was about to touch Iwen, she looked as scared as a lamb trying to escape from its predator. Her eyes were so big that they were about to fall out. Exhausted from the crying, she fell asleep against the foot of the bed frame. When Yi-Wei tried to carry her into bed, she furrowed her eyebrows and clenched her teeth the moment he touched her. Her puffy red eyelids looked like they were covered in eye shadow. It was the first time Yi-Wei thought that he had really done something wrong. She was so tiny in Yi-Wei's arms, and when she was in bed, her bent waist stretched out like a flower that only blossomed for him. Yi-Wei went to the living room to clean up. On the marble floor lay the watch he bought for her and a spilled-over cup of water. Cleaning up the shattered glass, he went back to the bedroom. It was very late in the night, and Yi-Wei noticed Iwen was awake. She lay there, blinking tears from her wide-open eyes as though not aware she was crying. It was like what he saw every time he came back home at this time. Yi-Wei pulled a chair next to the bed and asked Iwen if she wanted some water. She said okay and he helped her up. The way she sipped the water was so adorable. When she handed the cup back to him, she let her hand and the cup linger in his palm. Quietly, she said, "Yi-Wei, I'm pregnant. I confirmed with the doctor several days ago. I told them not to tell you first. It might have been the trip to Japan."

From that moment on, Yi-Wei and Iwen became the loveliest married couple in the world. Whenever Yi-Wei saw baby products, he would buy clothes in both pink and blue. Iwen laughed and said, "What a waste; if he were a boy, there would be nothing wrong with dressing him in pink." Yi-Wei would squint his eyes and say it also wouldn't be a waste if they had a second baby.

Putting toys in the cart, he would take the hand that Iwen was playfully hitting him with and bring it in for a kiss.

———

Si-Chi and Yi-Ting were both born in the winter. They had celebrated their thirteenth, fourteenth, and fifteenth birthdays with Iwen because she was also a winter baby. In their last year of senior high school, they celebrated their eighteenth birthdays. All that Si-Chi felt was numbness, as though she hadn't grown up. Of course, the word *birthday* was not an incantation that would guarantee anyone growth. But she knew that, no matter what, she was not going to grow up anymore. Everything on her mind was being fed into a supermassive black hole, the kind of black hole that would eventually belch chaos. Not to mention the black hole was living inside her. Everyone told her she was too pale, like a plaster sculpture. She always imagined a pair of hands reaching into her stomach and swiping a match into flame. Inside her stomach was engraved a sentence that Teacher Lee once said to her: "Sculptures are born from destruction."

Yi-Wei led Iwen to Mr. Maomao's shop to pick out a present for their expected baby. Mr. Maomao watched them come inside, hand in hand. The expression on Maomao's face was like the basket of mint candies that anyone could take from at the front of a barbecue restaurant.

"Ah, Mr. and Mrs. Chien, congratulations."

Iwen looked at Maomao like she was staring into an ocean. *I want to shout into the water, like that Japanese romance movie we used to mock. I want to cup my hands around my mouth and scream my name into the sea of your eyes.*

"I recommend buying an anklet; it's safer for your baby," said Maomao.

"We'll get an anklet then!" Yi-Wei immediately replied.

"Just something simple," Iwen said.

Maomao saw Yi-Wei put his hand on Iwen's thigh.

"Something simple . . . What about this?"

Maomao drew a new design in several strokes.

"We'll take it." Yi-Wei looked very cheerful.

"I've received a good number of requests lately. Would it be all right if I delivered it to you in a month?"

"You can take nine months if you'd like!" Yi-Wei laughed.

"Mr. Chien must be very happy!" Maomao replied with a smile.

"Oh, of course!"

"And aren't you so happy, too, Mrs. Chien?"

"Uh-huh."

When Maomao walked them to the store entrance, he noticed Iwen came only to Yi-Wei's chest when wearing flat shoes. Maomao had to lift his head to meet Yi-Wei's eyes and lower his head to meet Iwen's. *Your eyelashes are tickling my heart; my heart doesn't giggle but cries out of itchiness.* Yi-Wei had already entered the driver's seat, and Iwen waved at Maomao before seating herself next to him, which made Maomao feel like it was actually her eyelashes waving at him. Back at the shop, Maomao went up to the second floor, quickly made a decision about the number of carats and drew an even design. He carefully traced along the lines with an eraser while revising it, which gave his anklet drawing a distinctly domineering impression. *As long as you're happy, that's all that matters.*

Not long after that, Iwen visited Maomao's shop again.

"Aren't you so happy, Mrs. Chien?" he asked her.

He had asked her the same thing two days ago, but they both knew how the same question bore different meanings.

"Yeah, happy. So happy."

"I'm so glad." Maomao really meant what he said, but in the meanwhile, his entire body opened its eyes, with tears secretly streaming down. Only his actual eyes remained dry.

"I'm picking up pendants for my little friends."

"Little friends? Ah, yes, of course."

She was collecting a pair of platinum pendants. They were thin birdcages, each with a blue bird perched on a swing. The birdcage had a dome like that of a mosque; the body of the bird was made of sparkling, watery enamel; their eyes were made of yellow diamonds that resembled sunrise; the claws were engraved with meticulous patterns and nails; the door of the cage swayed ajar; the bird on the swing swayed along with it. Iwen dangled one of the pendants and observed from beneath, then put it back in Mr. Maomao's palm. When her finger touched the softest part of his palm, Maomao imagined himself as a tree on the top of a hill, split open by lightning.

"Mr. Mao is a real artist," Iwen said.

"Not at all. Mrs. Chien is too kind."

"Acting overly humble is also very artsy."

"Actually, I feel very proud of this piece after giving it a final touch."

They laughed together.

"Even being proud of your own work makes you really artsy."

You look so beautiful when you laugh, I would so like to weather that smile and seal it into a velvet box.

Iwen suddenly collected herself and twiddled her wedding ring over and over again. She had become even skinnier, and just with a slight push she was able to remove her ring. This was inauspicious. Her left hand stopped fiddling when she said, "I'm very sorry about my behavior the other day."

Maomao paused, opened his mouth, and spoke in a quiet yet non-secretive tone. "I'm the one who should apologize. I said something that troubled you. But now that I think about it, I seem to be overestimating myself to think I could cause you any inconvenience. I'm very sorry regardless."

Iwen quietly closed the pendant's velvet box with a *pop* sound. She closed the other one, too. Her four fingers and thumb closed together, demonstrating how she used to play hand puppets with the neighbor kids when she was a student; she would move her thumb and let the puppets speak. The kids would laugh out loud like a long, sweet dream. She knew Maomao understood what her hand gestures meant.

"Does Mr. Mao like children?"

"Oh yes." He laughed again. "But I've seen very few kids at the shop in the past ten years."

That made Iwen laugh.

"I've never really thought about the kind of jobs suitable for those who like kids. That and jobs where you see kids without having to discipline them," she said.

They laughed together. What Maomao didn't say was, *I'll always like your kid, even if your kid is Yi-Wei's.*

Mr. Maomao spent the entire day upstairs drawing a cocktail ring. The tiny, enamel flowers in various colors crowded around a large gem, their vines climbing from the ring up toward the gemstone. On the main gemstone, flowers stretched across the wings of the butterflies; smaller gems framed the edges of the petals. Having drawn for an entire day, he was sore all over his waist and back, and when he stood up to stretch, his spine made cracking sounds. *A cocktail ring that will never come into shape. This is the first time I've felt like my drawing turned out well, and this is also the first time I've worked a day for no rewards.* Maomao spent several days revising the cocktail ring design, and even created a 3D mockup. *Wasting time on you is better than wasting time on anything else. It makes time feel more real.*

Several days later, Yi-Wei entered Maomao's shop unexpectedly. Mama Mao sat in her usual spot. "Ah, Mr. Chien, do you want me to call Maomao to come downstairs?"

"Yes."

Mama Mao walked upstairs, intentionally stomping her way up. "Mr. Chien is downstairs."

"Mr. Chien? The young one?"

"Yeah, he's looking for you."

Maomao beamed toward Yi-Wei as he came downstairs. "What brings you here, Mr. Chien?" He immediately felt ashamed that his vocation required him to be so affectionate. *This is the man who wrecked you.*

It turned out that Yi-Wei wanted to buy a birthday present for Iwen. It was then that Mr. Maomao learned Iwen's age. He asked carefully, "Any preferences regarding the gems? How big?"

Yi-Wei just waved and replied, "The cost doesn't matter." And then he added, "Just give me something different from everyone else."

"Something more simple or more complex?"

"The more extravagant, the better—something dreamy. You probably haven't noticed but Iwen has been daydreaming all the time."

Maomao realized why he found Yi-Wei strange. Perhaps the world was too easy on him. Unlike Iwen, who would rather bear that guilt than disrespect others. Yi-Wei's major flaw was that he took everything for granted. Maomao thought back to when Iwen had told him how much she disliked Victorian novels: "If the word *classic* has a negative meaning, my definition would be: *an act of taking everything for granted*."

This guy is so classic. Maomao showed Yi-Wei several designs, but he kept telling Maomao they weren't enough. Maomao went upstairs to print his most recent cocktail ring design—he watched the light scan from left to right in the Xerox machine while his mother swept her gaze over him.

It only took a quick glance for Yi-Wei to say, "I'll take this one."

Maomao called the metalworking master in Hong Kong. As he pressed one button after another, he felt happiness. The kind without any dark humor or anticlimax. He simply felt that whatever belonged to Iwen would eventually belong to her.

———

A series of major exams were about to take place in the coming weeks. Yi-Ting received a lot of birthday gifts from her classmates. Mostly books. She thanked them and was hesitant to mention that she no longer read these types of books. On her way home with Si-Chi, Yi-Ting spoke to Si-Chi in a teasing, bratty voice. "Your present's waiting for you at home." When they got back, the girls exchanged cards and gifts. Yi-Ting received a silver bookmark, and Si-Chi received a book of collected photos from her favorite photographer.

Yi-Ting wrote on the card:

It seems like ever since we were little, we never got into the habit of apologizing to each other. Or we never really have the opportunity to apologize. It's hard to begin, so I would like to apologize to you here, even though I'm not sure what I should be apologizing for. The truth is, it breaks my heart to hear you cry in the middle of the night, although I don't know why you do. Sometimes, I feel so small in front of you, like I'm a tourist hiking along the edge of a dormant volcano. You're the deep crater, and I watch you, feeling the urge to jump right inside and the desire to see you explode.

When we were little, we boasted so much about romance, intense passion, ultimate happiness, treasures, paradise, and how they all relate to each other. We talked about these things more passionately than couples in love. Our prototype of a lover is Teacher Lee. I'm not sure if I'm jealous of you or Teacher Lee, maybe both. When I chat and do homework with you, I notice new expressions growing on your face, something I've never really experienced. I always thought: This must be a trace of what happened over "there." And then I would think, if I were in your place, maybe I could do even better? Whenever you came back from "there," I would hear you cry next door; I don't know why I'm even jealous of your pain. I feel like "there" doesn't exist elsewhere but lies between us. If you're not happy, why do you carry on?

I hope you try to sleep early and stop abusing alcohol

or coffee. I hope you spend some time listening to classes at school and come back home more often. Saying "it'll do you some good" sounds too conceited, but I have a feeling that you're heading towards complete estrangement. I'm not sure if it was you who abandoned me or me who abandoned you.

I still love you as always, but I know that my love for you right now is blind. It's the old you that keeps my love hanging on. Heaven knows how much I wish I could understand you better. Your eighteenth birthday is a big one, and my only wish for you is to stay healthy. I hope you wish yourself the same, and I'm sorry to have been so harsh to you the other day. I love you. Happy Birthday.

They opened their gifts and cards from Iwen. They both received the same exact thing: a special, intricate birdcage pendant. The intricacy of the artwork was so neat, it pained them. It reminded Si-Chi of Mr. Maomao wearing his blue polo shirt.

Iwen's handwriting resembled her—beautiful, determined, and audacious. In a card for Si-Chi, she wrote:

My dear, dear Chi-Chi, happy eighteenth birthday! Even though both of you are so far away, there's at least one good thing about it: now that I'm sending you presents, you won't be able to return them to me. What was I doing when I was eighteen? I used to fantasize that once I turned eighteen, I wouldn't just be smart but full of wisdom. I even dreamt of growing tall overnight.

When I was eighteen, I could memorize the whole Bible, *Fortress Besieged*, *The Divine Comedy*, and *Hamlet*. It sounds incredible, but it was what it was. When I was eighteen, I had never thought about who I would become. I've always been someone who lived one day at a time and thought life was all about memorizing my dictionary. If I memorized ten pages per day I would eventually memorize everything. I'm still the same now, peeling an apple one day and peeling a pear the next. I no longer know what's coming in the days ahead. The time we spent reading together is the closest I've had to an ideal future. In the past, I thought I would finish my PhD program and become a professor, or at least work as a teaching assistant at the university, or maybe a lecturer, an associate professor. I viciously took everything for granted while trying to acquire a higher position.

And then, both of you became my everything, you became my lecture. I often ask myself if I've ever hurt you girls without realizing—especially you, Chi-Chi.

In realist literature, falling in love comes from finding someone adorable; when someone dies, it's because he deserves it. The writer can kill the obnoxious character by setting fire to the attic and letting her fall—but reality isn't like that. Life is not like that. I've learned to understand the suffering, repentance, and trauma in this world through books. When these secondhand negative emotions assault me in reality, time never allows for me to fight back by flipping through some books and coming up with a thesis. Half of my body was always stuck between book pages, uncertain whether to curl back into the book or break free from it. Maybe I've grown to become an adult that my eighteen-year-old self would loathe.

But for both of you, there's time and opportunities to change. And you're both smarter than I am, really. Do you believe that? It's not too late for you. I've been experiencing some bodily changes recently, and maybe these changes are something similar to what eighteen-year-old girls experience. Maybe they're so similar, it's hard to believe. I'll tell you more about it in detail when I get a chance. I really enjoy getting your calls, but sometimes I grow hesitant, unsure if I should check in on you. Maybe I'm too weak. I fear hearing that you're not doing well, even more so that you would tell me everything's all right while it's not. Your senior year in high school must be a lot to handle, and sometimes I'm concerned if the calls are taking too much of your time.

I hope one day, I can ask you how you're doing in person and embrace whatever answer you give me. I miss our time reading together, and the time we spent at the secret base drinking coffee. If I list out all the sentences in my head about missing both of you, I'd definitely sound like I've been studying the sacred art of flirting, ha. Yi-Wei says hi. Last but not least, I want you to know you can tell me anything. Something as small as an ephemera or something as big as a black hole. I love how you're both celebrating your birthday, so I finally have an excuse to write letters to you. Happy Birthday! I hope both of you like your presents. P.S. Go buy yourselves a huge cake and eat every last bite! Yours sincerely, Iwen.

Fang Si-Chi took her two letters with her everywhere. Whenever she finished dressing at Lee Guo-Hua's place, she would take the letters out of her book bag and ask him, her voice a whisper, *Sometimes I think about why you would even start this. I was so young.* He simply lay there. It was unclear if he was thinking of an answer or simply thinking about not answering. In the end, he said, *You were a child at the time, but I wasn't.* She lowered her head, her fingertips tracing Iwen's handwriting on the letter. Teacher Lee asked why she cried. She looked at him and said, *Nothing. I'm just so happy.*

———

"Let's not throw any birthday parties this year. I want the two of us to simply spend time together," Yi-Wei said.

"The *three* of us," Iwen corrected him. She put her hand inside his sleeves and laughed. "We'll still get a cake."

Yi-Wei bought a small piece of cake from a long-established cake shop and brought it back home. Iwen opened the cake box like a small child would: she pinched the marinated cherry with her thumb and forefinger, lifted her chin, and brought it to her mouth. The cherry stem curled between her lips, seductive; the seed she spit out was full of deep wrinkles, just like the ones he'd find snaking down her pale, exposed belly to between her thighs. Iwen would try to close them up and murmur, "Yi-Wei, please stop staring. Really, I'm getting embarrassed."

Turning off the lights, they lit the candles. The heads of the candles gradually gained bald patches and dripped wax down their bodies. In the candlelight, Iwen looked like she was swaying, despite staying still. The way she pouted her lips and blew both candles looked like she was blowing kisses. Turning on the lights again, big drops of wax tears stuck to the two candles, like how sperm chases after an egg. Yi-Wei took out the cocktail ring, which made Iwen gasp in awe. "Oh, my god! I feel like I've been transported to the secret garden I see in my dreams. Yi-Wei, you know me so well. You're the best."

She received an express package sent from Taipei by the girls. It was a Hello Kitty stuffed animal bigger than herself. Iwen hugged it tightly, as though she were hugging Yi-Ting and Si-Chi.

Inside the package, she found a birthday card from Si-Chi:

My dearest Iwen, today, I turned eighteen. It doesn't seem different from any other day. Perhaps I should have given up the idea that it would be the most special day of my life. Maybe celebrating one's birthday, or mother's suffering day, is more absurd than how some Taiwanese burn incense and count Buddha beads to celebrate Jesus's birthday. I don't have what the Japanese call "a solid sense of existence." Sometimes I'm very happy, and that happiness is beyond myself, existing in the world in my place. And this kind of happiness is defined by a dictionary from a strange, faraway planet. I know on this Earth, my happiness is absolutely not happiness at all.

Something regretful happened recently. Teachers from our school have rarely assigned your average essay topics for us to write about. But I do want to write about my goals and my dreams. I used to feel that I shouldn't take up something I shouldn't do as a hobby. I already know that instead of listing "Becoming a writer" under "My Dream," I'd misplace it and list it under "My Goal." But I don't think about that anymore. I like the word *dream*. A dream is to think clearly about my daydreaming and give it a solid path. And my dream is to become someone like Iwen—this line is not your birthday present; it's a fact. You've told us the most beautiful thing about a sonnet is its shape: fourteen lines, iambic pentameter, one sentence with ten syllables. A sonnet is like a square handkerchief. If you were to use Shakespeare to wipe away your tears, then I can definitely use Shakespeare to erase anything else, even myself.

I really admire Shakespeare. His face is on the cover of all his books. Whenever I do math in front of him, I can use formulas to omit myself from the world. I write in my diary regularly these days, and I realized what you said to me before, that "Writing is a way to claim your authority," was totally true. When I write, my life becomes easy to let go, as easy as it is to close my diary shut. Iwen, I miss you very much. I hope everything goes well with you. I hope all the cliché blessings will come true for you, and that things go the way you want, and you'll live for a very long time. I wish you a spring full of wealth and happiness so overwhelming, it spills underneath your door. Happy Birthday. Love you, Si-Chi.

———

Lee Guo-Hua's instinct about people was almost always correct. But he had been wrong about Guo Hsiao-Chi.

After Hsiao-Chi was kicked out of Lee Guo-Hua's little apartment in Taipei, she opened an account on a dating website. It was easy for her to get to know someone. She was straightforward with the guys and expressed that she didn't want anything serious, and she only spent time with them at motels. Hsiao-Chi was determined and sometimes maybe too insistent. Whenever she took the subway to meet someone, the wind at the MRT station would blow up her skirt, which gave her this chilly feeling, like she was in some war-torn, windy, desolate place. Some of those guys smelled so stinky when they took off their pants, and some had such bad breath that the odor was worse than what emanated off his underwear. But this was what Hsiao-Chi was looking for. She wanted to trample herself. She spent half of her life accepting a demon, but that demon had forsaken her. She realized that the filthiest thing was not filth itself; it was more about how even filth became disgusted by her. Hell sent her into exile. *Where else could be more despicable and painful than hell itself?*

Most of the guys who met Hsiao-Chi were surprised, thinking that she might have misreported her weight or added inches to her chest size on the dating website. Someone even preached to her, "You're still so young and beautiful, why would you do this?" Hsiao-Chi opened her eyes widely and asked, "Do what?" The guy went silent and took off his clothes. Her time with these strangers was high-pitched. Her ears gradually failed to hear the lectures delivered by her college professors.

There was a guy who brought her to his place, where the walls were full of black silica ore. His tiny black leather sofa was so soft that the guy sank her into the cushions. He rested his head on the den of her neck. Hsiao-Chi tilted her head and smelled the calfskin. She thought, *So luxurious*. But she didn't think it was a luxury to let these guys trample her once-obedient self. Whenever the men finished, they quietly jerked off, as though they knew that she was absent-minded and were afraid to wake her up. After lying down, the first thing the guy said was in English: "My god." He stretched out the syllable for *god* the way someone yelled for their maid in a big house. It made Hsiao-Chi laugh.

Hsiao-Chi visited a famous bar for drinks. Holding a bottle of wine with a metal stopper, the owner made cocktails in exaggerated, parabola-curved gestures. Watching the owner's sturdy biceps, Hsiao-Chi thought about Teacher Lee. The owner looked up at Hsiao-Chi, who asked, "When do you close?"

"Early morning," he replied.

What time in the early morning? Hsiao-Chi didn't ask. The time she spent with Teacher Lee taught her tolerance. She continued sitting at the same spot, until drops of sunlight leaked into the bar. She didn't know why the glass looked to her more like wine-bottle glass than window glass.

The owner laughed and told Hsiao-Chi, "It's early morning right now; we're closing."

She became the lone person sitting at the bar. He spoke loudly behind the counter, as though they were situated on separate mountain peaks and what circulated between them was wilderness fog rather than smog from a sunlit tunnel. The owner happened to live above the bar.

One time, Hsiao-Chi remembered nothing but the guy's brown hair and high, thick eyebrows. His eyebrows were arched so high she could see them when she looked past her thighs as he went down on her. Teacher Lee never did that; his tongue always swam to her navel and stopped. Hsiao-Chi felt funny, as though she were a lake that allowed everyone to wash their faces and drink water. Teacher Lee always pressed her head, and she was as filial as a lamb kneeling for milk. She only remembered how

Teacher Lee's fingers crawled over her scalp, the way a hairdresser would when washing her hair; it felt like she was visiting a hair salon for the first time in forever. Thinking about her scalp made her forget to use her mouth. After graduating from high school, Hsiao-Chi stopped getting her hair washed at salons.

Hsiao-Chi very quickly entered the bedrooms of some seniors who had been pursuing her for years. These guys always asked, "Want to come over to my place and watch a movie?" When this one guy twitched, she lifted up her chin from his neck, tilted her head to the side of the TV and began watching the movie intently. Only when the passionate male protagonist kissed the seriously ill female protagonist did her tears quietly stream down. Staring at the screen, she began to understand the main difference between a movie and real life. In a movie, everything ends after the kiss, when in reality, the kiss is only just the beginning.

As she watched TV, her pale body withered. The light coming from the TV screen reached out its colorful hand in the darkness of the room, groping her.

The guy gave her a hangdog look and asked, "So, are we official now?"

Her body waved away the colorful hand from the TV, and the guy's facial expression was like a bonsai in need of water.

"You like me too, right?" he insisted.

She was unfazed and turned angry when the guy snapped the remote control away from her. "Don't you feel anything at all? You've already given it to me. How come you don't like me?"

Hsiao-Chi picked up the remote control from the guy's limp hand and changed it to a movie channel. She stared at the screen for a while, watching a blond father kissing his blond little girl. The blond father was going to save the planet. Hsiao-Chi thought, *If Teacher Lee knew what I'm doing right now, he'd definitely be smug. He'd understand that I'm hurting myself.*

The guy grew angrier and asked, "Are you just here to get laid?"

She turned her face back to him, combing her hair with her fingers, showing a beautiful, nonchalant face, speaking in a tone softer and spicier than the guy may have ever heard in his life.

"Don't you like it?"

And then her remark began to spread on campus.

Hsiao-Chi saw doppelgangers of Teacher Lee everywhere as she wandered the city streets. Some of them had Teacher Lee's hands, his neck, even his clothes. Spotting a dark-clothed shadow seemingly lit by stage lighting, her vision suddenly blacked out; as he walked, his dark arms swayed by her side, pulling her eyeballs, walking her like a dog.

"Teacher Lee, is that you?"

Her eyeballs pulled her body and, half staggering, she fell to the side of the man, as if she were clinging to the side of a cave in search of the light.

You're not Teacher Lee. Then why did you steal his clothes? Why do you have his arms? Her vision was disrupted. Standing in the middle of the street, through her tears she slowly watched the crowd in front of her melt away.

Hsiao-Chi's best friend asked her out to lunch. She felt a cold premonition, like she was entering the eatery knowing exactly what she would order.

"Hmmm, I don't know how to put this, but a lot of people at school have been shit-talking you," said Shin-Shin.

"What are they saying?" asked Hsiao-Chi.

"I've only heard this one thing. Someone said you've been out with a lot of seniors. Hearing that pissed me off, of course, so I told them you're not like that."

Hsiao-Chi placed her hand on the floor-to-ceiling window, letting the winter sunbeam project a shadow onto the table they were sitting at. Her fingers were already very skinny, and the shadows were even skinnier than her actual fingers—just like those rumors. Hsiao-Chi gnawed her straw.

"It's true," she said.

"Really?"

"I really did all those things."

"Why?"

"It's hard to explain."

"Oh my god, Guo Hsiao-Chi, do you have any idea how they said you're . . . *easy to fuck*? Do you know how hard I've tried to explain to them that they've got you all wrong? And now, you're saying everything is true? There must be a reason. Were you drunk?"

"No, I was very sober. Too sober, actually."

Shin-Shin started to cry when she heard this. Her tears immediately angered Hsiao-Chi, so she stood up and left. She couldn't understand how someone in her world dared to cry before she did.

———

When an expulsion letter was sent to Guo Hsiao-Chi's home, she announced to her family that she wanted to drop out of college. Mama Guo cried and asked where her obedient little child was. Hsiao-Chi replied that she had long been dead, since her last year of high school. Mama Guo asked what she meant by that, and Hsiao-Chi just burst out three words: *Lee Guo-Hua*.

The whole family went silent for two seconds. Cheerleaders on the TV screen were yelping; neighbors' pet birds were snapping food from each other; the sun was rustling through the trees. Within two seconds, so many people on the planet passed away, and more were born. After two seconds, Papa Guo's voice was a landslide, engulfing the entire house: "Do you think you'll be able to get married after having done things like this?"

"What do you mean by 'things like this'?"

"*Incest!*"

The word hit right between Hsiao-Chi's eyebrows like a stone, making her fall back on the long rattan chair.

The chair creaked, and Mama Guo growled with all the muscles of her throat, "You're a homewrecker. We don't have a daughter like you!"

Papa Guo began to growl with his fists. "He must be a fraud, lying to young girls to get their firsts!"

Hsiao-Chi's tears scorched her face. "We really love each other," she said.

"*You*—sleeping with an old man, making love, mating with him!"

The little squares in the screen window looked like a wire fence.

"Pa, Ma, I don't want to hear this."

"Why don't you turn to him? If you love each other, then ask him to take you in!"

Hsiao-Chi grabbed her phone and was about to leave. Mama Guo snatched her phone away and smashed it on the floor. Her pink flip phone opened its mouth wide and chomped on the tile, the notification visible on the front of the phone forming a jittery smile. Hsiao-Chi stuffed her feet in her shoes, but then Mama Guo pushed her away. "Forget about the shoes!"

Even though it was spring, the roads were still steaming from the heat. Stepping barefoot on the asphalt road, Hsiao-Chi felt like she was watching a pot of flowers die of dehydration. Hsiao-Chi walked all the way to Lee Guo-Hua's secret little apartment barefoot. Across the street from the apartment, she fell down to her knees against a pillar under the arcade, like a piece of feces on the floor; she would rot with the passage of time. It was not until afternoon that she spotted familiar leather shoes stepping out of a taxi. When she opened her mouth to call him, she realized she lost her voice. And then, a little girl stepped out from the other side of the taxi. She looked several years younger than her. Hsiao-Chi watched them enter the elevator and felt faint.

Hsiao-Chi hailed a taxi home. As the meter fare jumped, the car's red electric clock seemed to prick her until blood gushed out. The driver didn't know the way there, and she hadn't realized how much she wished the driver would get lost forever. Papa and Mama Guo said they were going to tell Teacher Lee's wife everything.

Lee Guo-Hua and his wife asked Papa and Mama Guo to meet at a fancy restaurant in a hotel. It was Lee Guo-Hua's pick; he claimed it didn't get much traffic. But the real reason was that he knew the Guo family relied on their food-stand business for a living, and they got intimidated by the very sight of hotel decorations. Having made the trip from Kaohsiung to Taipei, Teacher Lee's wife sat beside him, while the Guo family sat across the table. Papa and Mama Guo dressed more formally than they did when attending a wedding. Hsiao-Chi looked like she had shattered her most cherished glass. And even though she had so cherished that glass, it was nothing more than a gift bought with customer points she collected from the convenience store. *Everyone* had one.

"Does Teacher Lee love Hsiao-Chi?" Papa Guo raised his voice.

Lee Guo-Hua clasped his hands, playing with the wedding ring secured tight around his finger, which he hadn't taken off for years. The deep wrinkles on his knuckles seemed to hold more promises than a ring. He lectured in various tones, and one of the tones he used was to let his students know that they needed to put three stars next to a paragraph in their textbooks. With that tone, he said, "I love Hsiao-Chi, but I also love my wife."

Hearing this, Hsiao-Chi wished that she could be deaf and mute, and all the pores in her body were trembling; every hair that stood up was about to raise its hand and ask, *Who was that girl in the taxi?* Teacher Lee's wife started crying. Papa and Mama Guo kept apologizing to her.

Watching Teacher Lee slump his back, Hsiao-Chi could look into his open collar. On Teacher Lee's chest was a tiny red bud. She thought, *For years, whenever I spent time with him at his apartment and when he pressed that bud, he would transform into a man-eating monster and chase after me.* She thought about how Teacher Lee wrote "Guo Hsiao-Chi" on her pale, bare stomach over a hundred times, lecturing; *Naturalis Historia* said that he would be able to squirm into her heart like a worm this way. The bud was a worm squeezing out of Teacher Lee's body. When she lifted her head, she saw Teacher Lee's wife watch her with a pair of watery, sympathetic eyes that one could only find on your family's Buddha sculpture. Hsiao-Chi vomited.

In the end, Papa Guo fought with Teacher Lee for the bill. On their way back home, Papa Guo told Mama Guo, "Thank god I didn't pay the bill. Those hotel beverages are so expensive."

Lee Guo-Hua followed his wife and went back to their building in Kaohsiung.

Having arrived home, Teacher Lee's wife didn't want to sit down. She stood there, her head drooping, letting her tears stream down her neck.

"How many times?" Her voice was as salty as the Dead Sea.

Lee Guo-Hua stood in front of his wife and spoke with the same three-star tone, "Just once."

When he thought about the Dead Sea as a metaphor, it reminded him of what his chemistry teacher had said during his first year of high school: "Those who drink the seawater will die from thirst." He'd never understood what osmotic pressure was, so he studied humanities and languages. But the poetics of this line had been engraved in his heart. And now, that playful and obscure poetry had resurfaced.

"Why should I believe you?"

Lee Guo-Hua understood her undertone: *Please give me a reason to believe you.*

He splayed on the floor and said, "I've kept my nose clean for over twenty years. I'm a father; naturally, I aspire to be the kind of man I hope my daughter will encounter somewhere out in this world."

"Then why did that *once* happen?"

"Please, I beg you to forgive me. She seduced me. It was Tsai Liang who told me the girl wanted to ask me some questions, and she forced me to do it. It was just *once*," he emphasized, and that three-star tone began increasing its stars.

His wife's voice began to shiver. "How did she seduce you?"

He wiped his eyes with his big hand. "It's her. She initiated it, from beginning to end." His voice grew louder. "Oh my, it was such a nightmare!"

"But it excited you, right? Otherwise how would this ever have happened?"

"Yeah. My body was. She was very stubborn, and no man could resist. But I swear, emotionally I wasn't into it at all."

"But you said you love her. *Love?*"

"When did I say that? Like at the restaurant? I don't even love her. I said it to not anger her parents. You don't know what she's like, and I don't know why she's setting me up like this. She even threatened me, asking for a hundred thousand dollars to squander. She even demanded I buy brand-name purses for her."

"You could've talked to me about it!"

"Why would I? I've already made such a mistake, and I hate myself. All I could do was fill up that void."

"How long has this been going on?"

Teacher Lee cracked his neck and answered in a very deep voice, "Two years. She kept threatening me. It's been so painful. But I understand that you're in greater pain than me right now, and I'm the one who should apologize."

Teacher Lee's wife stood up and grabbed an embroidered box of tissues. "How come a tough man like you can't fight off a high school girl?"

"That's why I'm telling you I'm sorry. Oh my god, I don't

know how to explain this to you, but back then she was such a . . . I didn't dare move an inch. I was so afraid she would get hurt. She was really, really, she . . . she . . . she was a *whore*. She was being an absolute cunt!"

Drowning in his own big hands, Lee Guo-Hua began to sob without tears. "I won't say this is a mistake all men make. I was the one who couldn't control myself. I shouldn't have been so easily seduced. It was my fault. Please forgive me."

His wife sat across from him and quietly blew her nose. He continued, "Looking at you in such pain makes me feel like garbage. I shouldn't even have been tempted by her. I'm real trash, scum, good-for-nothing. I should go straight to hell."

While he spoke, he took a plastic bottle from the table and fiercely knocked it against his head. Eventually, his wife gently snatched the bottle away from him.

Sitting across from each other, they both looked inside the plastic bottle. The hyacinth beverage slowly came to a halt, as though it were about to die and was cherishing what joy remained. After half an hour, his wife said, "Let's keep this a secret from Xixi."

At home, Papa and Mama Guo discussed having Hsiao-Chi take a year off from college. God knows what would happen if she were to get tricked by *another* professor. In the kitchen, Hsiao-Chi numbly washed all the dishes. She felt like she was praying with incense, the way she rubbed and washed the chopsticks. She thought about when, one time, Teacher Lee took her to Longshan Temple. *The way Teacher explained folktales and myths was so beautiful, so pious.* She asked him what religion he believed in. He replied, "I only believe in you."

Teacher Lee really does love me, she thought. *But who was that girl in the taxi?* Her thumb turned a spoon around as she washed it. She thought about the years she spent visiting Teacher Lee's apartment. The elevator button to his floor was so often pressed that the number was nearly gone. *Who was that girl in the taxi?* When she put her hand into a glass, she thought about her first time taking a ride up to Teacher's apartment. In the car, the cram school manager, Tsai Liang, said to her that Teacher Lee liked her very much. She would learn what she meant by *liked* when she entered his apartment. *Teacher Lee, who the hell was that girl with you in the taxi?*

Hsiao-Chi slowly walked up to the second floor, her parents' concerned faces sticking to her body like gum. The medicine box at home was in a small cabinet in the hallway. Some were for headaches, some were for digestion, and others for skin rashes. Hsiao-Chi thought to herself, *None of them can cure me.* Her heart was shattered, losing all its patterns, unable to be pieced back together. Patching up a heart was harder than patching up a pool of water. The aluminum pack made popping sounds when she squeezed small pills out of it, like goldfish feasting on their fish food in the huge tank inside Teacher Lee's apartment. She squeezed all the pills out of the pack. It was like a mini trash mount, full of distinctive colors. A dirty illness like a dirty incest should be cured by equally dirty pills. Hsiao-Chi swallowed all of them and lay in bed. The only thing she felt was her bloated stomach. She had drunk too much water.

Surprisingly, Hsiao-Chi woke up the next morning. She'd never been so disappointed in herself. She went downstairs and saw her parents watching TV as usual. She tripped on her right foot and fell down the stairs, the floor slapping her cheek. With her phone kept in her sleeve, Hsiao-Chi told her parents she might need to go to the hospital. Later, she sat alone in her hospital room and made phone calls using her IV-less hand. After more than forty calls, nobody responded. She felt like a child standing in front of the beverage vending machine on a scorchingly hot day, inserting coins, only for the machine to reject them, leaving her unable to quench herself, rounding out her desperation. She became completely desperate and sent a text message instead: *Teacher Lee, it's me.* After a very long time, her phone vibrated, and the cover of the phone showed a marquee of notifications, one of which told her that it was midnight. The emergency room never turned off the lights, so she couldn't tell if it was day or night. She also didn't know how long she had been in that bed.

Once she flipped the phone open, she saw a message from Teacher Lee: "I've never loved you, and I've just been lying to you this entire time. How come you don't understand when everyone has been telling you what this is all about? Don't call me again, or my wife won't forgive me." Slowly, Hsiao-Chi read the message over and over, and an image of Teacher Lee popped into her head, texting on his phone with a silly expression, laughing and saying, "I'm a caveman living in the mountains. I don't know how to text." He'd never written anything to her before. After all, he wouldn't want her to keep any evidence. She'd loved him for so many years. Her tears dropped onto the screen, amplifying and distorting the two characters: 老師. *Teacher.*

After checking out of the hospital, Guo Hsiao-Chi took all the books Lee Guo-Hua had given her and dumped them into the ghost money stove, leaving them to burn. Wang Ding-Jun, Liu Yong, Lin Ching-Hsuan—one book after another, she tore the pages out and tossed them into the fire. The tongues of the flames looked like a phoenix, screeching skyward before descending back into the stove. Every single page was embedded with a golden halo, angelically surrounding the dark, eroding characters. Pages and pages about self-help, Islam, and a world of naivete all turned into ashes. The book covers were the hardest to tear off, especially those glued to the spines. Fortunately, Hsiao-Chi had cultivated her patience with Teacher Lee. The pages rocked, rushed upward, tumbled down, and tattooed a ring of fire. Then each page crumpled, just like humans do when they bring their worries to bed. Hsiao-Chi never really gave things too much thought, but at that moment, she had a feeling she too was deep inside that ghost money stove.

———

Chien Yi-Wei awoke from his drunkenness early in the morning and felt the quilt damp in his grasp. He tiptoed to not wake Iwen up. He patted his cheeks and entered the bathroom. When he turned on the light, he found bloody handprints on his face. It was a scene out of a Greek tragedy, when the protagonist, in disbelief, watches his palms held upward, but filled with emptiness. The lights in the bathroom were like lights for the stage; a bouquet of tulips hung upside down, enwrapping him. He washed his face immediately, ran back to his room, turned on the light, and flipped the quilt open, finding Iwen on the right side of the bed as usual, her lower half covered in blood. He thought about the night before, when he came back home and kicked Iwen fiercely with the toe of his leather shoes. The narrow toes of his shoes were like poisonous snakes surging out of him. Iwen had hugged his legs tightly, so he was only able to kick her in the back. He thought about how Iwen kept begging him: *no, no, no.* But as it turns out, Iwen had actually been saying something else entirely: *baby, baby, baby.*

Iwen was sent to a hospital founded by the Chien family. After they pushed her out of the surgery room, she entered the general ward. She woke up not long after and found Yi-Wei sitting at her bedside. Her hand was in his, and she was as pale as a pill. Outside the window, birds began to chirp, and the look on her face suggested she had just woken up from an unexpectedly good dream. It was then that she realized good dreams could be scarier than nightmares. She raised her voice and asked, as if out of natural curiosity, "Where's the baby?"

She was as pale as a forest full of cherry blossoms struggling to bloom, where people would take a picnic basket full of food only to find the blossoms on the muddy ground, already destroyed by rain. Heart-shaped petal fragments lay by their feet; their edges resembled a void, the kind that comes from being stood upon by someone. They were not in their original shape.

"Where's my baby?"

"I'm sorry, Iwen, my chouchou. We can have another one."

Iwen looked at him as though he was written in a language she could never understand.

"Iwen, babe? You're okay; isn't that all that matters?" Yi-Wei watched Iwen's body shiver, like a motor forced to its very limit. She looked like an engine about to start, but now her entire motor had been extinguished.

"I don't have the strength," Iwen said.

"I know. The doctor wants you to rest."

"No, my hand—I meant *my hand*. Please let go of me; I don't have the strength to pull it back."

"Iwen," Yi-Wei said.

"Let go of me, *please*."

"Can I hold your hand again later?"

"I don't know."

"You don't love me anymore?"

"Yi-Wei, listen to me. In my dream, I already knew I had lost my baby. Maybe this was destined to happen. I don't want to see a baby born to a family like ours. The baby's good, too good for me. They're letting me get back to my life alone, don't you understand?"

"You want a divorce?"

"I really don't have the energy to talk about this right now. I'm sorry."

With dull eyes, Iwen began to count the tiles on the ceiling. The birds continued to chirp outside; they sounded like the boys who whistled at her back in high school. She quietly listened to Yi-Wei walk out of the room, crying and growling in the hallway.

Then, Iwen made a call to Si-Chi.

"Hello? Ah, Chi-Chi, it's finally my turn to hear you answer. I'm so happy to hear your voice."

Si-Chi thought about how, every time she called Iwen, hearing her say hello reminded her of how she used to read to her and Yi-Ting.

"Chi-Chi, how did your exams go? I'm sorry, I've been thinking about checking in with you for a long time, but I didn't want to bother."

"Our grades are out. We could probably make it into all the

191

top schools' liberal arts departments. That is, if our mouths don't get constipated during the admission interview."

They both laughed.

"I'm happy for you, my dear. I feel even more nervous for you girls than I was for myself, way back when I was taking my entrance exams."

"How about you, Iwen? How have you been?"

Very slowly, Iwen said, "Chi-Chi, I'm moving out. I just lost my baby."

Si-Chi was shocked. She knew what Iwen meant when she mentioned moving out and miscarriage together. She also knew Iwen expected her to understand the situation right away.

"Don't worry about me," Iwen quickly said. "I'm all right; I'm really all right. Now I can eat cake for every meal."

Iwen could hear Si-Chi sob on the other end of the phone. She imagined how Si-Chi distanced herself from her cell phone, her tiny shoulders shivering up and down.

Si-Chi then said, "Why is our world like this? Why does etiquette mean those who are suffering must shut up? Why do people who beat others go on TV or show up in billboard ads? Iwen, I'm so disappointed. I'm not disappointed in you. I'm disappointed about this world, this life, destiny, or God, if that's what you want to call it—whatever it is, it's so lame. These days, when I read novels where the virtuous are rewarded and the evil are punished in the end, next thing I know, I'm in tears. I'd rather people admit the fact that some pain in our world can never be reconciled. And I hate how people say suffering makes you a better person. How I wish people acknowledged that pain can be destructive. I hate how lyrical people get about big reunions. I hate when a prince ends up marrying the princess. Positive thinking is so kitsch. But Iwen, do you know what I hate even more? That I'd rather be kitschy, that I'd rather know nothing than have to witness the backside of this world."

Crying hard, Si-Chi's words blurred together. Iwen could easily visualize her crying, snot and tears covering her writhen face.

Inside Lee Guo-Hua's apartment, Si-Chi closed her phone and heard the married couple next door making love. The wife moaned as if she were singing a pop song with a climax of a coloratura soprano. She listened, and her tears were stuffed away by the sound of the neighbors. She didn't find it obscene but satisfying. After all, she was waiting for Teacher Lee. She quietly sipped her orange juice and wrote in her diary. In the aluminum pack was concentrated juice with strands of orange pulp. *Being good-looking was homesickness for the counterfeit; it was almost like a pastoral poem, pretentious and unrewarding.* The noise from next door suddenly went away, the *ah* sound from the woman broken in midair. It turned out that it was just someone watching porn. Si-Chi felt miserable for that person, thinking that everything around her was trying to put a finger on the absurdity of her life. Hers was different from others'; her time didn't go straight but ran back and forth. Apartment to motel, motel to apartment, like a pen on paper, repeatedly tracing the same short line hard. In the end, the paper tore. Later, Yi-Ting would read this line from Si-Chi's diary: "Actually, I was already dead the first time I thought about death. Life is like clothes, so easy to be taken away."

Si-Chi went back to her and Yi-Ting's apartment. The color of the sky was that of a dead fish showing its white stomach. Yi-Ting was home, bent over the living room table doing her homework.

When Yi-Ting greeted her, she lifted her head, and Si-Chi could tell from her eyes that some glacier had caved in. Yi-Ting stopped her pen and mouthed to Si-Chi, "You smell like love"; the tiny stuffed animal dangling from her pen cap began to tremble.

"Why are you hiding behind English?" Si-Chi started to get a little angry.

"Oh, so you're back now?" Yi-Ting lowered her head.

"How do we talk if you won't even look at me?"

Si-Chi began to point around her mouth, which made Yi-Ting grow emotional. "It's like how most people can't understand why we talk like this, and nobody understands what we talk about. There's an invisible rope between you and me, and I have my own principles, my own pride. But what about the both of you? Do both of you have your own language? If we covered his eyes to pick one of us, would he be able to pick you without mistake? Or would he pick me instead? Could he see through your face and know that you're having a headache and not a stomachache today?"

Si-Chi's eyes opened wide, her eyelashes standing straight. "Are you jealous of me? Or him?"

"I don't know. I don't know anymore. When we were little, we talked about not learning new languages, but between us, isn't it all about language? What else could it be between the both of you, if not a language? I felt so alone in this apartment. Whenever you come home, it's like you're bragging that you speak some foreign language fluently, like a stranger."

"You don't know what you're talking about. All I could do *there* was listen to what he said. To *obey* was to learn a language, after all, just like the slogans and posters during the Chinese Cultural Revolution."

"You're right, this is *exactly* like the Cultural Revolution."

"When I was *there*, my wish was to be able to hope for something; my dream was to be able to dream."

"I don't want to argue with you anymore."

"Me either."

Yi-Ting continued, "Teacher Lee and his wife have been together for so long, he must have been able to imagine the painful looks on his wife's face. Even though it might be cruel to say so, I have to admit he's the one who's more responsible. He understood everything from inside out before he did anything. And we grew up sheltered. I'm so confused; you looked happier than I've ever seen you, and yet in so much pain. Are you unable to set yourself free, hiding behind our language?"

Si-Chi made a face as though her entire home had been looted. "Do you want me to whine to you?"

"If you're in pain, yes, but if you think that language can only evolve by spending time with Teacher Lee, then you haven't seen how I spend my time alone with Teacher, or you haven't seen him spending time alone with his wife. I guess if our building tumbled down into the ocean, he would only rescue Xixi."

Si-Chi shook her head. There was no pain, but there was no language, either. This was all about a student who obeyed everything her teacher said.

Yi-Ting began to exaggerate with her lips, as though her words were hard to chew. "It's not adding up! Are you telling me you're not disgusted, and that there's no such thing as true love? You're lying, lying, lying, lying. This is not for you to decide. You must love him to death."

"No, I don't."

"Yes, you do."

"No, I don't."

"Yes, you do."

"I said I don't love him."

"You surely do."

"You don't know anything."

"You can't lie to me; you two are too obvious. I can smell it when you enter the apartment."

"Smell what?"

"The smell of true love."

"What are you talking about?"

"It's all over you, that erotic smell, the flavor of the night, an odor from your underwear. You're nothing but a pair of panties."

"You better shut up!"

"Those smells of fingertips, saliva, and your lower body!"

"I said shut up!"

"The smell of an adult man's . . . se-se-semen." Yi-Ting's face was like a vast battlefield, her tiny freckles piles of wood smoldering in fire.

"You don't even know what you're envious of. You're so harsh. We were only thirteen years old." Si-Chi let herself wail, her tears slowly stretched out her face, melting, eroding the shape of her mouth. Yi-Ting really understood nothing at all.

———

After Iwen moved out of the building, she didn't return home. She couldn't stand the look of concern on her parents' faces. At home, when they said their good mornings and good nights, their voices were as bland as a piece of tile. Iwen moved to a three-story house under her family's name. Her parents had maintained the house very well. *This is great,* Iwen thought. She wanted to clean and arrange the house on her own to run herself ragged. *Was it five years, or six? The time I spent with Yi-Wei was like a dream. It wasn't all nightmares.* She did love Yi-Wei, and she held the same determination she had when, as a student, she decided on her thesis topic. Yi-Wei's world was all about taking things for granted, the way a child wanted mother's milk, sucking it until the age when differences between boys and girls became distinct. To deal with a kid as smart-mouthed as Yi-Wei, you had no option but to give him the very best pacifier.

The day she left Yi-Wei's building, she looked back. When the high and majestic building opened its front door, the sparkling chandelier inside looked like teeth. It opened its mouth wide as though it were about to swallow her.

Iwen was never able to fall asleep at night. The embroidered wallpaper met the ceiling, connecting the four walls around her like an exquisite box, locking her inside. She always went downstairs to the living room to watch movies on TV. She cried when the big white shark ate someone, and cried again when the shark was killed. When she cried herself to exhaustion, she fell asleep on the couch. The sofa emitted a soft leather fragrance. She leaned over it, supported by her breath, bobbing up and down. It was almost like the sofa was the one breathing. She imagined this was what it must feel like to lay on top of a cow. She fell asleep and woke up in shock. Whenever she woke up, she continued to watch TV. The female costar from the last movie was the protagonist in the following movie, made ten years later. She still looked the same. The years Iwen would spend here were much like the face of a Hollywood actress, oblivious to the passage of time.

And then one day, Iwen finally phoned Mr. Maomao.

"Hello?" he answered.

"Ah, Mr. Mao, did I bother you?"

"Of course not."

"What are you up to?"

"Me? I'm drawing. My hand is always holding a pen or is about to hold a pen."

You didn't laugh, Maomao thought. *Your silence is like a line drawn by a wrong pen, unable to be erased.*

Maomao had no choice but to continue. "I seem to have forgotten dinner. Whenever I'm in a rush to finish a project, I buy dinner from the convenience store. I suppose it sounds like a waste. We only live for a couple of decades, and we're only supposed to eat three meals a day. I should probably take your advice and eat whatever I want most for every meal. Have you eaten yet?"

Iwen didn't answer his question directly but said, "Can you come stay with me?"

When Iwen answered the door, the moment it opened, Maomao felt as if he were finally able to read a translated novel that he had been familiar with as a kid in its original language. *This is my first time seeing you wear glasses. I want to read you like a classic.* Iwen sat on one end of the long sofa, with Maomao sitting on the other. They watched a movie; during scenes where the director intended to make the audiences laugh, Iwen actually laughed out loud.

The container and solution for your eye contacts sit on the coffee table. Your slippers are uneven, with one flipped over on the floor, like jiaobei moon blocks turned upside down. Your jacket, hanging on the back of a chair, looks as if it had grown shoulders. A book written in a foreign language with a protruding spine is pressed down in a shape that resembles a 人 character on the table; the heavy, dark-patterned marble table is your bookmark.

After watching three movies consecutively, Iwen fell asleep. Her head tilted against the back of the sofa; the ice cream in the bucket she held between her thighs began to melt. Maomao gently took it away from her and put it back in the fridge in the same gentle manner. The fridge was empty, and when Maomao closed the door, he thought about the time when he saw Iwen in her light-blue pajama pants, the fabric in between her thighs moistened to indigo. Pieces of receipt were casually tossed in the big container on the table, like insects retracting their legs. They all were from either fast-food restaurants or convenience stores. On the armchair rested a thin, folded blanket; sitting in front of the chair was a coffee mug with coffee grounds dried up at the bottom, the edge of the mug stained with coffee kisses. As he pulled the drawer of the grinder and ground a spoonful of unused coffee, he spotted a water glass. *I bet you lay on the couch all day.* Maomao took off his slippers, his socked feet pressed against the floor; he was careful with the sound of his flip-flops to not wake Iwen up. When he turned off the TV, Iwen woke up from the silence.

He saw her tear up as she said, "Can you stay over tonight?"

Maomao didn't know how he should reply.

You're too vulnerable; I don't want to take advantage of you.

"My house has lots of rooms," Iwen added.

"All right then."

Every day after that, Maomao went back to his place to work, then grabbed some of his things before heading back to Iwen's apartment. He gradually moved more things over; some days he even drew his designs at her apartment. Iwen sat right across from him. He drew while she read. Between them was not the echoing silence within a mountain range but the silence of a gem-encrusted cliff. One day Iwen gingerly waved her hand in front of Maomao, as though he were far away. Maomao lifted his head and watched Iwen push a book toward him, her finger pointing at a specific paragraph. Maomao stopped his drawing hand and read the paragraph, then said, "It's so good."

Iwen told Maomao: "We're actually a lot alike. And you're a gentler me."

He resisted saying, *You're treating me the way you treated Yi-Wei. This is a layered metaphor for love; even with time, it'll never perish.*

When Maomao poured water for himself, he would pour some for Iwen, to which she would open her lamblike eyes widely and give an intent "Thank you."

When you say thank you, a pair of dimples ripples your cheeks; it's so adorable. Do you know the original meaning of dimple *is actually related to wine? In ancient times, when people brewed wine, in order to give it more exposure to natural air, they would blend the yeast with grains and patch them along the wall of the ceramic pot. That way, it would reveal what's at the bottom. I can almost see the very bottom of you through your dimples.*

But Maomao simply said, "Don't thank me." He held off from saying, *I'm happier this way. It's me who should be thanking you.*

Before entering her room upstairs, Iwen playfully imitated a soldier's salute. "Good night, roommate."

Gradually, I stopped hearing you cry in your sleep. In the morning, I see you coming downstairs in your pink athletic wear. You're always wearing those fluffy pink slippers. In my mind, I automatically zoom into your tiny eyes behind your thick glasses. After eating some quiche, I bring a sweet pie from the kitchen, which you pretend to be in shambles and say, "No way, Mr. Maomao is going to spoil me rotten." I'd be happy to fall into a hell made of dough, rolling in it one life after another. I spend my whole life rolling dough flat enough for you to safely walk on, tearing a mouthful to eat whenever you feel hungry.

They watched a movie that evening. When Iwen reached for the DVDs from the tall shelf, she tightened her muscles, stretched her body, and made a determined groan. Then she would squat and turn on the DVD player, pressing a button, and making a *biiiiiii* sound.

Sometimes I don't even know if I should help you. You're too adorable. When we watch French movies, you want macarons, and when we watch British movies, you want scones; when watching Russian movies, you want Russian soft candies, chewing them like marshmallows. When you chewed a dry, hard walnut piece, you looked like you had awakened from a disrupted dream; I swallowed back questions that sprang inside me out of nowhere—what are we, actually? You said when we watch movies about Nazis in World War II, we can't eat anything.

I love going to a coffee shop you know well and choosing coffee beans with you. When the owner scoops up the coffee beans, you tuck a strand of your hair back at your ear and try to smell the beans, then turn to me with a face full of infinite surprise. "This is honey, and that was walnut! This is Truffaut, and that was Kieślowski!" I really want to say to you, "Yes, Buñuel, and Godard." In this world, there is beautiful coffee with fair trades. I want to apologize to you for this world, for the past six years snatched away from you. I like how you're more curious than tourists when strolling at the night market. Drops of sweat that stick to your face don't look like sweat but dew. I like how you squat down, observing the capsule toy machine; the way your long dress sweeps across the floor like a sleeping tail. I like how you hold the six ten-dollar coins in your palm until they are drenched in your sweat, but even then you still can't make up your mind about which machine to insert them in. One time, we had a bet about which one you were actually going to get. The person who lost had to buy bubble milk tea for the winner. I like how you owe me hundreds of bubble milk teas and never want to buy me a single one. It was only when the owners said to me that I have a beautiful girlfriend that my heart wrenched a bit. I like looking at your profile at home, your face slanted by the refractions of your glasses. It is like learning as a kid why a straw looks bent and broken underwater. Once I learned, I would rather have never known about it. I'd rather believe that anything that is easy to bend and break in the world and the faults created can be easily mended. I've seen the dry crusts around your eyes in the morning and heard you flush the toilet. I smelled your sweaty towel and tasted your leftover plates. I know when you sleep, you have a small stuffed lamb at your side. And I know that I'm nobody to you. I simply love you too much.

Patting on the sofa, Mr. Maomao saw a slim, folded, wrinkled shadow. It turned out to be Iwen's long hair. Picking it up with his finger, he spun it around his finger twelve times. I like how you speak in Japanese: "Tadaima! I'm back!" I like it even more when you say, "You're home!" What I like most is you placing our tableware in a symmetrical manner. As long as everything goes in pairs, we've done more than enough.

When Guo Hsiao-Chi came home from the hospital, she immediately posted to an online forum and revealed Lee Guo-Hua's name. She wrote: "Lee Guo-Hua and Tsai Liang both lied to this one girl when she was in her last year of high school. But she was afraid, so she remained in 'a relationship' with Lee Guo-Hua for about two or three years, until Lee Guo-Hua found a new girl."

When spending time with Lee Guo-Hua, Hsiao-Chi had once thought that even if she equally divided her pain and gave a piece to every person living on Earth, all of them would be in so much pain that they wouldn't be able to catch their breath. She couldn't imagine that there were other girls before her, or even after her. She had always enjoyed watching American true crime documentaries about how the FBI dealt with felonies and caught murderers. To the FBI, killing seven people was a massacre. What about seven little girls who died by suicide? She pressed the "confirm" button to publish her post. She had only one thought: *These things should come to a complete stop.* There were over five hundred thousand people browsing the platform every day, so she received responses very quickly. They were completely different from what she expected.

- So how much money did you take from him?
- *Bao bao* for *bao bao*: scallop-vaginas for brand-name purses.
- Being a cram school teacher must be such a *joy*.
- Homewreckers should go to hell.
- That teacher's wife should be pitied.
- Probably a competing cram school part-timer posted this.
- Doesn't she enjoy his thing coming in and out?

For Hsiao-Chi, reading each of the responses was like receiving fatal stabs from a knife.

It turned out that most people lacked imagination for other people's suffering. Her post was a landscape for the most evil and barren languages: a man with money and power, a young and beautiful mistress, a wife in tears—people looked at it all as a dull stream of words, an 8:00 p.m. soap opera, because they didn't want to acknowledge the tangible existence of inhuman pain, so they denied the facts while vaguely understanding one thing or another. Otherwise even a little peace might seem unkind. In this era when everyone claimed to be losers, nobody would admit there was a group of girls out there who had really lost it all. Their minor pain seemed to mirror happiness: everyone indulged in minor happiness as they murmured minor pain with their lips, but when bare-naked pain was brought to their faces, the peace they enjoyed would immediately become ugly, their pain apparently frivolous.

The long stream of comments felt like thousands of knives chafing against Hsiao-Chi's body. Even though Teacher Lee was the guilty one, her body remained next to him.

Tsai Liang told Lee Guo-Hua about the online post. After reviewing it, Lee Guo-Hua came up with a short list of names. Tsai Liang asked someone to investigate, and they soon discovered that Guo Hsiao-Chi was the account holder. Lee Guo-Hua was infuriated. In the past twenty years, none of the girls had dared to do such a thing. Even board members from the cram school began to question him. *I should show her what I'm capable of.* When Lee Guo-Hua thought about this, he laughed. He laughed about how closely his interior monologue resembled the tête-à-tête between a cop and a bandit you'd find in a Hong Kong detective film.

A few days later, Tsai Liang reported that Guo Hsiao-Chi was still replying to the comments under the post, claiming that she was sexually groomed and that she finally understood why Lee Guo-Hua had given her a hundred thousand dollars.

Lee Guo-Hua sat on a sofa so soft one could sink into it like quicksand. Sitting across from Tsai Liang, he watched her feet shake mindlessly, the brand-name shoes he bought her kicking and dangling; her right leg propped up on her left leg, the flesh of her right calf bulging playfully, exposing her freshly grown leg hair. Each hair shot out its head like stubble. Now that he didn't have anyone in Kaohsiung, whenever he came to Taipei to meet Fang Si-Chi, he thought his beard grew especially fast. It must've been hormones or whatever. He thought about how his stubble rubbed against Si-Chi's tiny breasts, her pale skin peeling off with white flakes, and the red edema hidden underneath. It was like using cinnabar to draw natural landscapes on a semitransparent porcelain vase. *These silly girls. These bitches sure are daring, going around telling everyone they were raped. Even Tsai Liang doesn't care; she's in the bathroom smearing shaving cream on her legs.* Nobody understood him. The world's understanding of him couldn't hold a candle to how much his stubble understood him. Stubble wanted to stand out, and the hairs were more than just stubble; they had genuine value. In his mind, he was merely a poor student who had just graduated. He had to calculate his expense for every meal. He wouldn't let some idiot girl ruin his career like this.

Lee Guo-Hua started to reach out when he headed back to Taipei.

Before Teacher Lee's taxi arrived, Si-Chi and Yi-Ting were

talking about the first thing they wanted to do when they entered college. Yi-Ting said she wanted to learn French, and Si-Chi's eyes lit up. "Yeah, let's do language exchange with a French student. He'll teach us French and we'll teach him Mandarin." Yi-Ting said, "We can teach them all kinds of things with that newscaster accent—'Wo Aini' (I *short* you / I love you), 'Shei-shei' (Thank youuuu), and 'Duai-bu-ji' (I'm sowwy)."

They burst out laughing. Si-Chi said, "Yeah, whenever we learn a new language, we always learn how to say 'I love you' first. How the hell are we supposed to know when you get to know someone well enough to say that?"

Yi-Ting laughed again. "If we lost our passports abroad, we'd be on the street desperately murmuring, 'I love you, I love you.'"

"Well—*fraternité*," said Si-Chi.

They were beside themselves with laughter. Yi-Ting continued, "Other people beg for money on the street, and we beg for love." Si-Chi stood on her tiptoes and turned around, swimming her hands outward, blowing out kisses to Yi-Ting and mouthing, *I love you*. Yi-Ting laughed so hard she fell off her chair. Si-Chi sat down again and said, "Ah, in this world, people are either barren of love or overflowing with it." Half kneeling on the ground, Yi-Ting lifted her head and said to Si-Chi, "I love you, too."

The taxi honked downstairs.

Si-Chi's gaze began to sway as she slowly stood up. She pulled Yi-Ting up and said, "I'll be home tomorrow. Talking with you is always so much fun." Yi-Ting nodded, and when the car steered away, she didn't even look down through the curtains. Inside their apartment, she quietly smiled. *I love you.*

Bending Si-Chi at the waist, Lee Guo-Hua carried her on his

shoulder from the living room to the bedroom. In his arms, she said, *I can't do it today, my period, sorry.* Teacher Lee's face rippled with a mysterious grin; he wasn't just disappointed, but getting furious. Every wrinkled line on his face shivered. Once put on the bed, Si-Chi was a dried flower meeting water, flexing herself open. But she pressed her skirt tightly and said, *I really can't do it today, my period.* And then she asked provocatively, *Isn't Teacher Lee afraid of blood?* Lee Guo-Hua made an expression he had never shown her before. It was something out of a special effects–heavy Hollywood movie, with an antagonist about to transform into a monster; the muscles in his entire body swelled, with blue veins floating up against his skin; the thick blood vessels in his eyes were like sperm swimming toward an egg. He looked like a bag full of walnuts about to break. Right after that moment, he relaxed, turning back into the teacher that bears *gentleness, respect, humility,* the teacher who tore her underwear, giving her a papaya while being rewarded with a beautiful piece of jade. Si-Chi began to suspect she was hallucinating again. *All right.* She didn't know why he was saying *all right.* He leaned over and kissed her, patting her down there, making it loose, then covered her with a quilt. Her body was squeezed between the bedsheet and the quilt; one of his hands pushed against the doorframe of the bedroom, while the other hand turned off the lights. *Good night.* Si-Chi saw his face before the room went dark: half-angry and half-nonchalant, it had that same expression he'd make when he had just broken an expensive antique. It was childish. He said, *Good night,* but it felt like he was saying *Goodbye.*

After the door closed, Si-Chi kept staring at the ray of light leaking in from the living room through the gap beneath the door. Si-Chi thought that threshold of light, the horizontal line, was disrupted, making two slits inside the darkness: a golden 一 turned into two 一 一.

Apparently, Teacher Lee is still lingering outside the door while I lie here, in bed, my hands placed on the hemline of the side of my clothes, as though many hands are stroking my body, and inside my body, here and there, something is dashing around. I'm a paradise who lets anyone ride on me like a roller coaster. One that brings thrilling ascent to the edge of the clouds; the speeding cars never understand the thrill of the sky, or the thrill of humans. I can't fall asleep on this bed, and I'd rather know that my skin and my bodily fluids will remember nothing. Memories in my mind can be buried, but physical memories can't. Two 一 一 remain by the door gap. 一 一 what? We were exchanging exam papers to grade our classmate sitting next to us. I placed one check mark after another on Yi-Ting's paper, and then we exchanged back, and mine was also full of check marks. Surprisingly, exams with the same score lead to such different lives!

Teacher Lee enclosed me in his arms and mistook the origins of Emperor Han-Chen's gentle hometown for that of Zhao Fei-Yan. I seemed to have tolerated his hand for all this while just to wait for the moment he made that mistake. He's missing a step between his desire and his career, having tripped over the threshold that separates living room and bedroom. When I discovered how much I had been kneaded and wrung, I could still internally argue that it was Zhao Fei-Yan's younger sister Zhao Hede. I feel like my last remaining dignity is finally saved. During class, Teacher Lee is genderless. Clothed and unclothed, he hit and contradicted me while misremembering the details of the story; he wore the black shirt he often wears to class, but without pants. It was uncertain whether he simply forgot to take off his shirt or he forgot to put on his pants. But he only belongs to me, Teacher that falls with the entire body, crystal clear and transparent, between the cracks of time. One time I asked him, Why did you even do that in the first place? He replied, I was just expressing my love a little too roughly. Listening to his answer, Oh, the satisfaction. Nobody chose their words better than him, and there were no words that sounded more off than his. The vitality of literature came from the ability to parse out humor through a merciless situation, not boasting to anyone, but immersing oneself in a mysterious, silent happiness. Literature was about memorizing and chanting that one same love poem to a fifty-year-old wife and a fifteen-year-old lover. The first song I learned to memorize by heart during my upbringing was Tsao Tsao's "Short Song Ballad," and Teacher Lee often sings it to me while I translate it in my mind: Stars around the bright moon are few, southward the crows flew. Flying three rounds, circling a tree, where shall they nest? It was the first time I discovered that eyes were like birds. Looking across the tops of Teacher Lee's shoulders at the spots where arm and shoulder meet, I counted over and over the number of candles around the chandelier with numerous branches; it was round, as though walking on Earth, nothing but climbing down grids on an infinitely wide essay paper, like the round table the adults reunited around; Teacher Lee was on my left and also on my right; my eyes circled around the chandelier, counting one round after another. I don't know when everything started, and I don't know how to make it stop.

Si-Chi suddenly thought about Kwei. If I'd never been with Teacher Lee, I might have ended up being with Kwei. He's polite, a gentleman, and his family background aligns with mine perfectly. But he is so stubborn and hard to be persuaded. At the end of the day, he's that kind of guy. I remember when we were little; one time I spotted *the candies I had given him at his house. He had kept the box a year after, even though it wasn't a particularly beautiful box. He started to notice my gaze and began to stammer. It was then that I finally realized why Kwei had been so mean to Yi-Ting. Whenever I got his postcards from the US, all I felt was numb and I never responded back. I wasn't sure how forlorn or optimistic he was to be able to keep tossing stones into the infinitely bottomless and dark valley. Maybe he has been chasing other girls in the US at the same time; it's easier and heartbreaking to think this way. Kwei, there's nothing wrong with Kwei; actually, he's too good to be true. With time, the English in his handwritten postcards increased, like adding more spices to a dish, making the recipe gradually become more exotic. I could have fallen in love with him, but it's too late. I don't really think he's my type. This is nothing but nostalgia for a home I've never even encountered. I see, this is how it feels when I'm not loyal to Teacher Lee—it's so painful. I have to endure not thinking about it, but the scenes become more distinct in my head. There's a tall, strong man that I've never seen before, and on his face are traces of Kwei in his childhood. The eyes staring at the music sheet are as vivid as the black and white on the sheet itself; the black is like the shade of tuxedos, cocktail dresses, and the sea of dark silk in the symphony. I fell down into it from the bed.*

I will always remember that day in junior high. I walked home with Yi-Ting. I told her I would go accompany Iwen while Yi-Ting headed to Teacher Lee's essay lesson. I immediately regretted saying the word "accompany." I wasn't being respectful to Iwen's private wounds, nor her private pain. We ran into Teacher Lee in the lobby, and Yi-Ting pulled me toward her and we both nuzzled his side, talking about the Chinese teacher in our school who sang Beijing opera during class. The golden elevator resembled an exquisite gift box, enclosing all three of us. I couldn't be sure who was the one following the rules and who was the one being objectified. All I wanted was to apologize to Iwen. Faintly, I heard Yi-Ting say that the tone our schoolteacher sang with was "on edge," and I was surprised to see how much effort Yi-Ting made to talk to Teacher Lee; it was almost as if she were falling for him. Our necks rested against the golden railing in the elevator. We arrived at the seventh floor. "Why don't you head out with me?" Yi-Ting laughed and said, "We're seeing you off here. We're going downstairs now!" In a trance, I walked out of the elevator, feeling the rugged millstone floor; my shoes in front of my apartment looked so skinny. I turned my head back and saw the golden elevator door slowly close Yi-Ting and Teacher Lee in, like the final scene of a stage play. I watched Teacher Lee; so did Yi-Ting, but Teacher Lee only looked at me. This final scene was so very long. Teacher Lee's face didn't look like he was going to be imprisoned; it was more like the 「」 of the elevator door contained the elements of life that were to be shorn and trimmed by a superior existence, slowly moving in toward its center, and in the end, what remained was but Teacher Lee's face. Before the door closed, he mouthed, I love you, to me. When he twisted his lips, his smile folds became surprisingly sharp; his wrinkles tightened and loosened, loosened then tightened, like the way fault lines squeeze out a volcano, letting the volcano spout, loudly releasing until it's empty. I realized at that moment, this love was as impartial as lava; direct, saturated with the color of blood and texture of vomit, tumbling toward me. When his lips sucked on me, he broke right through my heart's virginity. Suddenly, it occurred to me: Teacher Lee really does love me. And it would forever look like I'm living on the seventh floor, when in truth I've perpetually been on the sixth floor. The me that stayed in Teacher Lee's sixth-floor living room is a counterfeit of

me in my bedroom; *the me in my home on the seventh floor is a counterfeit of me in his sixth-floor living room. After that, whenever he
wanted me to put his thing in my mouth, I always felt this unexpected,
maternal gratitude. Every time I thought to myself, Teacher Lee is*
handing me the most vulnerable part of him.

Which motel will Teacher Lee bring me to tomorrow? Si-Chi
flipped over, her body drenched in sweat. She was unsure if what
she had experienced was a series of dreams, or perhaps she had
just been lying there, pondering. She looked at the gap of the
door, watching the golden 一 character turn into two 一 一.
Teacher Lee must be standing outside the door.

Half drifting to sleep, she imagined the darkness of the room
wasn't contrasting the light, but the lit silhouettes of Teacher Lee
dragging his slippered feet. His shadow projected inside the room
and stretched very long until it submerged into darkness. That
darkness was ubiquitous, as though Teacher Lee's shoes could ride
on top of it, secretly climb through the door gap and sneak into
the bed, then give her a kick. She felt a startling fear.

She heard the hissing noise when the door opened. All the
main lights, recessed lights, and projected lights in the bedroom
were turned on simultaneously at full brightness; the door was
pushed against the wall fiercely—*hoooong.* It sounded like thun-
der right after a lightning strike. Teacher Lee climbed on top of
her quickly, snaking his hand into her skirt, stroking her, and said
cheerfully, *I knew you were lying to me. Didn't you say you just had
your period?*

Exhausted, Si-Chi said, *I'm sorry, Teacher, I'm really tired today.*

So when you're tired, you lie like a little kid?

I'm so sorry.

Without even taking a shower first, Teacher Lee began cracking fingers. He smelled like a zoo. She was shocked when he began taking her clothes off. He had never done this before. Teacher Lee had stubble all over his face, and they intertextualized with his wrinkles. It was like a labyrinth of thorns. She started coming up with dialogue in her head as usual. Suddenly, the production line of her sentences began to scream. The wheel and axle that bit into each other started to tear one another off with their sharp teeth; the conveyor broke, and dark blood flooded out. Was that a twisted rope in Teacher Lee's hand?

Open your legs.

No.

Don't make me beat you.

Si-Chi thought, *Teacher didn't take off his clothes; why should I open up?*

Lee Guo-Hua took a deep breath, admiring his own patience. *Gentleness, respect, and humility, President Ma's motto. Thank goodness I learned about it when I was doing my military service. An overhand knot here, and a square knot there.* Her limbs were drowning.

No, no!

Reveal what should be revealed. Make another figure eight knot here, and then another clove hitch there.

Her wrists and ankles were rubbed so hard they became swollen. *No! No! No! No!*

That's right, just like a crab. I can't stabilize her neck; it'll be no fun if she dies.

No, no. Fang Si-Chi's scream shot out from her organs and stuck in her throat. *Yes, oh yes, it's this feeling, this exact feeling,* she thought. Staring at the books on the shelf, she began to be incapable of reading Chinese characters there. And then gradually, she couldn't hear what Teacher Lee was saying. All she saw was that twisted mouth, the same one Yi-Ting and she made when they were both little, like rocks spilled out from spring water. *This is it, my soul is about to leave its body, and I'll forget this humiliation I'm feeling right now. When I return, I'll come back completely intact.*

It's ready. The crabs Mama Fang gave me the other day were also tied up like this.

Lee Guo-Hua laughed out of humbleness. *Gentleness, respect, and humility.* The bodily fluids were warm; sprouts and weeds of energy; menarche to be congratulated; condoms saved—life was given.

This time, Fang Si-Chi was mistaken. When her soul left her body, it never returned again.

After a few days, the metal shutter at Guo Hsiao-Chi's house was sprayed with a bucket of red paint. A letter lay quietly inside her mailbox: there was only one photo inside the envelope, a photo of crab Si-Chi.

PART 3

Paradise Regained

After she graduated from high school, Yi-Ting only went to Taichung once to visit Si-Chi with Iwen and Mr. Maomao. The nurse in white raised Si-Chi's limp hand, speaking in a baby voice to coax her: "Look who came to visit!" Iwen and Yi-Ting saw Si-Chi had lost so much weight that she resembled a skull embedded with a pair of eyes; they jutted out so cartoonishly, they looked like a famous rock star's wedding ring, six claws grasping a huge diamond. One eye, like a ring, was situated at the south hemisphere, while the other lay in the north hemisphere, but still bonded by eternal ties. Yi-Ting had never seen eyes that were so disconnected from

215

each other. The nurse waved her hand at them and said, "It's all right, come closer. She doesn't bite." It was as though she were talking about a dog. And it was not until they took out the fruits that Si-Chi began to speak. She picked up a banana, peeling it and immediately started munching. She said to her banana, "Thank you, you treat me so well."

Yi-Ting had finished reading Si-Chi's diary. She hadn't shown it to Iwen. *Iwen looks too content right now,* she thought.

Yi-Ting headed back to Taipei while Iwen and Mr. Maomao went south to Kaohsiung. After they said goodbye at the high-speed-rail station, Iwen finally burst into tears. She cried so hard she fell to her knees. The passersby stared at her exposed thighs that showed when she was trying to curve them back underneath her skirt. Slowly, Maomao took her arm around his shoulder and sat her down on a seat. Iwen cried so much her entire body was shivering, which made Maomao want to hug her, but instead he quietly gave Iwen her asthma medication.

"Maomao," Iwen said.

"What's going on?"

"Maomao, do you know how smart a little girl she was? Do you know how kindhearted and curious she was about this world? And now, all she remembers is how to peel a banana!"

"It's not your fault," Maomao said, haltingly.

That made Iwen cry even harder. "It's definitely my fault!"

"It's not your fault."

"Sure it is! I've been drowning in my misery, and there were so many times she was so close—so close to telling me what happened! But she was afraid to be a burden, so nobody knows why she turned out this way, even now!"

Gently patting Iwen's back, Maomao could feel her protruding spine.

He cautiously continued, "Iwen, I don't know how to tell you this, but when I designed that birdcage pendant, I could really feel your love for them. But it's like what happened to you; it's not your fault, and it isn't her fault, either. Whatever happened to Si-Chi is absolutely not your fault."

Several days after getting home, Iwen got a call from Yi-Wei. She picked up the phone and spoke blandly, like plain water, "What's up?"

She didn't say his name; she didn't know how to address him.

"I just want to see you. Can I go to you?" Yi-Wei used a voice lower than his height.

Maomao isn't home. "How do you know where I live?"

"I could guess."

Iwen's bland, plain water voice, was now mingled with ink, and that drop of ink started to bloom toward the geocenter.

"Oh Yi-Wei, why don't we let each other go? I just visited Si-Chi days ago."

"Please?" Yi-Wei faked a duck's voice. "Please?"

When Iwen opened the door, she was greeted by Yi-Wei's usual supercilious face. He quietly observed Iwen's home decor: books and DVDs stacked in two separate chaotic piles. As Iwen turned toward the kitchen counter, Yi-Wei sat down on the high stool in the kitchen, watching Iwen's large chunk of exposed skin between her vest and her shorts. She was as pale as a hotel bedsheet waiting for him to lie on. Yi-Wei smelled the scent of coffee. Iwen had to try very hard not to treat him too gently.

"For you. Don't burn your tongue."

217

The weather was scorching, but not only did Yi-Wei keep his blazer on, he even held the mug with both hands. Iwen buried her head in the fridge, looking for something, and Yi-Wei's eyes located a pair of socks that belonged to a man. Iwen sat across from Yi-Wei at the counter, and he reached his hand over, stroking the contour of her ear.

"Yi-Wei." Iwen jerked her head away.

"I've already quit drinking."

"Good for you."

Yi-Wei suddenly grew emotional. "I really did quit drinking, Iwen. I'm over fifty years old now and I can't bear to lose you like this. I really do love you. We can move away, live wherever we want. You can make our house as messy as your place, and you can stuff our fridge with your garbage fast food. Could you please give me another chance? Please, my pinky-pie Iwen?"

He could smell her breath.

Iwen thought, *It's really hard for me to hate him.*

Their arms and legs clasped together, converged together. On the sofa, it was hard to distinguish which body part belonged to whom.

Yi-Wei tried to rest, lying on top of Iwen's tiny breasts. The semen he had just ejaculated still lingered in her body, and he still felt the rhythm of her consistent cramping from her waist and back. She moaned *uh* when she arched herself up like a coming wave, *ah* when she arched back down like a receding tide; her fists held so tight her blue veins floated against her skin. But then she gradually loosened her grip, letting it go; her arm swept down beneath the sofa. Suddenly, he saw the heart of her palm carved with her pinkish fingernail marks.

It was like when they first moved in together, passing the glazed stone bottles back and forth. Iwen carefully moved Yi-Wei's head away and dressed quickly. She stood up and watched Yi-Wei, looking like a baby without his glasses. Iwen handed him his clothes and sat next to him.

"Do you forgive me?"

Iwen quietly said, "Yi-Wei, listen to me. Do you know what I fear most? If you hadn't woken up early that day, I probably would've died from blood loss. The time I've spent by myself has helped me discover how greedy I am about my own life. I can tolerate just about anything, but the fact is that you could've killed me. I can't bear to think about it. Everything has some leeway, but life and death are resolute. Maybe in another world, you didn't wake up, and I passed away. I think about all the photos of us in our house, surrounding you, widening their eyes, watching you. But even if I had died, would you get sober and live your whole life in spite of its emptiness? Or maybe you would drink even more? I know you love me very much, and that's exactly why I can't ever forgive you. Over and over, I pushed my boundaries to their very limit, but this time, I really do want to live my life to the fullest. You know, when I told my professor I was going to drop out of my program, he asked me what my fiancé was like. I replied, 'Oh, he's like a forest of pine trees.' I even looked it up in the English dictionary to make sure I was talking about the strongest and most determined kind of tree. Do you remember the collection of love poems I often used to read to you? Now that I look back at it, it was like reading pages of my own diary. Yi-Wei, do you know? I never believed in horoscopes, but I saw in today's newspaper that your luck will follow you all the way to the end of the year, including your luck for love. Don't call me harsh; I didn't even say how harsh you are. Yi-Wei, please listen to me, you're great; please stop drinking. Find someone who truly loves you; treat her well. Yi-Wei, I won't love you back even if you cry. I don't love you, really. Not anymore."

Maomao came back to Iwen's place and heard Iwen showering as he opened the door. He threw himself on the sofa and immediately felt something lying behind the cushion. A balled-up tie. Its gray color cast a shadow over Maomao's eyes. The sound of the shower was followed by the sound of a hair dryer. *I need to think this over clearly before you dry your hair,* Maomao thought. *I can see your slippers, calves, your thighs, your shorts, your top, your neck, and then your face.*

"Iwen?" Maomao said.

"Yeah?"

"Did someone come over today?"

"Why do you ask?" Iwen said.

He showed her the balled-up tie, which seemed to sigh in his palm, unraveling.

"Was it Chien Yi-Wei?"

"Yup."

"Did he touch you?"

Iwen looked infuriated, and Maomao realized he was yelling.

"Why should I even answer your question? Who are you to me?"

Maomao's heart began to pour; he felt like a wet dog limping, moaning, and whimpering in the rain. He lowered his voice. "I'm heading out."

Quietly, he closed the door, as though he had never once opened it.

Iwen cleaned up the house in silence. She suddenly felt like everything was a counterfeit. Everyone was demanding her to do something. Only Dostoyevsky belonged to her.

After an hour, Maomao came back.

"I went to get some groceries for dinner. Sorry for taking so long. It's pouring outside," he said, not knowing whom he was explaining to nor what he was trying to explain. He put the groceries in the fridge very slowly. As he shut the door, the smart refrigerator began to sing its special door-closing song.

When Maomao spoke again, his voice sounded like rain—not the kind of rain that passed by the display window or traveled outside the arcade, but the rain dripping down in front of someone who was waiting by the hallway. "Iwen, I'm just disappointed by myself. I thought the only virtue was to be satisfied with what I have. But I'm very greedy when it comes to you. Maybe subconsciously, I don't even dare admit how much I want you to sneak into my room whenever you feel empty and lonely. How much I hope I can just keep doing this without ever asking for anything in return. But I'm not like that. I don't dare to ask you if you love me. I fear your answer. I know Chien Yi-Wei intentionally left his tie here. Like I've told you, I'm willing to trade everything I have for you to look at me the same way you used to look at Yi-Wei. I really mean it. But maybe everything I have is only worth his necktie. We're both students of art, but I violated art's biggest taboo, and that is to feel self-satisfied with my humility. I shouldn't lie to myself about how being able to spend time with you is already enough, and that it would be enough if I can simply make you happy. Because in truth I want more. I really do love you, but I'm not selfless, and I'm sorry to disappoint you."

Iwen looked at Maomao, but paused when she was about to speak. It was like her tongue had fallen down and was unable to crawl up again. She could faintly hear the married couple next door curse while making love; she could hear seeds sprouting underground and an elderly neighbor from the other side dip his dentures into water, bubbling between its teeth, making popping sounds as they broke the water's surface. *I see your face gradually brighten up, like a topcoat over a nail.*

Iwen eventually made up her mind to say something. She laughed; her exaggerated, twisted lips seemed about to say something that was going to scorch her tongue. Like a child pointing at a street sign, she solidly, sweetly spelled out one character after another: "Jing 敬 Yuan 苑."

"Eh? How come you never said this before?"

"You never even asked. So why would I say this to you?" Iwen laughed so hard that the vanilla cake in her hand turned into a landslide, a mudslide, a fissure. Mao Jing-Yuan's upper and lower mustache hesitantly separated, and when he spoke with more energy, Iwen could see the skin underneath his mustache turn red, like when vegetation meant for red soil returned from their ochre plots, and their stomata would emit a strong fragrance. Mao Jing-Yuan laughed, too.

———

Yi-Ting was no longer the same person after she finished reading Si-Chi's diary. Her soulmate, her twin of the soul, no matter if she was downstairs or by her side, had been contaminated, defaced, and treated like leftovers. Her diary was like the back of the moon, never able to be seen. Yi-Ting finally understood that the rotten sores of this world were bigger than the world itself. The twin of her soul.

She read the diary repeatedly, to the point where she knew every page by heart. She felt like everything that had happened to Si-Chi had just happened to her. After memorizing the insides, she took Si-Chi's diary to Iwen. Yi-Ting saw Iwen cry for the second time in her life. Iwen's lawyer introduced them to a feminist colleague, whom they visited together. The office was small, and his body was so large that the whole office became nothing but his armchair. The lawyer said, "There's nothing we can do. We need evidence. Without any evidence, his team would sue you for defamation and he would win."

"What do you mean by 'evidence'?" Iwen said.

"Condoms, tissues, things like that."

Yi-Ting felt like she was about to vomit.

Yi-Ting and Si-Chi visited their college campus to preview student life. They observed guys on the basketball court and rated each of them. They scored them for their faces, body builds, and basketball skills. They stuck a to-do list on the wall of their room, listing things they wanted to try after their college entrance exams; each unchecked box resembled an eternally yawning mouth. There was a teacher that said in front of the entire class that Si-Chi was a psycho, and Yi-Ting made a paper ball and threw it at that teacher's face.

———

Yi-Ting thought about her soulmate. *Before our swimming competition, I didn't know how to put in a tampon, so you took me to the bathroom and helped me stuff it in; you carefully carried beverages in your bag and brought them to me when Lee Guo-Hua happened to have bought something I like. I said I didn't want to drink it, and for a second you looked destroyed. For the first birthday we celebrated after starting high school, we borrowed a senior girl's ID card to go to karaoke, and we jumped like two fleas inside a big room; when we were little, our families went to see lotus blossoms together, but the lotuses had withered and their leaves curled up like burnt tea leaves that died on their stems. That pond of lotuses, made up of all stems, looked strangely naked. You mouthed poetry to me: The lotus leaves have withered beyond keeping off the rain. So stupid—just like humans. I always knew we were different from the crowd.*

After all, what is poetry, writing, etiquette, enlightenment—the traditional six arts? When I escorted you out of the police station, I couldn't help but bow and thank the police officers. "Sorry for the trouble, officers." Oh my god!

If I hadn't expressed my disgust, called you dirty, would you still have gone mad?

Yi-Ting asked Lee Guo-Hua to meet in person, claiming that she already knew everything and that he should let her visit his little apartment. Once the door was closed, Yi-Ting felt a surge of fear, as though her hair wasn't growing out of her scalp but stabbing her head. There was a tank of goldfish in his apartment, numb to her waving hands. They seemed to have gotten used to humans teasing them. Si-Chi's little hand quickly came to mind.

Yi-Ting spoke in a newscaster's voice. She had practiced it at home so many times that it sounded natural.

"What made Si-Chi lose her mind?"

"She lost her mind? Oh, I don't know. I haven't been in touch with her in a long time. Is this why you're here?" Lee Guo-Hua spoke plainly, like water; his voice was unbreakable.

"Teacher Lee, you know I can't sue you. All I want to know is what happened to Si-Chi—what made her go mad?"

Lee Guo-Hua sat down, stroked his stubble, and said, "She's always been a little crazy. And why would you want to sue me?"

He smiled cheerfully, squinted his sorrowful eyes into a deep line; they looked like the tiny bubbles goldfish spat out of their mouths. Yi-Ting took a deep breath. "Teacher Lee, I know you raped Si-Chi when we were thirteen years old. Even the newspapers would report you."

Lee Guo-Hua's eyes became watery, puppy dog eyes. He spoke in the same manner he did when explaining the ancient Chinese history in class: "Ah, I'm sure you didn't know but my twin sister died by suicide when we were ten years old. I woke up without a sister—I never got to see her for the last time. I heard she hung herself at night with her own clothes. We slept in the same bed, and I was sleeping right beside her. There's an old saying that goes, *Evil must have something pitiful inside—*"

Yi-Ting interrupted him. "Teacher, stop acting; you're just quoting Freud. Your sister's death doesn't give you the right to rape someone. *Evil must have something pitiful inside it* is a line straight out of a novel. Teacher Lee, you're not the protagonist of everything."

Rescinding his watery puppy eyes, Teacher Lee made a blank face and said, "Mad is mad; there's nothing you can do about it. She won't return even if you make me pay."

Upon hearing that, Yi-Ting took off all her clothes, her eyes unfazed, unclouded, showing no wind, no rain, no sun.

"Teacher Lee, come rape me then."

225

Like what you did to Si-Chi, I want to feel everything she was feeling—her sincere love, her deep hatred for you. I want her same nightmares that lasted two thousand nights.

"I don't want to."

"Why not? Please—rape me. I was more into you than Si-Chi ever was!"

I want to wait for my twin of the soul. She was forsaken by you at thirteen years old. The same age I forgot about her. I want to lie there and wait for her, wait for her to catch up with me. I want to be with her.

She hugged Lee Guo-Hua's calves.

"No way."

"Why not? I'm begging you. I want to be just like Si-Chi. I want everything she has!"

Lee Guo-Hua kicked Yi-Ting's throat, making her retch on the floor.

"You should piss on the floor and see your reflection. Look at your face with those pimples and freckles. Fucking psycho bitch."

He tossed her clothes out the door, and Yi-Ting slowly crawled out to pick them up. As she crawled, she felt the goldfishes' eyes protruding against the fish tank, staring at her.

Papa and Mama Fang moved out of the apartment building. They never thought they were merely regular people. After their daughter suddenly lost her mind, they finally understood the platitude: "The sun will rise as usual, and those who live still have to live. Days will go by." The day they left the building, Mama Fang's powdered face looked like the smooth granite of the building façade: nobody could see what was hiding underneath.

These days, Hsiao-Chi stayed home to help her parents with their eatery. She kept busy most of the days—she sweat so much it was like she had spent time in a bun steamer. Before bed every night, she prayed, "God, please grant me a good guy, someone willing to spend the rest of his life with me and my memories." When she fell asleep, Hsiao-Chi would forget that she was not a Christian. She'd even forget that she resisted visiting religious temples with her parents. She simply fell into a quiet slumber. If Teacher Lee were to see her sleeping sideways, blue flower-pattern quilt clinging to her body, he would most certainly describe her as a blue china vase lying down and himself as the florist. But when she woke up, Hsiao-Chi couldn't remember anything at all.

Sometimes, in his secret little apartment, Lee Guo-Hua lowered his head to look at himself during his shower. He would think about Fang Si-Chi. He would think about how careful and crazy he was, carrying an ego so bright and bloated, leaving it entirely inside of Si-Chi. And then Si-Chi would be pulled by him, entangled, struggling so much her vocabulary would return to that of a kindergartener's. Because of Si-Chi's sealed mouth, his secrets, his ego, were all locked deep inside her body. Until the very end, she still believed that he loved her. This was the weight of his words. He thought about the time he enlightened one of his high school students who abused animals to the point the student teared up. The student poured oil on a mouse and set it on fire. Teacher Lee almost cried himself when he saw his student's tears. But in his mind, he took this running little mouse on fire and made it into a metaphor; it was a shooting star, hell money, a spotlight. Such a beautiful girl! Like inspiration, which could only be met and not requested; like a passion for poetry, the stanzas that hadn't been written, or couldn't be written, were always deemed the best. In the shower, Lee Guo-Hua rubbed white shiny foam on his curly body hair. He forgot about Si-Chi as he stepped out of his bathroom, silently repeating three times the name of the girl who was staying in the bedroom. He was courteous, and in his twenty years of teaching, he had never mistaken a person's name.

Iwen visited Taichung once a week, bringing peeled fruits for Si-Chi and reading literary works to her as she had done years ago. Once she sat down next to her, she'd stay there for a long time. When she lifted her head from the book, she saw the tilted shadows of the metal bars projected on the floor of the mental hospital, organized and equal. Compared to when she first arrived, they looked like two snapshots of the Chinese Cultural Revolution choir, one taken right after another, its members swaying and singing. Si-Chi always curled up, nibbling on the fruit. Iwen read aloud, "I started to realize one could feel bored in Auschwitz." She paused, looking at Si-Chi, and said, "Chi-Chi, you used to tell me this sentence was the scariest for you. Feeling bored in a concentration camp." Si-Chi showed that she was thinking hard, her tiny eyebrows furrowed into a ball, squeezing juice out of the fruit in her hand. She laughed and said, "I'm not bored. Why was he bored?" Iwen recognized Si-Chi's smile; it was the same one she herself would make before she married Yi-Wei, one that hadn't witnessed the world's underbelly. She patted her head and said, "I heard you grew taller. You're taller than me now." Si-Chi laughed and said, "Thank you." When she thanked her, juice trickled down from the corner of her mouth.

Iwen went on a date with Mr. Maomao in Kaohsiung. She

felt like a tourist in her own hometown. At the circular plaza, she said, "Jing-Yuan, let's not take that path—the one near that building."

Maomao nodded his head. Iwen didn't want Maomao to see her face, so she turned away. She also didn't want to see herself from the rearview mirror near the passenger seat. Neither left nor right, she felt like she had never looked straight in her entire life. Back at Maomao's place, Iwen finally said, "I'm so pathetic. I grew up here, but there are so many places that I never want to see again. They're like a piece of film strip; my unrolled memories become lines of yellow caution tape—"

For the first time, Maomao interrupted her, "You're not the one who should be apologizing."

"I haven't said anything."

"Then say nothing."

"I'm very sad about it."

"Maybe you can share some of your sadness with me."

"No, I'm not feeling sad for myself," Iwen said. "I'm feeling sad for Si-Chi. Whenever I think about her, I feel like I could kill someone. Really."

"I understand."

"When you're not home, sometimes I catch myself thinking about how to hide a fruit knife up my sleeve. I'm serious."

"I believe you, but Si-Chi wouldn't want you to do that."

Iwen's eyes widened and began to turn red. "No, you're wrong. Do you know what the problem is? It's that nobody knows what she wants now. She's nothing, gone! You understand nothing."

"I do, and I love you. Whom you want to kill is whom I want to kill, too."

Iwen stood up to grab some tissues, her eyelids swollen and red, as if she had patted on some rouge.

"You don't want to be selfish, so let me. Stay here for me, will you?"

Before the start of college, Yi-Ting and Iwen met each other again. From a distance, Iwen saw her stand up and wave at her from the outdoor seating of the cafe. Iwen was wearing a black dress with white polka dots; the dots were aligned as though wherever they pointed, a constellation would be found. This was Iwen in a nutshell, full of constellations. Their beautiful, determined, and audacious Iwen.

Iwen sat there, underneath the sunbeams filtered by the foliage. Her pale arms were like stars, sparkling. Iwen said, "Yi-Ting, you're only eighteen years old. You have options. You can pretend nobody in this world takes pleasure in raping girls, or that no little girls have ever been raped. You can pretend Si-Chi never existed, or that you've never shared a pacifier and a piano with anyone else. You can pretend nobody has ever shared the same appetite and stream of thought with you, and that you can live a peaceful, middle-class life, pretending there's no cancer eating away at the world's psyche, pretending that nowhere else in the world has metal bars, and that everyone behind those bars was reaching their terminal stage. You can pretend the world is one with only macarons, pour-over coffee, and imported stationery. But you can also choose to experience what Si-Chi has suffered. Learn the efforts she has made to fight her pain, from the time you spent together as newborns to the time you read from her diary. You must go to college, enroll yourself in graduate school, fall in love, get married, have kids, all in Si-Chi's place. Maybe you can get expelled, divorced, or miscarry, but Si-Chi won't be able to experience even the most vulgar, dull, and stereotypical life. Do you get it? You must experience everything and remember all her ideas, thoughts, sentiments, feelings, memories, and fantasies; even her love, hatred, fear, loss of balance, barrenness, gentleness, and desire. You must hug Si-Chi's pain tightly, and you can become her. Then, live in her place. Live all the parts of your life fully for Si-Chi, who can no longer experience any of it."

Yi-Ting nodded. Iwen straightened her hair and said, "You can write everything down. But, writing isn't for salvation, sublimation, or purification. Even though you're only eighteen years old, even though you have a choice, if your fury is always present, that's not because you're not charitable, kind, and empathetic enough. Everything has its reasons; even rape and contaminating others has its own psychology and sociological excuses. In this world, being raped and humiliated doesn't need reason. You have a choice; think of it like synonyms—you can let it go, step over it, and walk out of it. But you can also remember that it's not that you weren't forgiving enough, but that no one should ever be treated this way. Si-Chi wrote everything down before ever knowing her end. She doesn't even know that she is gone. But her diary is so clearheaded; she has helped so many people—people like me—who couldn't accept all this to learn acceptance. Yi-Ting, I ask you to please never deny you're a survivor, the twin who continued to live. Whenever I visit Si-Chi and read to her, I don't know why I keep thinking about the scented candles in my house: the tears from those fat, white candles always reminded me of the word *incontinence*. Then I'd think, *Si-Chi, she has really loved before. Her love simply lost control. Tolerance isn't a virtue, and taking tolerance as a virtue is a way this pretentious world tries to maintain its depraved sense of discipline. Rage is a virtue.* Yi-Ting, you can write a book about rage. Think about it: your readers will be so lucky to read what you write. They won't even need to experience anything to learn this world has a dark side."

Then, Iwen stood up and said, "Jing-Yuan is here to pick me up."

"Iwen, will you live happily ever after?" Yi-Ting asked.

She saw a tan line around Iwen's ring finger when she lifted her bag. Yi-Ting thought Iwen was pale enough as it is; she didn't know she was even paler before.

"Not a chance. That kind of life doesn't exist anymore. Anyone who is honest will never be able to feel that happy," Iwen said.

Yi-Ting nodded again, and in an instant, Iwen's nose turned red. Tears began to trickle as she said, "Yi-Ting, I'm actually really afraid. Sometimes I feel truly happy and content, but right after feeling so, Si-Chi flashes in my mind. Am I turning into everyone else, just with that tiny piece of happiness? It's really hard, you know? Loving Si-Chi almost means not loving Jing-Yuan. I don't want him to be stuck with some disgruntled woman for the rest of his life."

Before Iwen entered the passenger seat of the car, she took the last sip of her iced coffee. She looked like a bird nibbling on a petal.

Iwen rolled down the car window and waved at Yi-Ting. The fingers of the wind blew through Iwen's hair, which flew like the flames of the sparklers Yi-Ting and Si-Chi used to play with when they were little. With the growing distance, the car became smaller, fainter, almost extinguished. Yi-Ting realized that her

232

and Si-Chi's first impression of their building's inhabitants was completely wrong: Iwen, after all, was the one who was decrepit and frail; the one who was still strong and audacious was Teacher Lee. Whenever she learned a new term from a dictionary or a book, she would accidentally come away with the opposite meaning. She suddenly realized that wasn't the fault of people who learn literature; rather, literature itself let them down. Before the car disappeared past the corner of the road, Yi-Ting turned her head away.

———

Everybody thought a round table was the best invention in the world. It could save time for those deciding who gets to sit at the head of the table and effort for those pushing each other for the seat. Such things went on long enough for someone to eat each of a crab's eight legs as well as its pair of pincers. At a round table, everyone had that irresponsible air of a guest and the imposing manner of a host.

Mr. Chang didn't care about table manners; he simply reached out his chopsticks, skimmed the vegetables on the plate to the side, and picked up meat to put in his wife's bowl.

At the sight of that, Mama Liu started to raise her voice. She elbowed her husband and said, "Look at Mr. Chang, still spoiling his wife after all those years of marriage."

Mr. Chang replied right away, "*Aiya*, this is different. Our Wan-Ru has been married for so long, and yet we're still getting used to relying on each other. Your Yi-Ting has just gone off to college—of course Mr. Liu hasn't gotten used to it."

Everyone at the table laughed and tumbled their wineglasses.

"Look at this; what is it? Is this what the young people call . . . what *do* they call it?" Mrs. Chen asked.

Teacher Lee finished her sentence. "Being flashy!"

Grandma Wu laughed out more wrinkles. "You can't beat being a teacher. Spending time with young people makes you even younger."

"The kids are growing up so fast, so fast we have no choice but to age," Mrs. Chen said.

"Why didn't Xixi come today?" asked Mr. Hsieh.

Teacher Lee's wife felt laid-back next to people she knew well. "Xixi said she's going to her classmate's house to do homework," she said. "Whenever she goes there, she always comes back with all these bags—big bags, small bags. She must do her homework at the department store!" And then she cast an annoyed glance toward Teacher Lee. "He spoils her too much!"

"It's better that the girl spends money on herself than on her boyfriend." Mrs. Chang laughed.

Half-joking and half-dejected, Teacher Lee's wife continued, "Isn't a girl who is wasting time dressing herself up just as bad as one who is spending her money on her boyfriend?"

"Well, when it comes to our daughter, it's like she's already gotten married. She's just entered college, but you would think she had gone to Mars! She doesn't even come back home during the holidays," Mama Liu bellowed.

"It's not like we don't put food on her plate. She doesn't even like what we serve," Papa Liu murmured.

Mrs. Hsieh watched Mr. Hsieh as she continued, "He keeps saying America is far, but I've been telling him, if he wants to come home, America is as close as Taipei!"

"Perhaps she's got her eye on someone in Taipei? Whose boy is so lucky?" Mr. Chen laughed.

Mr. Hsieh laughed as well. "Whether they live far away or right around the corner, American daughters-in-law aren't as easy to manage as Taiwanese sons-in-law."

All the in-laws laughed together.

Grandma Wu's wrinkles seemed to bear an air of authority. She cleared her throat. "I used to watch the girls; Yi-Ting doesn't look like the type who falls for someone that easily."

The girls.

The round table turned silent.

On the table lay a giant braised fish with sharp little teeth; it looked like it wanted to say something but was holding back. In its eyes was some kind of grievance. The fish lay sideways, as though pressing its ear to the table, listening to the movements underneath.

"Yeah, our Yi-Ting has high standards." Mama Liu raised her voice, then laughed dryly. "She doesn't even fancy any rock stars."

Mama Liu's voice was as loud as a dog barking at a stranger.

Having just tightened her wrinkles, Grandma Wu loosened them again. "It's very rare for young people to not chase a star these days."

And then Grandma Wu coughed up some laughter and spoke to Teacher Lee's wife. "Last time you came to my house, Xixi sat right down and turned on the TV. I asked her why she was in such a rush; she answered she had just missed watching a very intense scene downstairs before coming up." Grandma Wu looked around, laughed out loud and said, "How much could she have missed out on just by taking the elevator upstairs?"

Everyone laughed together.

Mrs. Chang cupped her hand around Teacher Lee's ear and whispered, "I told them to not let the children read literature. See? It drove someone crazy. Even I would rather watch a soap opera than read a novel in translation. Only someone as strong as you can study literature, don't you think?"

Upon hearing that, Teacher Lee slowly nodded, with a sorry expression on his face.

Mrs. Chen stretched out her long fingers; the green emerald on her ring showed a hint of conspiracy. She bellowed, "*Aiya*, Mrs. Lee, Mrs. Chang and Teacher Lee are telling secrets!"

"No secrets are allowed at this table," old Mr. Chien said.

Mr. Chang chuckled and tried to smooth things over. "My wife was just asking Teacher Lee for his opinion. She asked if we were to have another baby, would we be able to match her with your young Mr. Chien. Do you think it's too late?"

Only Mr. Chang had the guts to make fun of the old Chien family.

Old Mrs. Chien yelped, "*Aiyo*, aren't you being *flashy* again? Wanting to have another kid with your wife and using Yi-Wei as an excuse!"

All the husbands and wives screeched and laughed out loud. Red wine began to spill, gradually spreading across the white tablecloth. It looked like the tablecloth was blushing.

In Teacher Lee's eyes, the tablecloth looked like a bedsheet. He laughed cheerfully.

"They're not just being flashy; they're being outright flagrant!" Teacher Lee said.

Everyone laughed so hard, it sounded as though they were screaming in fright.

When the sommelier came to refill everyone's wineglasses, only Yi-Wei nodded and thanked him.

Yi-Wei thought, *In fact, this sommelier looks young*.

And then he felt a surge of pain. He'd never used the words *in fact* like this before.

Mrs. Chang began to blush, which was rare. She said, "He's like this all the time. Acting so attentive outside, but back at home—oh, look at him—when I look at him, all he has is his mouth!"

Grandma Wu had long passed the age to be timid. "It's not like you can't get busy with just a mouth."

Everyone laughed and raised their glasses to toast Grandma Wu, saying, "After all, aged ginger still tastes spicy."

"She's Ximen Qing in the living room and Liu Xia Hui in the bedroom," said Teacher Lee in a low voice.

Everyone considered whatever they couldn't understand must be something that made sense. They all turned to Teacher Lee and said, "Cheers."

Mrs. Chang changed the subject: "I'm not saying studying hard is a bad thing."

Old Mrs. Chien considered herself a studious person. An expert at adapting to changes in conversation, she nodded. "It depends on the kind of books one reads."

And then she turned to Mama Liu and said, "You should've let her play in the park instead of letting her read those books back then."

Her words pained Yi-Wei. He knew that by "letting her read those books back then," what she really meant was "the books Iwen used to let the girls read."

Yi-Wei resented his memories. His chest was as heavy as it was when Iwen used to lie on top of it.

He remembered how Iwen wouldn't stop blinking, and how her eyelashes would tickle his cheeks. She would hold the end of her ponytail, write calligraphy on his chest. One time, as she wrote, her tears began to stream down her face. He had sat up immediately, shifting her onto the pillow, where he wiped away her tears with his thumb. She was fully naked with a pink diamond necklace around her neck. The diamond shone, forming a ring of spotlights around her face. When her nose had turned red, Iwen looked even more like a little lamb.

"Remember me forever," Iwen had said.

Yi-Wei's eyebrows had furrowed, squeezed together. "Of course, we'll always be together."

"No, I mean, before you really own me, I want you to remember me right now. Because you'll never see her again, you understand?"

"All right," Yi-Wei had said.

Iwen had tilted her head and closed her eyes. When her neck moved sideways, her necklace slightly tingled.

Sitting at the table, Yi-Wei looked around. Everyone's high-pitched laughter caused their tongues to come in and out of their mouths like bills in a cash dispenser. When they laughed, tears gathered in their eyes; their crystal clarity was like looking into a pool of golden coins. Their dark eyes held its reflection, bringing that same eternal sense of peace he felt when he first met Iwen.

Yi-Wei couldn't be certain if this feeling was what Iwen called "Not knowing senescence is around the corner," or "Avoiding death at old age is an act of thievery," or "Even though I walk through the valley of the shadow of death, I will fear no evil, for you are with me."

In his formal dress, Yi-Wei sat there, faintly feeling Iwen's cold, tiny hand carve her fingernails deeply into his bottom, trying hard to please him.

"Say you love me."

"I love you."

"Say you'll love me forever."

"I'll love you forever."

"Do you still remember me?"

"I will always remember you."

The last dish came to the table, and Mr. Chang was about to pick up food for his wife again.

Mrs. Chang waved her claws and spoke loudly to the entire table, "If you keep giving me all that food, nobody will be able to see the ring you just bought me today!"

Everybody laughed. Everyone was gleeful.

Their building remained extravagant and abundant; it was majestic, an ancient Greek temple that looked as though it had sprouted from the ground. The pillars remained the same without their thinned-out middles, even after so many years. When passersby drove past on their scooters, they always turned their heads, lifted the face guards on their helmets, and told their significant others holding on behind them, "If we could live here one day, our lives would be complete."

Epilogue

The younger sister who awaits an angel." I had just married B. I often told my psychiatrist, "From now on, I'm really going to try and stop writing."

Eight years have passed since my senior high school graduation. I've been wandering between my apartment, my college, and the local cafe. At the cafe, I put on my earphones; when I write articles, I like to observe the customers at the next table over. Through the way their lips and tongues move, I try to guess what they are talking about. Sometimes I guess they are a couple that look like they could be mother and son, or sisters that look like they could be a couple. Self-serve cafes are my favorite. They allow me to watch a man in a suit speak to his smartphone to the point his golden teeth almost fly out of his mouth, only for him to carefully bring his coffee back to his seat the very next second. A tiny cup of coffee could control a giant man like him. That was the moment when I looked life in the face. I saw the expression he wore back in his mother's water. It made me think about when I was a teenage girl.

I always flash back to the break we had that day back in high school. My class was scheduled in a different building from the other class so I walked to the other building, waiting for the girl I'd been interested in since junior high to finish her class. The courtyard in front of the building had dense clusters of tropical almond trees. Under those trees was a table set made of fragmented, powdery black and white silica cores; the dust on them seemed to bear an air of waiting. It was around summer; the tree leaves were so lush that it looked like the unwanted ponytail of some boyish girl; her mother was commanding her to keep that tail abundant. The sunbeam filtered through the foliage, creating needle dots of lights on the black surface of the table, each of them round and shiny as a coin. I thought about how I would send her text messages after school, or after cram school, back and forth, then insist that she had to send the last message, claiming it was only gentlemanly. One day, half-angry and half-joking, she told me her phone bill was going to explode. I was happy. What I didn't mention was, *I don't want to text you goodbyes. Even though we are bound to see each other again, I don't want to say it*. At that time, I faintly understood that love could be so innocent that it became calculated.

Lifting my head to look at the almond tree, I could see its thick leaves teasing and slapping each other. They moved in a way that was distinct from the yellow leaves whispering and swishing by our feet; green leaves in the summer seemed a little oblivious to their noises. In junior high, to enter the best high school's elite class, I never took any breaks. I was always nailed to my seat doing assignments. Whereas she was expressive, active; whenever there was a break, she yelled for people to join her at the volleyball court. My eyes would stare at math formulas while her voice entangled with my colorful hormones, digging into my ears. However, my answers were all the same, determined, and were in the state of nirvana. Her voice was metaphorical, aligning with my sore, slumping back, which suggested a sense of suffering. When the wind started, it brought the fragrance of the almond trees, conjuring a polynomial ham and egg tropical almond tree sandwich out of my breakfast of math questions and bread; my seven orifices hummed with the surrounding scent. When I looked inside her classroom, the chalk hitting the black-board sounded like someone knocking on a door. In front of the teacher's podium, everyone wore white shirts and black skirts. A mountain and sea of people spread out before my eyes, and I was unable to distinguish one from another. But I knew she was among them, and that reassured me. The volleyball court was on the other side of campus. People over there would yell like shepherd dogs and flocks of lambs; whenever a dog began to rush the flocks, the lambs would throng together. I thought about the way she played volleyball, and how her sweat would stick to her face. I don't even think that it was sweat, but rather dew. What abundance! That day, I told her I couldn't wait for her anymore. I didn't know then that losing my temper and bragging about my self-esteem was how I meant to say farewell.

That day, you told me your story, and I ran out the door like I was running for my life. I ended up at a cafe I visited often to write articles. When I approached the door, I realized I had brought my laptop with me. The whole season poured down from above like boiling water; it felt like I was being tortured in a cooking pot, as in ancient times. I looked up at the sun; it looked like a golden clump of fat smothered on the bottom of a pot of soup. The moment I was lewdly scorched, I realized the flaming, burning kernel in this entire world was myself. I walked into the cafe, ordered an Americano without milk or sugar. I placed my hands on the keyboard and let myself cry hard. I didn't know why I still wanted to write at that moment, and I spent half of that year unable to recognize any written characters at all. Ugliness and evil were a kind of knowledge, and they were very different from my knowledge of beauty, which kept regressing. But the former is irreversible; sometimes, I would wake up at B and I's home and realize I was standing, attempting to hide a fruit knife up my sleeve. I could forget ugliness and evil, but they would never forget me.

I often tell my psychiatrist, "From now on, I'm really going to try and stop writing."

"Why?"

"It's useless to write about these things."

"Let's define what is *useful*."

"Literature is the most useless thing and the funniest kind of uselessness. I've written so much, and yet I can't save anyone. I can't even save myself. I've been writing for so many years, but I'd rather take a knife and rush over to kill him. I mean it."

"I believe you. I'm grateful that we're not in America. Otherwise I'd have to call him up and warn him."

"I really mean it."

"I really do believe you."

"But I wasn't born just so I could want to kill someone."

"Do you still remember why you wrote in the first place?"

"At the very beginning, it was like a physical need, because it was too painful, and I needed a way out. It was like eating rice when you're hungry and drinking water when you're thirsty. And then it became a habit. I don't even write about B now, because I only write about ugly things."

"Is it merely a habit to write them into a novel?"

"I met her after that, and my whole life changed. Melancholy is a mirror, and rage is a window. It was she who pulled me away from those funhouse mirrors—their illusions, their voices. It was she who stayed with me to get a view of the landscape through a clean window. I'm very grateful, even though that landscape was a hell."

"So you had a choice?"

"Like what Iwen said in my novel? Can I pretend no one in this world takes pleasure in raping little girls, and that the world is only full of macarons, pour-over coffee, and imported stationery? I don't have a choice. I can't pretend; I can't do it."

"What do you fear most when writing your book?"

"I'm afraid of consuming any of Fang Si-Chi. I don't want to hurt them. I don't want to hunt for particularities or bring emotional sensations. I write eight hours every day, and that process is beyond difficult. I'm often a crying mess. What's most scary when reading my finished draft is to find out: in my writing, the scariest things I wrote about turned out to be things that really happened before. All I could do was write them down. There are some girls who were harmed; others are being harmed the moment readers read this conversation. But the perpetrators are still hanging out on the billboards of some famous places. I hate that I only know how to write."

"Your prose has a secret code inside of it, did you know that? Only women who have been through such circumstances will be able to decode it. Even if just one person, just one among hundreds and thousands of people, reads this, she'll no longer be alone."

"Really?"

"Absolutely."

"The younger sister who awaits an angel," you're the one I want to hurt least. Nobody deserves more happiness than you do. And I want to give you a hug so soft you'd think I was made of hundreds of marshmallows.

In junior high, whenever midterms and final exams were over, our group always caught a matinee at the mall. It was during the week, so it was just us in the movie theater. The most daring of us took off her shoes and put her feet up on a front-row seat. We looked at each other and followed her lead. That was the worst, naughtiest thing we did. And I'll always remember taking the escalator after the movie. The girl with a ponytail resting her arm on the hand railing, fatigued but cheerful. I stared infinitely at her outstretched arm. The shape of her fingernails was like an ecliptic of the Earth orbiting the sun; the wrinkles on her knuckles were like a spinning galaxy. My hand rested right next to hers; my hand that did assignments, my hand that wrote articles but never held another's hand. Time passed as we rode the escalator six floors, and I completely forgot about the movie we just watched. The distance between us was that of a fist, and because of some childish self-esteem, it made that distance so far, so slim.

After that, we grew older, and I attempted suicide for the second time. I swallowed a hundred pills of Panadol and they had to insert a tube up my nose to pump activated carbon into my stomach. The activated carbon was the color of asphalt, and because of that, I was unable to defecate within my control. My entire bed at the hospital was covered in vomit, piss, and poop. They put up the railing next to my bed and pushed me to the ICU. I could feel the floor of the hospital stream behind me; it flowed like a poem for children. To clip the pipes to monitor my blood oxygen, the nurse removed nail polish for me, like another metaphor, a Chinese cross-talk show. The nurse's hands were so warm, and the remover so cool. I asked the nurse if I would die. She asked me why would I even attempt suicide if I was concerned about death. I said I didn't know. I really don't know. Because of the activated carbon, my poop was as dark as the road. My body was full of pathways made of intersecting tubes. In such a small hospital bed, once I lost my way, eight years passed.

If she were to snake her hand between my fingers; if she were to drink the coffee that I've drunk; if she were to hide a tiny photo of mine between her cash or to gift me a childish book that I would have never read; if she were to remember every food that I avoid, and her heart would palpitate upon hearing my name; if she were to kiss me, to love me back. If I could go back. All right, all right, it'll be all right. I would like to lie on a Hello Kitty bedsheet with her, to watch the polar lights, with a doe nearby giving birth to a baby deer covered with a thin rainbow membrane, with rabbits in heat and long-haired cats predicting their death, walking to somewhere untraceable. Inside the ancient bone china cup crawling with blue flowers on the outside, fortune-telling coffee grounds would tell us: *Thank you.* Although I'm always missing out on everything. Self-esteem? What is that, even? Self-esteem is nothing but a nurse closing my curtains, pushing a bedpan under me so that I can aim my shit right inside it.

Translator's Acknowledgments

As a translator and a writer, I find that languages contain the most vital and intimate parts of me. These languages are beyond the Mandarin Chinese, Hakka, Taiwanese Hokkien, English, Spanish, and French that I speak and breathe every day. My translation of short stories, poems, and books wouldn't be possible without the years I've spent across Taiwan, France, the United States, and Latin America. That love for languages and literature took me around the world. That love led me to my encounter with Lin Yi-Han's novel. The process of translation itself is a process of rebirthing a language, of retelling a story over and over for us all to remember.

Without Lin Yi-Han's voice, the #MeToo movement in Taiwan would never have been the same. Every touch of her words, every breath I share with this book, becomes a language that continues to change me, and will change so many others who come across it in ways we would never imagine.

I remember sitting in my dimly lit New York apartment, watching the rain. My hand smoothed across the cover, and I inhaled the fresh beginning of the book before starting my translation. It was 2020, in the midst of the pandemic, and as I sought to survive, this novel opened a new chapter in more ways than one.

Translator's Acknowledgments

Fang Si-Chi's First Love Paradise is a story about my home, about a world that I share with many others, a world that has been long overlooked. The idea that first pulled me into this story is this parallel—about all of us coexisting in the same physical space, but sharing such different experiences. Issues of gender, the LGBTQ+ community, violence, and trauma are squeezed together into dark, narrow spaces in Taiwan, and only voices like Yi-Han's open a new pathway to a world where identities and personal stories confirm transformation is possible.

The English translation of *Fang Si-Chi's First Love Paradise* was made possible because of so many incredible people who I share meaningful connections with, whose languages inspire me in every moment we spend together. I hope that no matter where you are in the world, you will know that you are important to me, and that because of you all, my love of language is possible.

To Isaac Sarmiento, who understands my language the best, who for almost a decade has stayed close to me whenever I need him the most. He is vital and irreplaceable, someone who believes in everything I do as a writer, translator, artist, and human being. I want him to know that without his language, perspective, and the consistent ray of sunshine he brings into my world, I would never find my language, nor would I find home.

To Hilario Menéndez and his family, who bring wonder to my world. Again and again they have offered me positive energies and the best time in Guatemala, where many of my magical stories, translations, and inspirations have been born. I'm forever grateful for all their kindness and hospitality, which will always remind me that I have a home in another corner of the world.

Translator's Acknowledgments

To Kao-Ying Chen, my globe-trotting buddy and a good listener to my stories. His brotherly support, thoughtfulness, care, and friendship make me thrive as an artist. I hold memories of our time spent exploring the world's natural wonders—Machu Picchu, Salar de Uyuni, the San Pedro de Atacama desert, and many more close to my heart. Without you, my life in New York would have never been possible.

To Isabella Corletto, who I bonded with through languages, whose bubbly presence and understanding brightened up my dark days in New York without her even noticing. I want to let her know that I cherish our newfound friendship deeply, and that I hope our friendship continues to celebrate our shared love for many languages and literature.

To my therapist, Madelline Zaiter, who shares my dislike of oranges and who provides infinite understanding to all the stories I tell. Her company throughout my time translating this novel meant so much to me.

To Tuan Doan and Nguyen Tran, whose home and kitchen have brought me so many days full of comfort food, good shows, and thoughtful conversation that made America feel like home during my hardest of times.

To the entire HarperVia team, with special thanks to Lisa Zuniga, Liz Asborno, Yvonne Chan, Laura Gonzalez, Alison Cerri, and especially my editor, Alexa Frank, who provided infinite support and time for this story to travel across the world. Without her, this book would have never made it to the English-speaking world. You're the best editor to work with, Alexa!

To author Lin Yi-Han and her family, for entrusting me as the translator to bring this story into a new language. Their perseverance, strength, and understanding has made Yi-Han's novel vibrant and alive no matter where the book travels.

To the Bardon Chinese Agency team and Guerrilla Publishing in Taiwan: Mengying Hsieh and Yu-Shiuan Chen, who have been a pillar of support throughout the years, and dedicated so much time trying to let Yi-Han's voice be heard around the world.

To the Grayhawk Agency team in Taiwan: thank you Gray Tan, Catrina Liu, Canaan Morse, and Jessie Hsieh for giving this novel a space in *Books from Taiwan* magazine, and being part of an important process for letting this title be seen.

To my extremely patient and inspiring mentor, Mike Fu, who has guided me and had so many conversations with me about *Fang Si-Chi's First Love Paradise* during our nine-month mentorship. He has never ceased to encourage me to keep moving forward with this book. I want him to know that what he's done for me has meant a lot.

To Rachael Daum, Kelsi Vanada, Elisabeth Jaquette, and Sean Gasper Bye at the American Literary Translators Association, as well as Yan-Ju Chou and Huichun Jo Chang at Taipei Cultural Center in New York, who made the 2021 ALTA Emerging Translator Mentorship Program in Taiwanese Prose possible to support this project. They have built the kindest, most inclusive community for me to grow as a translator.

To Sandy Chang-Chien, who joined the Taipei Cultural Center in New York to continue supporting translators of Taiwanese literature. I'd like to thank her for her infinite support in making this book travel far and wide. To Ju-Ting Felicia Cheng and Te-Yuan Mark Chien at the Taiwan Academy in Los Angeles, who are crucial to my journey as a translator coming from Taiwan.

To Natascha Bruce, who inspired me to become a literary translator.

To Jeremy Tiang, Julia Sanches, and Bruna Dantas Lobato, whose timely guidance, patience, and generous support have shaped me as a translator. Their warm encouragement and presence have made the literary translation community a real home.

To Anton Hur, the translator I admire most in the world. Thank you for always staying by my side, offering so much guidance, support, wisdom, and humor. We are both translators who frequently travel, and I hope to be able to meet you in as many parts of the world as possible. Without you, the English edition of *Fang Si-Chi's First Love Paradise* wouldn't be possible.

To May Huang, one of the most talented translators I've ever met.

To Soje, I would like to thank you for translating Choi Jin-young's *To the Warm Horizon*. Your poetry, translations, and infinite creativity have been extremely inspiring and brought me lots of joy during my years in New York.

To Stine An, who brought peaceful Korean indie music to my everyday life in New York. I miss our time being neighbors, cooking, and exploring new places to eat together. Thank you for being such a supportive friend and making me feel less alone in the city.

To Lisa Hofmann-Kuroda, whose voice is so vital in the translation world. Thanks for standing by my side, fighting inequity, discrimination, and more. Without you, this battle would be even more challenging, and I want you to know that I have your back as well.

To the collective members of the Bitten Path: Lya An Shaffer, brenda Lin, Lilian Huang, and Evian Yiyun Pan, who are all joys to be with, and whom I hope, with our shared love of languages, to build a world with.

To Umair Kazi at the Authors Guild and Ambre Morvan at the Society of Authors. This book would not be possible without their legal support and expertise in requesting the best contracts for translators and writers.

To my Bread Loaf Translators' Conference community: special thanks to my past workshop instructors Padma Viswanathan and Anton Hur (have to thank you again!) for their insightful guidance. Thank you to my best friends Hannah Allen and Yoojung Chun, who have become some of my strongest support. Thank you to the Bread Loaf Conference team at Middlebury College, who have made all these encounters possible.

To K-Ming Chang, Jami Nakamura Lin, and Hannah Bae, who value languages in such unique ways and persistently advocate for literary translation as writers. I am constantly inspired by them, and I hope that, no matter where we are, our paths will cross again.

To my editors Daniel Simon and Michelle Johnson, who have provided a beautiful space in *World Literature Today* for my translation of Lin Yi-Han's prose "Love of Stone."

To Sophie Haigney, Amanda Gersten, and *The Paris Review* team, who have dedicated their time and effort to giving one of my most precious translations a wider platform.

To Soleil Davíd, my editor at *Asian American Writers' Workshop*, who has dedicated meaningful time and space for my translation of Lin Yi-Han's prose "Once Upon a Time."

To my editor at *Catapult*'s "Don't Write Alone" column, Stella Cabot Wilson, whose knowledge and insight about language will forever inspire me.

Translator's Acknowledgments

To the Us & Them Reading series team: Sam Bett, Todd Portnowitz, and Molasses Books for providing a physical space for Lin Yi-Han's novel to be heard on a winter night; to Michelle Mirabella and Larissa Kyzer for including my translation at the Jill Reading series, Emerging Together, in 2021.

To my New School MFA writing community: Victoria Dillman, Vanessa Chan, Gina Chung, Danny Mangrove, Lauren Browne, and so many more. I hope our languages continue to shape each other in the years to come.

To Leon Peng, who so many years ago encouraged me to try at least touching the brim of a dream, and consistently believed in me despite all the years that passed. I hope he is well and that someday he will achieve his dreams, too.

Special thanks to my many aunties and uncles: first to uncles 湯元泰, 湯元貴, and 湯元和, who left way too soon but whom I still hold dear to my heart; to 古秋蓮, 湯玉秋, and 湯玉香, who keep me well-fed with their outstanding cooking and raised me; to my uncle 湯元財, who keeps me close and who I hope to keep close for as long as time allows.

To my father 湯元祿 (Thom Yen-Luh), who gave up everything for me to become a writer and translator, who never complains about having a hot-tempered girl in the house, and who, despite everything, reminds me over and over that he'll always be there for me.

To all of you, you, you, and you.

To all the readers who have opened this book.

Jenna Tang

A Note from the Translator

Literary translation exists in many shapes and landscapes. It brings the possibility of translation to an internal, personal level. Translation brings us closer to intimacy, unlocking its imaginative capacities—ones that bond us with awareness, with the capability of living in felt experiences, in memories, and in one another's story.

Lin Yi-Han's language is a beautiful remembrance of the many classical references in Sinophone literature. She was so well-read she was able to think in the ancient poetic lines of Li Bai; she let Eileen Chang's spirit palpitate in her characters' blood, and so much more; through her stories and the voices Lin sought to bring us, the most beautiful sentences of each Sinophone writer comes alive.

I have encountered many readers back in Taiwan who have expressed a certain level of fear about reading this novel in its original language. *It's too close to us, we're all living in this world.* Taiwan is such a small island, and many of our worlds intersect without us even noticing. Midway through my translating of *Fang Si-Chi's First Love Paradise*, I had been asked over and over, *How did you come to translate this book?*

Despite the global #MeToo movement and our growing awareness of how to respond to conversations about sexual

violence, I have witnessed many who live with a cruel ignorance to the topic. *As long as it's not me*, they think. Perhaps
half of the world shares such an egocentric perspective. Many
consider the issue of sexual violence to be too delicate, something to be discussed in a measured manner, something to be
forgotten. It is these same passive dismissals that push away
necessary voices and help enable the violence to continue.

Part of the most important discussions around sexual violence
is understanding the idea of sexual grooming, which is central to
what this novel wants to bring to our attention. It is the idea of
a monster trying to make sense of the world for those who didn't
understand what situation they were in, and therefore, through its
crooked logic, that monster convinces its audience that certain
sentiments, certain emotions, exist for a reason—ones that may
be romantic, ones that may bring hope, and ones that those never
put under such circumstances may find hard to decipher. For Fang
Si-Chi, her grooming became a love paradise, a place that existed
only for her, and somewhere she would always be destined to return to. It is not just a paradise of love, but a paradise borne of a
love for literature that speaks deeply from within her.

With the rich number of classical references in this novel, I
have found myself having to re-translate and even intentionally
reinterpret many poems, lines, and quotes in ways that corre-
spond with the narrative voices. These references may very well
be lost to a certain audience, and there was the added challenge
of not being able to converse with the author about her choices.
I had so many questions about the intentionality of her language
to begin with. To translate these references on my own meant
bearing the risk of disconnection to certain languages, and that

disconnection, sometimes, lies in the threat or monster of translation: the fear that something won't come through. By retaining traditional Mandarin Chinese characters, I hope to present the direct visual impact of the language in some parts of this novel.

Translating this novel also meant translating multiple streams of consciousness filtered through a convoluted timeline and complex headspaces. As the story unfolds, we as readers find ourselves in Fang Si-Chi's and Liu Yi-Ting's consciousness, a visitor to the literary paradise they share together. At other times, we find ourselves observing the back-and-forth, circular conversations Fang Si-Chi and Hsu Iwen hold with their monsters: Lee Guo-Hua and Chien Yi-Wei. Through traveling inside and outside of these characters we find that their monsters remain omnipresent within these girls, these women. Translating such streams of consciousness also meant I had, in a way, translated the monsters resting within it.

————

When I first learned about this book, I was on the train heading from Lyon to Paris. I bookmarked the title on my phone and got myself a copy when I returned to Taiwan that summer. A lot was happening in the Taiwanese media back then. A lot was happening with the publication of this book. My sun had dwindled a little bit as I headed back home, hearing here and there what people (having read the book or not) had been discussing regarding this book and sexual violence. I thought about you, and you, and you, and how before I decided to go abroad, a lot of you had disappeared.

When we were eleven years old, you used to peek into the

window of my classroom, staring at my homework, wanting me outside with you in the sun. We used to complain about how bad the school lunches were—the vegetables were so saturated in dark salty sauce—but we still enjoyed school because we had each other. Because there was sun. You never told me why you preferred to come home with me after school, why you disliked heading back to your place. You just stayed by my side, asking to watch hip-hop videos in my living room until very late, but sometimes I heard you on the phone, crying on the stairs of my house. I never understood your language.

When we graduated from grade school, I was sent to a private junior high school, and you disappeared forever. I heard classmates talk about you as though you had already given up on something. I heard you had gone elsewhere, somewhere we didn't know or understand, somewhere that only made sense to you. At that age, it was hard for you to tell me what happened, and now, every time I am bathed in sunlight, I think about you, and I hope you are somewhere under the sun, too.

One afternoon in New York, you told me about that house you ran away from. You told me about wanting to never go back. Our faces were numb and pale as we heard the ambulance and fire truck sirens. You told me more stories, and I listened. A part of me started to fear answering calls late at night, and to avoid salty-tasting food because they reminded me of others' blood. I remember all your stories, and I hope that you've finally gotten away.

That spring night, you disappeared in the intermingling of lights, leaving me in the red of your absence, my heart desperately searching for you, for fear that you might disappear, afraid that my momentary absence had pulled you a world away from me. My thoughts blared with the music surrounding us, and I threw myself in the frosty air of early spring to look for you outside. But still, something had disappeared.

And you, and you, and you, and you.

I translate with all of you in my mind. I think about all the instances where certain experiences were so close to me, and yet I became the listener of these stories. Having translated this novel, I often find myself thinking: *What does paradise mean to us? What is paradise, after all? And what makes a paradise?*

The author, in so many imaginative ways, has rendered a certain freedom and paradise in embracing her own languages; her intentionality to redirect or recalibrate the many voices is visible on the pages. She left certain logics and rules of writing, even narrative conventions and literary stylings, behind to find a paradise of her own making, in her very own words, and such ways of storytelling have come in parallel to my own personal journey finding another home somewhere in this world.

Looking back at my encounter with this novel in Mandarin: every Taiwanese landscape that the author incorporated in this story is a place I've walked through myself. We were in the same university around the same time, although we never had the chance to get to know each other. Knowing that there's such a parallel, this coexistence in the same little island, brings me closer to her book. It makes me want to share and bond with this story, so closely tied to our home.

As a translator, I tend to think about ways to translate that would let the book be reborn into another language. Translation, in a way, pulls the translator so near to the story that the process itself is a felt experience. While rendering Fang Si-Chi's story into English, I came to inhabit these characters' experiences; their thoughts, consciousness, trauma, and living heartbeats seemed to become a part of me, and through finding these words in English, I expressed the pain and rage that have been undermined in retellings of this story.

Upon reading *Fang Si-Chi*, one may wonder, what does paradise feel like? What is it like to let paradise live inside us, despite all the trauma and pain we feel?

———

After almost three years of translating this novel, at times I have found myself in a vulnerable place. Various questions dwell in my mind: How do I let others know how important this story is to me, and to many others? How do I talk about it when this book lived inside me for so many years? What will make people care? And when would this book reach its destination? What is its destination, after all? Having spent years with a novel about trauma and violence, something faded inside me, and I desperately found myself looking back for that interior language that was once so vibrant. I found myself looking for my own paradise, one that will make me come alive again.

In late spring, a year before this book was published, I tossed away all my belongings in New York and moved to South America, searching for a chance to reconnect with a language where I found home.

Home languages are languages we find emotional connections with, languages we acquire as we grow, due to our many moves, due to the many people we meet, and the meaningful experiences we have found through the flow of time. Home languages don't have to be our first or second languages; they are the languages that make us alive. They are the emotional expressions that make us who we are, and that is what gives us a home.

The manuscripts in Chinese and English have traveled through New York, Buenos Aires, Santiago, San Pedro de Atacama, Bogotá, Quito, and Guatemala City. The story has received many loves from many languages. The English final first-round edits were finished in New York, while the copyediting and this essay were both finalized in Colombia, where I find my heart fully belongs.

To me as a translator, a paradise means the many languages I acquired, and the possibility of finding new homes within all the languages I speak.

Fang Si-Chi's First Love Paradise is brimming with the author's love for language, her passion for literature, and a longing for home, however home may be defined. It is a meaningful voice that aims to bring more voices forward. Every time I read this book, I find solace in the gentleness of her language, like how my skin feels the warmth of a sunbeam whenever I need it the most.

I hope that through reading Lin Yi-Han's novel in translation, our languages will, in a way, become your paradise.

Jenna Tang
Bogotá, Colombia, June 17, 2023

Here ends Lin Yi-Han's
Fang Si-Chi's First Love Paradise.

The first edition of this book was printed
and bound at Lakeside Book Company
in Harrisonburg, Virginia, April 2024.

A NOTE ON THE TYPE

Designed by Frederic W. Goudy in 1915, Goudy Old Style is admired for its elegance and surprising flexibility, which makes it a timeless choice. While it may appear reminiscent of classic Italian typefaces, this font is entirely original, featuring graceful curves and delicate strokes that add a touch of warmth to documents that might otherwise seem overly formal in a more run-of-the-mill typeface.

HARPERVIA

An imprint dedicated to publishing international voices,
offering readers a chance to encounter other lives and other
points of view via the language of the imagination.